MUCH TOO VULGAR

Viggy Parr Hampton

First edition, 2024
ISBN Paperback: 979-8-9898755-2-8
ISBN Ebook: 979-8-9898755-3-5
Book Design by Nuno Moreira, NMDESIGN

MUCH TOO VULGAR

Viggy Parr Hampton

For Camille and Wyatt, whose impending births gave me the pushes
I needed to finish and revise this novel.

CHAPTER ONE

You Don't Get Fraps Often, Do You?

I'm sitting behind the reception desk in the Chaplains' Office of Georgetown's Healy Hall trying to pierce my skin with a letter opener. If it looks bad enough, I can go home and scream without anybody hearing me. The cramped office reeks of peppermint tea and Airhead Ani's lavender eucalyptus candle, and it's starting to give me a headache. I'd rather breathe in the fumes of industrial-strength antibacterial cleansers all day, every day—because that would mean I'd be working in one of Georgetown's labs, setting a course for medical school, instead of wasting my summer here, in this meaningless campus job.

My co-worker, Anica Ableman ("I go by Ani, like AH-nee"), will be back from the bathroom soon. To be honest, I've never met someone less able in my life. The girl's parents were clearly fans of alliteration, and so am I—so I've dubbed her Airhead Ani.

The laxative I slipped into her venti caramel Frappuccino was just a small dose. If she stays on the toilet any longer, she's just malingering. Not that I'm surprised, the girl spends the whole time we're in here texting or scrolling on Instagram. Of course, she looks up with those vapid blue eyes whenever a Jesuit or a professor or somebody with authority walks in. She hides her phone under the table and purrs at them like a street cat, asking if she can help them with anything, maybe get them some of that disgusting tea. It's gross to watch, actually. I want to scratch those eyes right out of her face.

I twirl the letter opener around and around in my hands, my fingers flirting with its sharp point. The sudden creak of the door opening startles me, sending the blade slicing through the pad of my left thumb. A small bead of crimson wells up from the cut, and instead of sticking my finger in my mouth like I normally do, I grab a tissue from the box on my desk to absorb the blood.

Airhead Ani walks in, her lips looking dry and chapped instead of pink and pouty, and it makes me smile for the first time all day.

"Are you alright?" I ask, my mouth contorting into something resembling concern.

"Yeah," she says, smiling weakly. Everything she does looks weak, even when she hasn't just emptied herself over the toilet for an hour. "Just a little stomach thing. Maybe I should stop drinking Frappuccinos."

"That stuff is horrible for you," I say, knitting my brows together in an approximation of sincerity. "Just think of all the sugar you're sucking down. I read in *Cosmo* that Fraps have a special kind of genetically modified sugar that goes straight to your ass. Oh, and it gives you cellulite like you wouldn't believe." I don't even read *Cosmo*, that senseless drivel, but the horrified look on Airhead's face gives me a rush. Her lips get even paler and those mold-blue eyes go wide.

"Seriously?" she says.

"Seriously," I say gravely. "It's a real shame they don't tell you that. You don't get Fraps often, do you?" I twist my mouth into an expression of mock horror.

"Only every day!" she cries out, her eyes now filling with tears—so pathetic.

"Jesus," I say. "I'm really sorry. I don't know if it's possible to reverse the damage once it's done."

For a second, I think she's going to cry, and I desperately want to see that. Instead, she sniffles once, pulls herself together, and says, "I'll just get diet ones from now on. I'm sure it's not as bad as *Cosmo* makes it sound. That magazine is always selling sensational stuff."

I don't want to push it further. I'm bored with her now. "You're probably right," I grumble, turning back to the paperwork on my desk— but then I spy a pouch of sugar-free Extra gum in the side pocket of her purse. "At least you don't chew that sugar-free gum," I say. "Then you'd really be in deep shit. Neurologically speaking, that stuff is basically pure poison for your brain."

Her face snaps back to me with a look of pure terror. For me, this is the best high there is.

CHAPTER TWO

The Pencil Goes All the Way Through

I can feel the swampy D.C. heat of the asphalt through my flip-flops as I slap back home from the Safeway with a new jar of peanut butter and a carton of blueberries swinging in the plastic bag against my thigh. I wouldn't have needed to make this Saturday morning trip at all if the blueberries I bought yesterday hadn't already molded in my fridge. While I was at Safeway, I figured why not get some more peanut butter, since I'll be out of it soon and you never know when a new test subject will walk right into your cage trap.

"Hey, Keely!"

I'm so lost in contemplating the contents of my fridge—e.g., a tub of expired yogurt I'm keeping as an experiment in growing different types of fungus, the aforementioned nearly empty jar of peanut butter I use exclusively for the rodents—that I don't even notice Roger sitting in the middle of his postage-stamp lawn until I'm about to pass him and he shouts over to me in his foghorn voice.

"Roger," I say.

"What you got in there?" he says, gesturing to my grocery bag.

I shake the bag, as if that will tell him anything. "Peanut butter and blueberries," I say.

"Yum. Good for oatmeal, right?"

"I don't eat oatmeal, but sure, I guess so."

Roger shifts in the dry grass, pushing his fingers into the earth. I stand there motionless, waiting for him to do something else.

"Keely," he says after a few more moments. The soles of my feet are growing uncomfortably hot.

"What is it, Roger?"

"What's in the bag?"

"Unicorn farts and leprechaun boogers," I say without a hint of sarcasm.

Roger laughs, the kind of blissful, uncomplicated sound that can only come from someone who does not have the capacity for worry.

Normally, I would never speak to a stranger, much less a male stranger who lives on my street. Nobody needs entangling relationships, especially not me. The first time Roger called out to me, he spilled his entire life story. I wanted to leave, but what he said was so fascinating I found myself itching to take notes. Roger told me he'd suffered a freak accident four years ago, something involving a piece of exposed rebar in a parking garage, that had left him with a very unique traumatic brain injury. His doctors didn't think he'd survive the night, but he managed to pull through, making a recovery—but not a full one.

"How's the head today, Rog?" I ask.

"The same, the same," he says, shaking his cornsilk hair. "You know those doctors wrote a case study about me. It was published in the *New England Journal of Medicine*." He smiles with pride, just like he does every time he tells me this, which is often.

"I know," I say. In fact, as soon as our first meeting concluded when his live-in caregiver called him inside for dinner, I went home and Googled his ass. People lie all the time, but I was delighted to discover Roger wasn't lying. I found the case study—anonymized, of course, but simple enough to uncover given all the details I had about Roger. I also read several news stories about the accident, the most interesting tidbit being how his family sued the owner of the parking garage and ended up with millions. That explains how he can afford this Georgetown neighborhood and a full-time caregiver.

"I've told you that before, haven't I?" he says, a small frown creasing his boyish face.

"Don't worry about it, Rog," I say. Beneath me, my feet are starting to burn, and I shift back and forth to alleviate the pain, wondering how long I can take it.

"You know I don't remember very well," he says.

"It's okay," I say. The *NEJM* case study went into great detail about Roger's traumatic brain injury, about how he is unable to form new memories of much substance. His injury is so unusual that doctors are still studying him. It's one of the reasons I don't hate him like I do most other people. He can't remember anything about me besides my name.

"What do you have there, Keely?" he says, pointing at my bag yet again.

Instead of answering his question, I ask one of my own. "What color is this bag?"

According to the case study, one of the effects of his brain injury is intermittent color blindness. The last time I asked Roger to name the color of a red tulip, he said it was blue. Roger is endlessly fascinating to me, like a live experimental subject.

"Looks green to me," he says. The bag is actually white, but whatever.

"Good job," I say.

Roger smiles, and I look around, making sure nobody else is within earshot. Roger's medical condition isn't the only reason I willingly speak with him.

He's also the best secret keeper.

"You know what, Roger? Yesterday was funny and everything, messing with Airhead Ani and getting her to throw away her gum like it was poison—I had to do it; the girl popped that gum constantly. If I hadn't put an end to it, I would have come way too close to stabbing a sharpened pencil into her thigh. Which of course I couldn't do, because that would leave a mark. It's really hard to get graphite out of skin once it's in there." When I pause to take a breath, I'm panting. I've stopped shifting around, and I no longer notice the pain in my feet.

"How do you know that?" Roger asks.

"That's what I heard from my cousin, who told me the graphite is still in her hand from the time I plunged my pencil into that soft part between her thumb and pointer finger when she was four and I was eight. I just wanted to see if the point would go all the way through, or if some combination of skin or muscle or vein would stop it."

"Did it?"

"Well, if she hadn't started screaming and calling for her mom, I would have had enough time to find out. Instead, I had to wait two years before I had another research opportunity. That time, I made sure the repulsive boy who pulled my hair never did it again. You want the spoiler alert, Rog? The pencil does, indeed, go all the way through—if you push hard enough."

Roger stares at me for a moment, his eyes unfocused. Then he says, "Hot out here today, huh?"

I'm not done. This past week has been a pustulating sore, throbbing against my psyche, threatening to burst. Meanwhile, my feet have lost all feeling, and I wonder if I've singed the skin on the soles or if this is a run-of-the-mill pins-and-needles numbness. I don't care about the potential damage; I'm more interested in the outcome of this little self-experiment. How long until I can't stand it any longer? "Talk about hot. Professor Demetri can go to hell right here."

"Who's Professor Demetri?" Roger asks.

"The nitwit who rejected my application for the Hughes summer research program."

"What's the Hughes summer research program?"

"It's the only direct path to the best medical schools in the country. I should be spending my summer in a research lab, analyzing samples or running electrophoresis gels or dissecting tumor-ridden mice, but instead I'm stuck throwing tea parties for lapsed Catholics in the fucking

Chaplains' Office. I'm not even religious!"

"Me neither," Roger says.

"I belong in that program more than anyone. I have the grades, I have the drive, I have the curiosity every great researcher needs. Professor Demetri only picked students from her freshman seminar, which is total bullshit. I know for a fact most of them didn't get anything higher than an A- on their biology finals—and let me tell you, Rog, I got an A. It should have been an A+, but the question was worded poorly so it really wasn't my fault."

"Sounds like you should have gotten in," he says, shrugging. If only Professor Demetri could see things as clearly as Roger Pally can.

"That's not even the worst part. When I had the Hughes interview with Demetri, she told me all the spots were filled, and that's why she couldn't accept me. Right after I left her office, I saw this girl waiting to talk to her after me. She breezed right past me, like I wasn't even worth her time. So, I stood outside the office and listened, and once the door was closed, I heard Demetri say something like 'Erica, I was so impressed with your application. Even though the program is full, I'm making an exception for you. We're going to find a way to fit you in. Congratulations, and welcome to the Hughes summer research program!' Can you believe it? There's no way Erica has better grades than me, and how could her application have been that much better than mine?"

"That's not right, Keely," Roger says. I'm impressed. Usually, his attention span doesn't last this long.

"It's absolutely not. You know what I did after that? I left that antiseptic-scented scientific paradise and spent the day dissecting the sparrow that broke its neck on my window. The vertebrae had been crushed and mangled. Kind of like a kid's macaroni necklace."

I stop, still panting, pain now flaring up in my sternum. Even though I've never had a licensed medical professional diagnose me, I'm fairly certain I have costochondritis. I get those characteristic sharp chest pains whenever I'm too excited; if it were really a heart attack, I'd have died multiple times over by now. As it is, I've come to rather enjoy the pain—it reminds me I'm alive.

The ice-pick stab in my chest starts to dissipate as I stare at Roger. For a second, his brow furrows with concern, then his entire face smooths out like pancake batter. "I like macaroni," he says. "But only the Kraft kind, Keely." His eyes brighten. "Is that what's in your bag?"

I've found a new limit to Roger's attention span. I'll have to make a note of that.

"I'll bring you some the next time I go to the store," I say. It's easy to make promises to Roger—he never remembers them.

"You're the best, Keely!" he says.

"I am. I really am, but I'm still not in Hughes. I tried to be in the study groups with all those Hughes-bound kids, tried to align myself with people going in my direction—but Mother was right. I shouldn't have helped them. Everybody is either going to drag me down or try to compete with me, and if I'm helping them, I'm hurting myself."

"Don't hurt yourself, Keely," he says.

"It's just not fair. The Hughes kids get everything handed to them—a stipend, free housing, iPads for the summer. Those kids roam around campus like they own the place, drunk off their asses, hooting and hollering. I wouldn't trust one of them to deliver a pizza, much less pipette reagents or excise tumors from mice. Would you?"

"I don't think so," Roger says.

"That's right, you wouldn't," I say. "You're a smart man, Roger."

Roger beams, then his face goes blank again. A welcome breeze ruffles his cornsilk hair, which is starting to thin at the top. He's about to say something when his caregiver opens the front door and hollers, "Roger—breakfast!"

Roger jumps up from the ground with surprising agility. His brain injury clearly did not affect any of his motor skills. "Bye, Keely!" he says, hustling inside and letting the door slam closed.

With a sigh, I start walking again. The pins-and-needles feeling creeping up my calves confirms my feet have fallen asleep instead of being burned. When I reach my basement apartment, I climb down the stairs somewhat unsteadily, unload my meager groceries, then go outside to poke the anthill in the minuscule backyard. I'm feeling riled up after spilling my guts to Roger, and watching the industrious way the ants scurry to rebuild what I've damaged helps calm me down. I'm about to make another deep jab when I hear a rustle against the wire-mesh of the cage trap I keep hidden under the deck stairs. A squirrel, scrawny and nauseatingly ratlike, is cowering inside. Its eyes are milky with fear.

For weeks I've been trying to catch something bigger than a mouse. At first, I told myself I needed a companion, just like anybody else. A fluffy little creature I could own, one that would be happy to be owned, too, maybe sit by my side as I wrote papers and analyzed data. Then, as I grew more and more frustrated by my lack of success, I realized I didn't want a furry companion at all—I wanted an experimental subject. Just because the Hughes program won't take me doesn't mean I can't advance my education on my own.

With extreme caution, I transfer the entire cage to the glassed-in shower in my bathroom, where the squirrel has an even smaller chance of escape. It's a skinny little thing, its ribs visible as it cowers from me, panting. I sit on the closed lid of the toilet, watching the squirrel and taking notes on its behavior in my lab notebook. I've turned up the volume on my speakers, blasting bubblegum Taylor Swift so the girls upstairs don't hear the squirrel scrabbling around. My basement apartment connects to the rest of the house, but it has its own entrance, so I wouldn't call those four girls my roommates. They're housemates, nothing more, and they're certainly not my friends, even though they talk to me like they are.

The runty squirrel is a dusty gray-brown, and I've already given him a name. People say you shouldn't name animals you're going to kill—I guess because it makes it more emotionally difficult or some other such nonsense but I find it's a useful way to catalogue my experiments. This particular subject I'm calling Dodge, because he always tries to dodge my hands when I reach out for him. Not that I blame him, because he can probably see the scalpels next to me. They should be glimmering in the light, but their shine is dulled by the corrosion creeping up the steel. Most of my equipment is liberated from disused science labs around campus, and hey—beggars, or in my case thieves, can't be choosers.

My next year of pre-med coursework involves a rat dissection. I want to be ready, so I need to practice. I'm not going to go in there with clumsy hands or a sensitive stomach, feeling around blindly in an open abdominal cavity. I'm going to be perfect.

Keeping one eye on Dodge, I roll out my tarp on my kitchen table and get my mismatched knives and pins ready. Now, all I have to do is wait for him to calm down enough for me to grab him. It's not like I want to torture him—his death will be quick. I'm not a monster, but I also don't want to give him a chance to cry for help.

I wonder what Mother would think if she saw me right now. She wouldn't be proud, she never is, but maybe some small part of her would respect my ingenuity, my drive. More likely, she would only see my unpainted nails, limp hair, and ill-fitting clothes. The sight of my unwashed bedsheets, stained yellow with my night sweats, would repulse her, as it does me. We all have our priorities, though, and making a nice home out of this hovel is not on my list.

I shake my head to clear it of any thoughts of Mother. She'll be proud enough when I'm a Dr. Rexroth, too. Maybe then I won't feel so empty, like a deflated balloon made of human flesh.

With a surgeon's sure hands, I grab Dodge, cradling him against my stomach. He doesn't fight me when I secure his tiny limbs to the tray. He doesn't even squeal when I make the first incision.

CHAPTER THREE

What's So Great About Harvard?

Monday morning rolls around, and Dodge's blood is still under my fingernails. I'm digging it out with the pointy end of a nail file, scooping the little rusty flakes into a pile that I'll sprinkle into the crevices of Airhead Ani's keyboard. It's almost 10 o'clock and she's still not here, but that's not unusual. With a name like Anica Ableman, she's always been at the very front of the line alphabetically. She's used to being prioritized by her parents, too, I bet, and even now, she still walks around like she's special.

People like that take everything for granted. Not me—as much as I hate it here, having this job means I don't have to go home this summer, don't have to wither under the white-hot glare of Mother's disapproval. It's painful enough over the phone; in person, it's excruciating.

The heavy door leading into the foyer creaks open, and footsteps pad up the red carpet to the Chaplains' Office. Instead of Airhead, a middle-aged woman with mid-length brown hair, a business suit, and a self-important air pokes her head through the doorway.

"Excuse me," she says, "could you tell me how to get to Regents Hall?"

This isn't the first, nor will it be the last, time someone comes in here looking for directions, wanting everything done for them and gift-wrapped with a pretty bow. It's like these dumbasses don't understand everything can be Googled. I hide my blood-caked nail file under a pile of papers on my desk and plaster on a smile. "Sure," I say. "I can show you on the online map." It's hard to keep the irritation out of my voice, but she doesn't seem to notice. She steps up to my desk, and I swivel my monitor so she can see it before Googling "Georgetown campus map."

As I click around, the woman rests an elbow on my desk. "Thanks for your help. I've been to Georgetown before, but not since Regents Hall was built."

I click again, and the map pops up on my screen. "Are you an alum?" I ask, only because she seems to require a response.

"No," she says, pulling her phone from her pocket as though that very action wouldn't have provided her with the directions she needed before she hustled in here and disturbed my peace. "I'm a recruiter for Harvard Medical School." She pauses for a moment, as though waiting for me to ooh and aah over her affiliation with Harvard, that arrogant school that clearly didn't have the good judgment to accept my undergraduate application. When I say nothing, only giving her a blank stare as though I've never heard of Harvard before, she continues, slightly flustered. "I'm—I'm here to talk to the Hughes research program students?"

I continue to stare at her. Harvard and Hughes combined? I wish I could pick up my pile of dried blood flakes and blow them into her face like they were granules of scopolamine, that drug that turns people into zombies. Maybe that would make her less of an asshole.

She tries to recover some of her confidence by leaning hard into pomposity. "You know, Harvard Medical School is only looking for the best and brightest. Georgetown may not be Ivy League, but we're always interested in the Hughes program students. They're very impressive. They automatically get interviews with us."

While she's blabbering, I'm digging my nails into my denim-clad thigh so hard I'll have bruises later. Through clenched teeth, I say, "Well, if they're that impressive, I'm sure they could go to any med school they want. What's so great about Harvard?"

I'm not daft. I know Harvard has the number one medical school in the world, but I hate the smug look anybody associated with that university always wears, as though they are part of an elite group that operates on a plane far higher than everyone else. I think about mentioning the human remains trafficking scandal to knock her down a peg, but decide instead to keep my mouth shut. Even with a morgue manager who couldn't keep his sticky fingers off of other peoples' body parts, Harvard is still the best.

At least my thinly veiled insult pierces her self-satisfied facade, and her face twists into an ugly sneer. I can see a smudge of aubergine lipstick on her two front teeth that looks like the world's worst coffee stain. "Harvard has the top-ranked medical school in the world, honey."

"I'm not your 'honey,'" I say. I can feel my breath starting to come in shorter spurts, which means the chest pain isn't far behind. I want this woman out of here before that happens.

She looks taken aback, but quickly recovers that smile-sneer that showcases her inability to apply makeup properly. "Can you please just tell me where Regents Hall is?"

My smile doesn't reach my eyes as I navigate my cursor over the map on my screen and speak quickly. The labels on this map are so small you can't really read them. "Just turn right out of here, then take another right at Lauinger Library, then go down the hill. Regents is just to the left of the dining hall."

Without saying thank you, she spins on her heels and marches out of the office. By the time she realizes I've sent her to the wrong side of campus, she'll be so late for her meeting with the Hughes kids that they might have to cancel. That thought tickles me, a dark glee blooming in the center of my chest—but it's quickly dampened by Ms. Harvard's reminder that the Hughes kids get everything any budding scientist or medical professional could want, while the rest of us, even if we're smarter than those Hughes kids, are stuck with whatever scraps are leftover.

My thigh aches where my nails dug into my jeans, and tiny ice picks are stabbing my sternum, but I don't care. My fingers find the nail file where I hid it under the stack of papers, and I get back to chiseling out the dried blood as I try to slow my breathing. Outside the Chaplains' Office, I hear the heavy door of Healy creak open and bang closed. I shove the nail file back under the papers and unceremoniously dump the little rust-colored pile onto Airhead's keyboard.

Airhead Ani barges in and plops down into her chair, dropping her overstuffed Louis Vuitton tote under the desk. "Oh my God, Keely," she says. "We have to talk about last night's episode of *The Bachelor*!"

This is going to be a very long day.

CHAPTER FOUR

Everything Is For Sale in This Dump

It's almost 6 o'clock in the evening, and it's been a while since I've been this on edge. I'm walking along O Street, away from the Chaplains' Office, where Airhead was sucking down diet Frappuccinos all day. When she wasn't gulping, she was chewing gum—"But don't worry, Keely, it's the kind with regular sugar instead of fake sugar!" she proclaimed. It took all the strength I had not to hold her down and rip her teeth out one by one. I know how I'd do it, too. I'd just take the sharp little staple remover from the drawer, dig it into her gums, and pull—really hard.

Instead, I wadded up reams and reams of toilet paper and, using a plunger handle, stuffed the balls deep into each of the first-floor ladies' commodes, hoping the combination of too much liquid and out-of-order toilets would make Airhead wet her pants. No such luck—I guess the YouTube tutorial I watched about deliberately clogging toilets didn't take into account the surprising strength of the old building's plumbing, which swallowed the boluses without so much as a cough.

As I stroll, I can feel my shoulders lower from their perpetual hunch. My fingers uncurl, my pulse slows, my breathing evens out. The streets are quiet, the heat radiating off the brick and asphalt like the steam from a fresh kill.

One of my favorite things about walking the streets of Georgetown is peeking into other peoples' lives. Right now, it's dinnertime, and I can see people in their fancy townhouses cooking—that's generous; from what I can tell, most of them are just stuffing Lean Cuisines into overworked microwaves, congratulating themselves on 'healthy eating,' and picking up forks in front of glowing TVs. I've always hated television. Movies I can stand, especially the R-rated ones where all the good, gory parts aren't cut out, but something about the inanity of TV shows makes me want to yank my own eyeballs out and leave them dangling on my cheeks by the optic nerves like bloody yo-yos.

The smell of greasy pizza wafts out of a hole-in-the-wall, but even though I haven't eaten since before dawn, I don't feel hungry. The smell is sickening. It permeates the entire street, as though the proprietor thinks everyone is dying for a piece of that nasty pizza.

I'm about to turn onto Wisconsin Avenue when I spot it.

These streets have become hauntingly familiar to me since I've been living in Georgetown and finding some solace on my meandering walks, but I guess I've never taken this particular route, or maybe I was just preoccupied before.

I stop in front of the cramped storefront. It's clearly a thrift shop, but it has the gall to call itself an antique store. The facade looks derelict, but the sign in the glass door, spiderwebbed with cracks, says 'Open'.

A bell overhead tinkles as I push the door inward and step onto the scarred wood floor.

Most people would probably find the musty smell off-putting, but I far prefer it to the stench of acne-inducing pizza. The shop is barely larger than my basement apartment, and every inch of every surface is covered in cast-off junk. Old typewriters, broken radios, dirty mink coats, busted tennis rackets, crooked picture frames, and abandoned dolls form claustrophobic tunnels. A tiny trail weaves through the piles. It looks like a hoarder's home; the way each item looks deliberately staged amidst the clutter intrigues me.

I take a few steps into the jumble, keeping my arms close at my sides. It'd be far too easy to knock something over, and I'm in no mood to haggle with some old bastard about a 'You Break It, You Buy It' policy. If you don't want things to break, don't junk up your shop with way too much useless crap for people to bump into. Or, I suppose, it could be a calculated way to make money on things nobody would buy. If that's the case, I can't help but feel a grudging sense of respect.

"Hello," a calm, creaky voice exhales from somewhere behind my left shoulder, making me catch my breath.

"What?" I say, holding back a snarl at the last minute. There's another person here, and it's time to put my nice girl mask back on. I hate the feel of that fake face smiling on top of my real one. The pretending really wears you down, and I've been pretending for so, so long.

"Welcome to Trudeau's Antiques," the voice says. I hear shuffling from behind the piles of junk, and a shriveled old man rounds the corner. He reminds me of Judge Valkenheiser in that movie *Nothing But Trouble*—stooped, gnarly, wrinkled, revolting. I touch the sharp edge of my apartment key in my pocket, ready to plunge it into his throat at the slightest provocation.

To my left, a single giraffe leg has been taxidermized rather poorly, topped with a circle of fake-looking marble, and turned into a cocktail table. I kind of like it, even though the fur is decaying in spots. It reminds me of the animals I dissect. I've tried to keep them before, but I'm no taxidermist. Preservation is not my forte—at least, not yet.

To my right, a stack of dusty leather-bound books rises up almost to the ceiling. A quick glance at the peeling spines tells me all I need to know. these are clearly the type of books rich, old geezers stick on their shelves to look cultured. I've seen bookshelves full of them in the mahogany-paneled studies leering out from behind those naked townhouse windows. Nobody actually reads them. It's all a signal of mock erudition and moneyed status to make everyone else feel small and stupid.

When I don't respond to the old windbag's greeting, he glances past me to a stack of flat rectangular boxes.

Looming up in front of me is a grime-caked tower of children's board games. I see Sorry!—a game I hated, because I'm never sorry—Trouble, Monopoly, Yahtzee. Mother tried to engage me in games, but it was never for fun. It was always a test—who would win and be glorified, who would lose and be ridiculed. She would always find a way to make me the loser one way or another.

A faded orange box on top of the stack catches my eye. There's a black embossed face on the lid, its eyes glowing an almost impossible shade of scarlet. Its tongue is hanging out in a way that strikes me as pornographic. The letters above the face spell out 'Ouija Board.'

"Ah," he wheezes, his breath smelling of old garlic and something rancid, like hot dogs left out too long in the sun. "You've found a hidden gem, my friend."

I want to shout at him, tell him I'm no friend of his, but instead I smile so sweetly it hurts my cheeks. "Yes, sir," I manage between clenched teeth.

"What's a nice girl like you doing looking at a Ouija board?"

If only he knew what kind of girl I really am.

"I'm just browsing," I say, wondering if he can tell my voice is sweetened with Splenda instead of the real thing.

"I always knew this thing would sell. I just didn't think it would be to a nice young lady," he says.

"Oh, I don't think I'm buying anything," I say with a sneer, twisting on my heel to leave. Unfortunately, the old lump of desiccated dog turds has shifted closer to me during our conversation and is now blocking my path. There's no way around him, and my fingers tighten around my keys.

He laughs, the sound like someone choking on their own tongue. "I've heard that one before," he says. "Missy, people don't come in here just to browse." He laughs again, and it sounds like frogs dying. "Well, at least, they may think they came here to browse, but they always end up with something."

I really want to leave now, because he can't force me to buy any of his shit, but something about what he said makes me pause. Maybe there is something here for me.

He must feel a sale coming on, because a chuckle squeaks from his throat. "Did you see *The Exorcist?*" he asks.

Of course I saw *The Exorcist* that's practically an admission requirement for getting into Georgetown. The movie was filmed right in front of the John Carroll statue in the middle of Healy Lawn, and that set of ridiculously steep stairs just a block off of campus draws almost as many tourists as the Declaration of Independence. "Yes," I say, trying to keep the hiss out of my voice. He's still blocking my path, and despite being a sack of rotting offal, he's bigger than me.

I was six and home alone when I first saw the movie, and I remember just laughing and laughing and laughing when Linda Blair spewed pea soup all over Max von Sydow. I must have looked ridiculous, sitting in that stupid frilly room my mother designed for the perfect pink cupcake of a daughter she hoped for, howling with hilarity. I was laughing so hard I didn't hear my parents come home, but then I heard Mother's quick footsteps on the stairs. I snapped off the TV just as Father Karras plummeted to his death. I yanked a borrowed Judy Blume book off of my nightstand. Mother asked me if I was being good, and I said something silly like, "That Judy Blume, she's just too funny!" Mother smiled, her teeth like needles, her eyes hard. "Judy Blume is too puerile for you," she said. "Pick something better, Keely. The library is full of more appropriate reading material. This is just embarrassing." Before she left, she crossed the room to my dresser and placed her palm on the back of the TV. She must have felt its warmth, because she bent over, unplugged it, and hefted the entire thing into her arms, the plug trailing behind like an umbilical cord. She left, slamming the door with her foot. Shortly after, I heard the click of Mother locking the door from the outside. I finally fell asleep on the floor five hours later, my fingernails shredded from clawing at the solid oak.

The old man snaps his fingers right in my face, and I barely manage to keep myself from biting those wrinkled digits off. "Hey, girlie. You in there?"

"Yes, sir," I say quietly. He looks relieved, but unsettled. I'm glad I make him nervous.

"Ouija boards are a great way to get possessed," he says, laugh lines wrinkling his already-creased mouth. He gives me a watery-eyed, calculating look that makes me want to peel off my own skin. "You know, demons can help you get whatever you want." He winks, a grotesque gesture, and I wonder if the police would ever find me if I slit his throat right here.

I don't need more demons. When I don't respond, he prods, "You want it or not?" He extends one of those gnarled fingers toward the Ouija board.

"No," I say, and I'm ready to shove him down and trample him just to get out of here, but a glint of sharp metal makes me stop before I can so much as take a single step. On the floor, to the right of the old man's threadbare house slipper, is a black leather duffel bag, about the size of a miniature poodle. It's propped open, and I can just make out the tip of a scalpel nestled inside, shining despite the dim light. I move my hand toward it, but the old man grabs my wrist.

"That," he says, "is not for sale."

That's ridiculous. I rip my wrist out of his grasp, my skin feeling itchy where it rubbed against his. Through clenched teeth, I ask, "And why is that?"

"It was my father's," he says, picking it up. "You know what this is, girlie? It's a surgeon's bag. It's for doctors, not for little girls like you." As if to emphasize his point, he pulls the bag fully open, and my mouth starts to water at all the sharp objects. My hand reaches out to touch the jagged teeth of a bone saw, but before I can get within reach of it, the old man snaps the bag shut, sending a whoosh of dusty, antiseptic-scented air into my face.

My eyes go wide and I can feel myself smiling, but it's not a nice smile. My vision turns red, and it takes all the strength I have not to plunge my apartment key into the soft flesh of his flabby neck.

"Well, in that case," I manage to say, "I'll take the Ouija board after all. How much?"

"Ten bucks," he says, his puffy rat-eyes gleaming.

"Fine," I say. "But I only have a twenty. Can you make change?"

"I'll have to go back to the register," he grumbles, which is exactly what I was hoping he'd say. As far as I can tell, the register is somewhere at the back, beyond the piles of junk.

I dig into my pocket and pull out a wrinkled bill. He sets the doctor's bag on the giraffe leg table and grabs the money, his eyes glistening with greed. "I'll wait," I say, pulling the orange box from the top of the stack of board games.

With a look of distrust, he turns and ambles away through the labyrinth. As soon as he's out of view, I toss the box back down, a cloud of dust erupting with the force of the impact. As swiftly and silently as I can, I scoop up the doctor's bag and fly out of the store. On the way out, I yell, "I changed my mind, but you can keep the twenty! You clearly need it!"

The door whistles closed behind me, and then I'm back out in the pizza-perfumed air, the worn handles of my prize clutched in my curled fist, my fingers starting to ache with the effort. Adrenaline pumps through me, and I run down Wisconsin toward M Street, dodging dimwitted, sauntering pedestrians shoving trendy cupcakes into their mouths.

I don't slow down until I hit the canal. I take a sharp right onto the narrow path that borders the dirty water. There's an empty bench in a spot of shade, and I collapse onto it, pulling my stolen goods into my lap.

There's no one around, and it better stay that way. I'm in no mood for tourists' goggle-eyed stares. The leather of the bag is cool on my thighs. With greedy hands, I pull the bag open. That faint, sweet smell of old carbolic acid antiseptic wafts out, and I breathe deeply. Immediately, I can tell this bag was worth the petty crime. A veritable goldmine of doctors' equipment sparkles up at me: scalpels of various sizes, delicate suture needles, tiny glass vials with powdery residues caking the bottoms. Forceps, a trocar, and—I can't believe it—a trepan, used to drill holes into peoples' skulls. Any of these tools could help me remove Airhead Ani's teeth better than a staple remover, and they make my current set of surgical instruments look like bad stage props. I'm not aware that my mouth is hanging open in awe until a fat blob of drool falls from my lip into the open maw of the bag. I snap the bag closed and drag my sleeve across my face. With a bit of sharpening and some light cleaning, these tools will be as good as new.

I'm going to be able to learn so much. A budding doctor needs genuine doctor's tools. Whoever said good things only happen to good people was so very wrong.

CHAPTER FIVE

No One Is Beyond Help But Me

It's still light out as I make my way back up Wisconsin to M Street, the doctor's bag bouncing against my side. I love it so much I want to pet it, feel the smooth, aged leather under my palms. Instead, I hold it close, swerving around tourists in matching tie-dye shirts and students in cliquey clusters. The sidewalk is tilted and cramped, teeming with the kinds of people who are simply not worth my time. I know it would be so much worse if Georgetown had a Metro station disgorging even more human refuse into the avenues and alleys, but the current density makes me angry anyway. It's not entirely my fault when I slap the hand of a snot-nosed little boy who reaches out to touch my doctor's bag. His father, gripping the boy's other hand, looks up at me with shock and rage in his piggy eyes.

"Did you just hit my kid?" he says.

"You should teach your brat to keep his hands to himself," I spit back, clutching my bag to my chest as the steady flow of people squeezes in between and around us on the sidewalk.

"Excuse me?" he says, his jowly cheeks turning red.

"Is your hearing as bad as your son's manners?" I know I should stop—but this man and his son don't matter.

He sputters, yanking the boy back into him and away from me. The boy yelps like a wounded animal.

The man's face turns an even deeper shade of crimson, and his fingers curl into fists. I'm not afraid of physical confrontation; if this man hits me, I'll scream. The crowd will turn on the big man assaulting the innocent young woman, the police will come, I'll give my statement, and the man will spend a miserable evening in jail, separated from his precious, handsy boy.

His cheeks are shiny with sweat, and his arm is starting to pull back. Even though I know I can play this assault to my advantage, I decide I'm not in the mood for a black eye or a broken nose today. Swift as an alley cat, I turn and bolt for a rough wooden door behind me, sandwiched between the Michael Kors and Victoria's Secret storefronts. The door gives way with a squeal, which pairs nicely with the man's scream of "Fuck you, lady!"

I slam the door closed and shoot the deadbolts. Meaty fists pound against it, along with more muffled cursing. I take a step back into a small, shadowy foyer, but I don't even have time to figure out where I am before someone above me clears their throat with enough force to dislodge a tooth. I ignore the banging on the door behind me and look up to the top of a flight of witchy purple stairs, where a woman stands under a sign reading 'Madame Leila, Psychic.' I stifle a laugh and grip my doctor's bag closer to my chest.

Madame Leila really leans in to the whole 'fortune teller' aesthetic—big, frizzy gray hair, Coke-bottle glasses, layers of junky necklaces and bracelets festooned with symbols that lose their meaning when applied in such great quantity. She's swathed in frayed scarves, and the crotch of her harem pants sags almost below her knees.

She looks me up and down, eyeing my doctor's bag for a few seconds longer than appropriate. When she meets my eyes, her face is tight and pale.

Finally, she says, "Come on up here. I can tell you're in need of help." Her accent is all deep South, molasses-thick, but I refuse to get stuck in the syrup.

My face contorts into a smirk, but I go up the stairs and follow this woman anyway. The banging on the door behind me has slowed, but I'm not ready to go back out there until that man and his snotty urchin are long gone. Plus, even if the coast were clear, I'm now too curious to turn around and leave.

The lair of Madame Leila (although I'm sure that's not her real name, she looks more like an Edna or a Gertrude to me) looks straight out of a made-for-TV movie. The smell of something sweet with decay, like potpourri or rotting gardenias, hits me like a wave. Reproduction tapestries line the walls, gauzy curtains cover the windows, and the floor is lousy with layers upon layers of carpets. In the center of the room, a small bistro table supports a crystal ball. Two chairs flank the table, and Madame Leila settles into one. She gestures for me to take the other.

I hesitate. I should be able to find better things to fritter away my money on. Syringes and barbicide don't buy themselves, after all. Plus, there's no way this woman can say anything to me that would provide any value—but I need somewhere to wait out that asshole, so I don't have much of a choice but to play along.

"Please. Come sit… Kandy? Kelsey? No, that's not it…" Madame Leila lifts a hand toward me, as if she's hoping to pluck my name out of the air. I keep my expression neutral, giving nothing away. I know how these kind of people operate, but I still take my place in the chair opposite her, placing my doctor's bag in my lap.

"There's a darkness surrounding you," she says, pausing to give me time to react. I'm not impressed. Everybody carries around at least a little darkness. When I say nothing, she continues, "I've never seen an aura as threatening as yours…Kelly? No… that's not it either…"

"I've never seen a fortune teller as clichéd as you," I fire back.

She's unfazed, which bothers me more. She nods at the crystal ball. "People come here expecting a certain experience. I give that to them. If, on the other hand, they come here expecting nothing, I can give them so much more." The scent of decomposing flowers irritates the back of my throat, making me want to cough, or maybe scream.

If she thinks she can impress me with mysterious babble, she's sorely mistaken. Spending so much time with Jesuits has inured me to that kind of nonsensical drivel. If she's intent on following through with this charade, I'm not going to give her a damn thing to work with.

"Give me your hand," she says. It sounds more like 'hay-und.' "I'm going to read your palm."

"For how much?" I say. This is how they get you; people like Madame Leila butter you up, then go in for the kill. Not this time—I like to know what I'm getting into, and I like throwing her off her game.

Without missing a beat, she says, "You need this more than I need the money."

My eyes narrow in suspicion. Not unlike the wrinkled windbag from the antique store, there's no way a buffoon like Madame Leila can pay rent on this M Street apartment even if she charges every customer an arm and a leg. There's a catch here somewhere, and I'm going to find it.

"You have no idea what I need."

She still doesn't look rattled, and it's starting to make me angry. "Let's stop this, okay? If you don't want to give me your palm, then don't. I just thought it would make you feel more comfortable. I already know everything just from looking at you—you want to be a doctor more than anything. You want to impress your parents, mostly Momma. You tend to get in your own way, and you care far too much what others think, even if you push everyone away."

Confusion and rage pop behind my eyes like exploding balloons. This woman doesn't know anything about me, about what I've been through. In my lap, I squeeze the handles of the doctor's bag so tightly I might actually break a finger. "You don't know what the fuck you're talking about," I hiss.

"Be angry if you need to be, but listen anyway. There's a girl you know, and she's everything you want to be. She has opportunities that have passed you by, she has friends, and she's free of the darkness that sticks to you like glue. Instead of hating her, try to learn from her."

The pounding from downstairs has stopped, and I can no longer feel my hands. I don't know how she's doing this, how she's cracking me open and peering inside as though my layers of armor are nothing but smoke. Hot tears flow down my cheeks, pooling at the base of my neck. She's talking about Erica, the girl who took what should have been my Hughes fellowship spot. I want to leap across the table and strangle Madame Leila, but I also want to wrap my numb fingers around my own throat and squeeze until the pain goes away.

"Learn, my ass," I say, spitting the words out like sodden cherry pits.

Just when it starts to feel like I'm dreaming this shit completely up, Madame Leila sighs and leans forward. With a whip of her palm, her frizzy gray wig is gone, replaced by a slicked-back blond helmet. She puts her elbows on the table and starts talking faster, the syrup in her accent replaced with vinegar.

"I hate having to wear this thing," she says. "You don't want to listen to me? Fine. But you're only hurting yourself. It's not too late for you… Keely. Yes, that's it—it took me a moment, but I knew it would come."

I scowl, even though I'm more startled than I'd like to admit that she actually got my name right. Although, the way she pronounces it with her honky tonk accent—'Key-uh-lee'—bears only a passing resemblance to my actual name.

She's not done. "You can still do research, and you can still be in a lab. I know you want to be a doctor, but you have to put in the hard work. Not just academically—I mean hard work on yourself. Let people in. Let them help you."

The difference between 'Madame Leila, Psychic' and whoever this woman really is without the hideous wig and the layers of fraying fabric is so jarring, it takes me a moment before I fully comprehend her words. I'm so tired of feeling like I'm not working hard enough, when all I do is put in the time, put in the effort. Nothing has been handed to me, but I'm still running on a never-ending treadmill. If I stop, I'll fall off and fly across the room to smash against the wall in one big bloody heap.

"No one can help me!" I finally bellow, leaping out of my seat, the doctor's bag falling from my lap to the floor. My cramped hands find the crystal ball, and I heft it above my head. Before I have a moment to reel myself back in, I hurl the ball across the room. It doesn't shatter; the tapestries and carpets cushion the blow. The ball thuds against the wall, then rolls, coming to a rest back at Madame Leila's feet. She stares at my greasy handprints smudging the clear glass, then looks back up at me. Her slicked-back blond hair shines in the low light.

"No one is beyond help," she says quietly, running her fingers through her real hair to loosen it. That dying gardenia smell wafts toward me again, and I almost gag.

Without another word, I hawk a glob of sticky spit onto her carpet, lean down, and grab my doctor's bag. I'm furious at Madame Leila, or whoever the fuck she really is, but I'm even angrier at myself. I can't afford to lose control like that. I need to leave before I do something I can't take back.

"You don't have to be perfect, Keely! No one is!" she hollers as I start running down the stairs.

She doesn't know what she's talking about. She never had Ellen Rexroth for a mother.

CHAPTER SIX

How Am I The Weird One?

"Keely!" Roger startles me when he calls from his perch on his front stoop. I haven't seen him all week. A plastic CVS bag full of Lysol and rubbing alcohol for my surgical tools swings back and forth from my hand as I walk.

"Roger," I say, slowing to a stop in front of his house.

"Lovely evening, isn't it?"

I haven't noticed. It's Saturday, which means the girls upstairs are going to have a party. I don't care; I have plans of my own.

"I guess," I say.

"My mother is coming to visit," Roger says, even though I know for a fact his mother died two years ago in a boating accident.

"I would never want my mother to come visit me."

"Why not?"

"Not every woman is qualified for motherhood."

"What do you mean?"

I sigh and shift my bag with the cleaning supplies to my other hand. "You want to know the last birthday present Mother ever gave me? I was three years old—and yes, I remember this clearly—and we had just finished my cake when Mother handed me a bag. I pulled out the tissue paper and found a stethoscope. Can you imagine?"

"Like what doctors use," Roger cuts in.

"Right. But this was no toy; it was a real, working stethoscope. My father looked at Mother and said something like, 'Ellen, is that really suitable for a child?' A decent question, no? But Mother turned to him and snapped, 'She's going to be a doctor, Howard. Doctors don't play with toys.' Then she looked at me and said 'Go on, darling'—I remember that specifically, those exact words— and pointed at the stethoscope. Like I was supposed to know what to do with it, at three years old! But I wanted to make Mother happy, so I reached for it. I had no idea what to do, and eventually I just put one of the round pieces in my mouth, hoping for a little sweetness. I can still taste the rubber, feel the cold of the metal on my tongue."

"I like birthday cake, too," Roger says.

"That wasn't good enough for Mother, though. She ripped the present out of my mouth, which hurt quite a bit. Then she yelled, 'Sylvia Murso's three-year-old is already reading chapter books, and here I am, stuck with a daughter who thinks a piece of medical equipment is a lollipop.'" I haven't thought about this in years, but the memory sits at the forefront of my mind as though it only happened yesterday.

"Do you have a lollipop in your bag?" Roger says, eyes hopeful.

"What kind of mother punishes a three-year-old for not knowing what to do with a fucking stethoscope? Ellen Rexroth, that's who. She never made me another birthday cake after that. Or gave me another birthday present, either." Something salty is pooling in the corners of my mouth. I flick out my tongue and lick the tears away.

"My mother is coming to visit," Roger says.

I take a deep breath. "Bully for you," I say, then give Roger a wave and continue walking to my apartment.

*　*　*

Upstairs, the party is in full swing. The thumping music drowns out the creaky cries of the large rat I've got secured to the kitchen table in my basement apartment. I don't love the inescapable cacophony, but I'll never complain to the girls upstairs. The Dean made it very clear that if I have another roommate 'situation,' as he called it, the University will be forced to put something on my permanent record. His use of 'the University' pissed me off. Let's face it, if he liked me more, or maybe if my parents had donated money to the school, I'd barely get a slap on the wrist. I've got an 'attitude problem' and a bit of a 'victim complex,' according to the Dean—as if that limpdick bastard is qualified in any way to judge me, much less diagnose me.

On the table, the rat squirms, but his—I've confirmed it's a boy—struggles are getting less and less violent. He was a fighter when I first trapped him, but even that little brain of his can sense he's out of luck, especially when he saw me sharpening my new toys from my doctor's bag. The scalpels, surgical needles, trepan: they're all arrayed on my tray, shining and sharp, so much better than my motley collection of corroded, stolen knives. I really should go antiquing more often.

I survey my gleaming equipment and write a few more observations in my lab notebook, hyping myself up while simultaneously trying to push all thoughts of 'Madame Leila' and her opinions about my life and my relationships out of my head. Mother made it very clear to me from a young age that my successes mattered to her—only my successes. My failures, attempts, second places, try-really-hards meant nothing. My feelings meant nothing. My personality meant nothing.

The rat lets out a shrill squeak that sounds eerily similar to the keening of the music upstairs.

My smudged water glass is nearly empty; I walk over to the kitchenette and fill it up to the brim. Cutting is thirsty work, and I've got a long night ahead of me.

The rat looks up at me, eyes seeming to plead. His nose twitches, the whiskers whipping through the stale air. He was almost too easy to trap; the girls upstairs always leave garbage all over—oily pizza boxes with one or two slices congealing inside, half-empty cups of some alcohol-spiked soda, gallon containers of ice cream with a few bites melting at the bottom. It's no surprise the mice, rats, and other vermin are attracted to this place. Those girls are just as much animals as they are.

"Don't worry," I coo at him, even though the rat has every reason in the world to worry. Pharmacies don't sell surgery-grade anesthetic to undergraduates.

I shouldn't be judged too harshly, though. I bought some marijuana off a dude in a back alley near M Street. I'm not a smoker—I think the habit is disgusting—but it'll take the edge off for old Mr. Rat. The rat's eyes flick back and forth, watching me pull a pinch of the skunky grass from a balled-up baggie and grind it into a fine powder between my fingers. The open jar of peanut butter in my fridge is almost empty, so I sprinkle the weed directly into the container and stir. When I bring a spoonful of the foul mixture close to Mr. Rat's face, his jaws grab at it like a shark biting off some unlucky swimmer's leg. He almost takes the spoon right out of my hand, but I'm faster than that, and my fingers are strong. I give him a few minutes, and then he stops struggling and squeaking entirely. This will still hurt, but not nearly as much—and it will keep him quiet.

I take a sip of water, then reach for my new-to-me scalpel, the largest from the doctor's bag. Tonight, I'm going to learn about the circulatory system. I've tried this before, but I wasn't successful. I'd had a late night studying, and by the time I got around to dissecting the mouse, it had been dead for several hours and was therefore useless to me, the body stiff with rigor, the blood cold and congealed. My own damn fault, but it was still a disappointment.

I've got a battered but sterilized cookie sheet under Mr. Rat to catch all the blood, and I start with a quick cut to his jugular. This cut also has the benefit of severing his vocal cords, so even if the marijuana doesn't fully do its job, old Mr. Rat can't tell a single soul about it.

Eventually, I want to be able to pair one rat's circulatory system with another's in an operation called parabiosis, a tricky surgery if there ever was one. I can already imagine the application essay I could send into medical schools. No school could say no to a student who taught herself how to make a hybrid creature—especially a hybrid creature that lives.

I move to cut open Mr. Rat's belly, and that's when I realize.

Somehow, I made the jugular cut too deep; maybe my new scalpel is sharper than I thought. Now, the stupid rat is bleeding out all over the cookie sheet, and it's about to overflow and stain my table. This table is rented, just like everything else in my apartment, and my landlord demanded three months' worth of rent as a security deposit, which should be criminal.

The damn rat's head is nearly off, and all the blood is spurting out, and this is a lost cause.

"Goddamnit!" I nearly scream, stifling it at the last second into a harsh whisper.

As carefully as possible, I balance the cookie sheet with dead Mr. Rat on my flat palms and carry it over to the sink. His body makes a wet plop as it slides off the sheet. I'll deal with that later. Right now, I just need to wash away all the blood.

After a few minutes, every last drop of scarlet has disappeared down the drain. I grab Mr. Rat by the tail and toss him into my trash can. If, for some reason, somebody notices, I can just say I have a rat problem in this vile basement and somebody needs to please do something about it so I don't have to do it myself. I rip the page of observations about Mr. Rat from my notebook and crumple it into a tight ball, then throw it in the garbage on to top of the exsanguinated carcass.

Finally, I set the cookie sheet to dry on my dish rack, and now I have nothing to do. My cheeks feel wet, but I don't think I'm crying.

It's hot as hell in this basement, but I shiver anyway, reaching for the laptop perched on one of my kitchen chairs. My fingers fly over the keys, asking Google how to properly dissect a live rat. Instead of anything helpful, content warnings fill my screen. I'd rather be subjected to pop-up pornography than these ridiculous judgmental warnings.

I slam my laptop shut so hard I worry I've broken the screen, but that's something I'll deal with later. The music is still thumping away upstairs, and my eyebrows feel like needles. I'm starting to pull them out hair by pointy hair when I realize: maybe 'Madame Leila' wasn't a total pustulating wad of sphincter after all. Her words float back to me: 'You can still be in a lab.'

On the table in front of me, my pile of eyebrow hairs is growing as my brain boils with ideas. Just because the Hughes program shut me out doesn't mean I can't work in a lab without their support. I don't need the stipend money. The Hughes kids may get special treatment, but they don't have a monopoly on undergraduate research. I want to smack myself for my oversight, but there's no need. I just keep pulling at my brows, relishing the plucky pain.

I grab my laptop and pull it toward me again, scattering scraggly hairs all over the keys when I open it. I'm relieved to see it's not broken, after all. I've been myopic, thinking there was only one way to do research, only one path toward the future I deserve. I'm done being sloppy.

I spend the next several hours researching professors, and by the time I close my laptop, the noises from upstairs have lapsed into silence. Monday, I'll pay Dr. Gunderson a visit. Besides being the top publishing professor on campus, she's got a reputation for welcoming undergraduates into her lab. Plus, I have an academic soft spot for neglected tropical diseases, how they can ravage a body so completely—even though, in most cases, treatment is so simple, but just out of reach. Dr. Gunderson's research into schistosomiasis definitely scratches my itch. I won't leave without a spot in her lab, even if I have to take it from someone else.

CHAPTER SEVEN

Schistosomiasis Is a Stupid Disease

I love the smell of Regents Hall, the brand new science building—like disinfectant, but with the faintest undercurrent of biological decay that no amount of cleanser can scrub out. I take the stairs two at a time to the fourth floor, where Dr. Gunderson's office sits right across the hall from her massive lab. It's still early—8am—so I'll have plenty of time to talk with Dr. Gunderson, get a tour of the lab, and get my things in order at my new bench before I have to report back to the Chaplains' Office for what will be my last day working there.

There's a GOCard swiper at the entrance to the hallway containing the labs and offices, and I pull out my student ID to gain access. The soft swick of the plastic through the swiper is oddly satisfying.

My hand is already on the door, pulling, before I realize something is wrong. The damn thing won't open. I give it another hard yank, but nothing happens, not even a metallic rattle. Frustrated, I launch my GOCard through the swiper again, but there's only a small flash of red light. I know what that means: access denied.

I want to curse, scream, and throw one of the heavy lounge chairs at the glass-fronted door, but I can't risk somebody seeing me doing any of those things. Instead, I clench my teeth so hard I feel my jaw pop.

"Need a swipe?" a voice asks over my shoulder. I whip around and come face to face with Erica, of course—the very same Erica who took the Hughes spot that should have been mine. She doesn't seem to recognize me. I suck in a harsh breath, mindful of the ever-present threat of pain in my sternum.

With a Herculean effort, I manage to contort my face into something resembling a friendly smile. It feels so unnatural, but it must pass muster, because she smiles back, revealing two rows of perfectly white, beautifully aligned teeth. "Your GOCard not working?"

I shrug. "Oh, you know, it's just one of those mornings, I guess," I say.

"I feel you," she responds, swiping her own GOCard and reaching for the handle. The door glides open without protest, and I resist the urge to kick it until the glass fractures.

She gestures for me to head in first, saying, "Are you new to the lab? I don't think I've seen you around here before." She takes a sip of coffee from the cup in her hand. The label reads 'Uncommon Grounds'—the undergraduate-run coffee shop in the Leavey Student Center, which is directly connected to Regents Hall. I start breathing through my mouth, because nothing is worse than coffee breath at close range.

"Yes, I'm new," I say, walking into the hallway. "I actually need to speak with Dr. Gunderson this morning about my position."

"Gotcha," she says, her hot breath hitting my face. I accidentally inhale, and the halitosis I expect is absent. Instead, I only smell the warmth and light spice of freshly ground coffee beans. My stomach growls. "Well, Dr. Gunderson's office is the third one on the right. She should be in—she usually gets to her office by 7:30 most days." Erica pauses, cocking her head at me. Her piercing green eyes look like sparkling emeralds in the fluorescent lights, and her hair shines in a way that absolutely cannot be natural. Her face is unmarked by acne scars, pimples, moles, or stray hairs, even though it appears as though she's wearing no makeup at all.

"Gotcha," I say, almost stumbling over the word. Erica smiles again, and my heart flutters in my chest. Even though I don't want to offer this girl a crumb of gratitude for a single damn thing, my lips betray me, eking out the words, "Thank you."

"Sure," she says. She flips her shining sheaf of hair over one shoulder, letting it waterfall down her back. I can't help thinking this is the daughter Mother would have wanted—not just beautiful, but effortless. I am under no illusions that I am beautiful or effortless. "Have a good one," Erica says, turning left into the lab, leaving me slightly dazed in the hallway. As the door swishes closed behind her, that circus show psychic's words come back to me: "There's a girl you know, and she's everything you want to be. Instead of hating her, try to learn from her." I call bullshit, 'Madame Leila,' because you can't learn what comes naturally to some people. I can't 'learn' prettier eyes or clearer skin or shinier hair or straighter teeth.

As I walk the short distance between where Erica peeled off like a scab and the door to Dr. Gunderson's office, I take a moment to smooth my hair, pull the wrinkles out of my clothes, and breathe deeply, trying to refocus myself.

I rap on Dr. Gunderson's door with my knuckles.

"Come in!" she shouts, and I do just that.

Dr. Gunderson gives me a quick once-over. "Hi," she says. "Can I help you?"

Even though she hasn't asked me to sit, I do it anyway, trying to push down the pulse of nerves in my stomach and look more confident than I feel. "Hello, Dr. Gunderson, my name is Keely Rexroth. I'm a rising sophomore, a pre-med biology major with a 4.0 grade point average, and I'd like to join your lab as an undergraduate research assistant."

Dr. Gunderson's gray eyebrows fly up into her severe topknot. I can't help thinking she looks like one of Mother's colleagues, Dr. Trent, whom Mother disdained for her 'lack of feminine grooming' because she always pulled her prematurely silver hair back in a bun instead of keeping it colored and beautifully styled at all times like Mother did. "Um," she says, clearly uncomfortable. "You want to join my lab? Now?"

I thought Dr. Gunderson would be a smart woman, but people can surprise you. She obviously requires me to spell things out for her, which makes me think she probably needs me more than I need her. God knows this woman isn't making discoveries on her own.

I arrange my face into a nonthreatening smile. "Yes," I say. "I'm working in the Chaplains' Office for the summer, but I really should be in a lab instead. I'm a hard worker, and I have a 4.0 GPA, as I mentioned. I'm extremely interested in the metabolism of trematode worms, and I'd love to study schistosomiasis in live mouse models."

The look of foolish surprise has left her face, and she's leveling a curious gaze at me. "I see you've done your homework," she says.

"I've read every paper your lab has ever published."

"Impressive," she says. My fingers are already itching to grasp pipettes and prepare microscope slides.

Time to go in for the kill. I lean in conspiratorially. "Dr. Gunderson, to be frank, if you let me work in your lab, I won't be partying all summer like those Hughes kids. I'll actually do the work."

Dr. Gunderson leans back, that gobsmacked look returning to her face. "Pardon?"

Reflexively, I gulp. The sound is loud enough to echo around the small room. "You need me in your lab. I will work more diligently than any other researcher you have."

She raises one silvery eyebrow and regards me for a long moment. "Why do you want to work in a lab, Miss Rexroth?"

What a silly question. Labs are stepping stones to medical school, to where the real discoveries are made, to the work that actually matters—but of course I'm not going to say that. An answer to a question like that requires some bullshitting. "To make the discoveries I know I'm meant to make," I say instead. At the slightly pinched look on her face, I try to backtrack, "I mean, that we're all meant to make, together, you know…" Under the desk, I squeeze a chunk of my thigh between my fingers, hoping to relieve some of the queasy vertigo creeping over me. This isn't how this meeting is supposed to go.

She leans back even farther in her chair, and I half-wish she would fall back and smack some sense into herself. "My goodness," she says. "You have a very high opinion of yourself."

A ball of saliva catches in my throat, and I swallow hard around it. I'm losing her, but I can't stop myself. "If you don't have a high opinion of yourself, who will?" I think I see a tiny sparkle in her eye, the barest hint of a smile, so I take a risk. "Cut the fat around here and give me the job." At my side, the fingers not currently pinching my leg are curling into a fist.

Her eyebrows draw together in consternation—she's probably going to have a headache after this, what with all the facial calisthenics. She'll need Botox before too long if she wants to stave off those deep furrows. "I'm sorry," she says. "All of my undergraduate research positions have been allocated to Hughes program students. There's no funding for another student researcher."

"Not a problem," I say. "I'll work for free."

Her lips curl into a pouty sneer. "That wouldn't be ethical, I'm afraid."

"What about all those other unpaid internships out there? Most employers, Dr. Gunderson, have zero problems with free labor." Why can't I make her see the obvious?

This time, it's her nose that's scrunching up. "It's not just the 'labor,' as you put it. We don't have the funding to buy all the equipment and supplies for another student researcher. It just doesn't work that way."

There's a hot wet patch growing under my left eye. "Then get rid of one of your other researchers," I say, hating the whiny sound of my own voice.

She rips a tissue from a box on her desk and tosses it at me with a look of disdain. "I will not be doing that."

Another wet patch blooms below my right eye. I must be crying. *Get a grip, Keely,* I tell myself. *Mother would be ashamed to see you blubbering in front of this woman who can't even be bothered to care for her physical appearance.* "I—"

In a voice as severe as her tight bun, Dr. Gunderson cuts me off before I can get another word out. "I'm sorry, but I think you need to leave, Miss

Rexroth." When I don't budge, she adds, "Now, please."

My lips are quivering and my chest is starting to hurt again, but my words still come out clearly. "Fine. I don't need this. One day, you'll be begging me to join your lab. You'll see." I get up to leave, then make a show of blowing my nose into the tissue she threw at me. With a flourish, I ball it up and purposely miss dropping it into the trash can by the door. "Schistosomiasis is a stupid disease to study, anyway—it's not even the most devastating parasitic infection. And it's barely fatal! Go spend all your precious funding studying something that actually kills people."

I don't look back at Gunderson's face, but I'm sure it's some wicked mask of contortion, twisted and knotted up on itself in anger and surprise.

I just want to get out of here, but I can't help looking into the lab as I storm down the hallway. Erica's in there, pipetting a sample into a small cylindrical tube. She's smiling while she works, chatting with someone I can't see from my vantage point on the outside. She looks fulfilled, gorgeous, happy. She's doing everything I should be doing.

Even if I wanted to follow 'Madame Leila's' advice to 'learn from her,' it's too late. I've burned that bridge; there's no way Gunderson would ever let me into her lab after that. They can all go to hell—'Madame Leila,' Dr. Gunderson, Erica—and burn.

CHAPTER EIGHT

I Know Where to Find Two Canoes, Babe

It's been twelve hours since my meeting with that unreasonable harpy Dr. Gunderson, and my mind can't settle. Without a conscious idea of where I'm going, my feet lead me to the Tombs, the bar near campus where all the Georgetown students go. It's quieter during the summer, of course, but there's still a decent crowd. I take a seat at the bar and tell the bartender to surprise me, but make it strong. I want to lose myself tonight, enough so I don't have to think about research, or medical school, or Erica, or Dr. Gunderson, or the girls upstairs, or, most of all, Mother and her scrutinizing gaze that always finds me wanting.

The bartender doesn't disappoint. The first sip of the ruby-red liquid burns my throat in the most delicious way, and I take a second large gulp.

"Whoa, slow down," he says, winking.

To spite him, I rip the straw from the glass, toss it aside, and gulp down the rest of the drink in one go. A gag rises up in my throat, but I shove it back down.

I slam the glass down on the sticky bar top and give the bartender my oiliest smile. My skin feels slick, and I wonder what he sees when he looks at me, because his entire face is an O of shock tinged with something like amusement.

He swallows, and I see his Adam's apple bob like a fishing lure. I imagine sinking a hook into the cartilage, pushing harder and harder into the rubbery firmness until I pierce his vocal cords.

"Another?" he finally says, and now I see it: the fear in his eyes, as if he sensed the horror of my thoughts. Good.

I just nod, and he floats away to get me what I asked for.

"You really pounded that one down," comes a squeaky voice from over my right shoulder. I turn to find a slightly pimpled, gangly guy who might as well be wearing a sign that says 'Looking for a hookup.' For some reason, he oozes a sort of unearned confidence, and I scowl.

"What's it to you?" I say.

Without invitation, he sits down on the empty stool next to me. "I'm Steve."

"I'm uninterested."

His face falls, but only for a second before regaining a greasy glow. "Do your friends call you something shorter?"

I do not laugh, because his joke is not funny. I want him to go away—possibly permanently. Maybe he would be a good subject for me to experiment with Adam's apples. I'd like to remove it and see how the loss affects that pitchy voice of his. "I don't have friends."

"Aw, don't say that," he says, and he even starts to put a heavy arm around my shoulder, as though I, of all people, look like easy prey.

"Hands off," I say, pushing his sweaty palm roughly away.

"Okay, okay," he says. "Man, for a girl who just sucked that drink down like it was water, you're pretty tense."

As if he could ever understand feeling truly 'tense.' It's time to send Steve's entitled ass packing once and for all.

"You want to know something interesting, Steve?" I ask.

Those eager eyes widen; oh God, he thinks I would actually engage with him. That'll make this even better. "What's that, babe?" I imagine him bound up on my bed, sweating and wailing as I run my knife down the length of his body.

"Have you ever heard of scaphism?"

"No, can't say that I have," he says, but light flicks behind his eyes in a way that indicates he thinks I'm about to tell him about some sort of arcane sexual practice.

"No?" I lean in closer, and he does, too. Our heads are almost touching. "It's this really intense experience that the ancient Persians used for people who'd been… naughty." I give him a wink to really drive it home.

The tiniest groan escapes his lips, and I wonder absently if he just blew his load. That wouldn't surprise me at all. "Keep talking," he says, in what he probably assumes is a seductive tone. It's not; his voice cracks on the last syllable, making his command sound like a question.

"So they'd take the person who'd been, well… naughty, and put them in a canoe with their arms and legs dangling outside the boat. Then they'd get lots and lots of honey…"

"… yeah?" He's almost drooling now.

"… and they'd pour it all over the person's naked body…"

His breath hitches and he mutters, "Oh…"

My voice speeds up: "And then they'd also force-feed them the rest of the honey, plus a ton of milk, cover them with another boat to seal them in, set them adrift far from rescue, and let them piss, shit, and vomit all over themselves until flies and maggots rotted their flesh and ate them alive."

It takes a moment for the eager, sex-starved sheen to leave Steve's eyes. When it does, he sits up so fast he almost slips off the stool—I wish he had, that would have been funny—and presses the back of his hand to his mouth, as if he's in danger of vomiting all over himself. I wish I had two canoes and my own private boathouse right about now. I'd quite like to see Steve shit himself to death under a mountain of buzzing flies.

"What the fuck," he finally says, looking at me like I'm some sort of wild animal he's coaxed into feeding from his palm before biting him savagely.

I shrug, reaching for my second drink that appeared while I was toying with Steve. "I think it's kind of hot."

He starts to stand and nearly stumbles again. "There is something seriously wrong with you," he says, a timid sort of anger crossing his unlovely features.

"Me? Am I the one who pushed my skinny little boy's body on a violently uninterested woman just trying to enjoy drinking alone?"

"Fuck you," he whispers, and coughs into his hand.

"Right back at you," I say, smiling sweetly.

He finally turns to leave, and I call out after him, "I know where we can find two canoes and some honey if you change your mind, babe!"

He yells something unintelligible, and I feel serene for the first time in weeks, maybe months. I didn't cut him physically, but I'm sure I left a psychic scar. With glee, I raise my glass to the bartender staring guardedly at me from behind the bar in a sort of cheers, and I down the rest.

Today has been a massive, pulsating frustration. Ignorant twits keep putting barriers up in front of me, blocking my path to research, to med school, to being the doctor I deserve to be. I'll knock down those barriers soon enough, along with the people who put them up, especially Erica—but not right now. Tonight, I'm just going to do what feels good, which usually makes someone else feel bad. I've earned it.

CHAPTER NINE

The Best Hangover Cure

Somehow, I make it back to my rathole of an apartment that smells like rusty dried blood all the time and, for now at least, vomit as well. I didn't make it to the toilet; the kitchen trash can is splattered with most of the alcohol I consumed at Tombs. I'm sitting at my kitchen table, pressing my forehead into my hands, hoping to physically force the dizziness out of my body.

After I scared off Steve, I felt invincible, powerful, like I could drink a whole handle of vodka by myself and still feel just fine. Clearly that was a mistake, because my head is pounding, my mouth tastes like bile, and my lips are starting to bleed from all the acid in my vomit.

There's a bottle of Advil at the top of my medicine cabinet, but if I stand up right now, I'm going to fall—and I probably can't keep the Advil down, regardless. It's not like there's anybody here to help me. I've always had to help myself. Even when I was a child sick in bed with the flu, Mother refused to 'coddle' me because 'I brought this on myself, hanging around with all those disgusting children.' Even if my father tried to creep in with a bowl of soup or a mug of tea, Mother would swat him away like a fly. He must have seen how much I needed him, but he shrank away under Mother's iron-hard glare.

To avoid knocking myself unconscious on the floor only to end up choking on my own vomit, I stay seated until I feel confident I can move. I hate the idea of having an actual roommate who shares my space, but right now it wouldn't be horrible to have someone who could offer a little assistance.

A wave of nausea rises, crests, and falls, leaving me dry-heaving, hunched over the table with its coppery scent. There can't be anything left in my stomach; the last thing I spit into the trash can was little more than phlegm.

I don't even know where my eyes are looking until I recognize the smooth leather of the antique doctor's bag. Without feeling fully in control of my hands, my fingers land on the bag, the leather soft and buttery with age. I caress it like most people would pet a puppy or the fuzz-soft head of a baby, neither of which I have much use for.

I blink and the bag is open, the instruments glittering inside. My fingers are moving on their own, like fleshy spiders skittering over dead bodies.

Reality skips for a second, and now a squirming rat is laid out in front of me like a gift, its body duct-taped to a metal tray. I don't remember trapping a rat, much less securing it to the tray. My arachnid fingers scuttle over my newly sharpened instruments. A laugh escapes my hoarse throat, nearly turning into a gag again, but I manage to stay upright. I don't want to puke anymore; it's starting to hurt.

I'm about to stand up to chug some water even though it's a bad idea, when a retch-like sob grabs hold of my throat and doesn't let go. Before I can choke it back down, I'm wailing like an abandoned Dumpster infant, snot dripping down my lips, salty water leaving my cheeks tight and red. The rat stares at me, seemingly shocked into silence by my disgusting display. After what feels like an eternity, I press the heels of my hands into my eyes, forcing the tears back inside. Eventually, my breath evens out.

I feel exorcised.

With a speed that leaves my drunk mind reeling, my fingers grip my tiniest scalpel, the one meant for delicate, small work. I shouldn't be doing anything like this tonight, when I'm still reeling—but here I am, and here's the rat, and I'm never one to pass up an opportunity to learn. My mind feels too jittery to write anything in my lab notebook, so I don't. I'll document everything later.

The rat is squirming again, but it's getting weaker. That duct tape isn't budging—not my normal restraint of choice, but whatever, good job, drunk Keely. The rat's eyes stare into mine, black and oily, and that's when I decide: this rat is going to live. I'm still going to cut him, but he's going to live. It's called vivisection, and it's hard—but, like most things in life, the hard ones are worth it. Maybe it's the alcohol giving me an extra gush of courage. I'm going to slice open the rat's chest and watch his heart beat, his lungs inflate, his stomach twitch. Then I'm going to sew him back up. That's what surgeons do to people all the time, and this is my chance to get a jumpstart on what I'm going to spend the rest of my life doing. As I put the tip of the scalpel to the rat's furry clavicle and press, I realize I haven't used the marijuana on him, but things are too far gone now for that. I press harder, committing to working quickly. My hands don't even shake.

Mother used to talk in great detail about her experiences performing surgery on live human patients. My father would say stupid things like, "Maybe this isn't the best subject at dinner?" or "Ellen, does Keely really need to hear about the teratoma you found in your patient's left breast?" But I relished every anecdote, tried to commit every word to memory. Mother's eyes shone with pride and joy when she talked about the surgeries she performed, something that never happened when she talked about me, even when I aced my AP exams, became a National Merit Scholar, and got into Georgetown.

A spurt of blood splatters my eyes and startles me from my reverie. I'm blinking hard, trying to wash away the gore that is tinting my vision crimson. The rat has stopped squirming.

I blink again, red trails running down my cheeks.

The rat is, without a doubt, dead.

If my vision weren't already scarlet, it would be now. Rage consumes me—rage at myself, at Mother, at my father, at Dr. Gunderson, at Erica, at

Professor Demetri—at every person who hurt me, every person who gave up on me, every person who dragged me down.

I stab the scalpel hard into the rat's rapidly cooling heart, spearing it like a kabob. Mother would be so ashamed of me, not because of what I've done, but because of what I haven't done. I haven't succeeded—yet.

CHAPTER TEN

I've Always Been More Comfortable in the Dark

I wake to the smell of sour meat some time later. You'd think after a night of heavy drinking I'd feel like a pile of actual excrement, but I don't. When I lift my head off the kitchen table, my thoughts are clear, and my vision isn't blurry or spinning.

In front of me, the partially dissected rat is still taped to the metal tray, the scalpel protruding from its shriveled heart like the sword in the stone. There's a wet sucking sound as I pull it out.

My doctor's bag is open on the floor, and I can't help but wonder if the pedo from the antique store has noticed it's gone yet. Even if he has, he doesn't know my name, and there's no way that shitty little shop has functioning security cameras. I almost want to go back to the store to check on the fallout from my theft, but I'm not sure I could control myself a second time around if he got close to me again. I certainly won't be torpedoing my life for a creep like him. I wouldn't be surprised if, when the cops search his premises to find his corpse when he inevitably dies amid his piles of junk, they find bits of mummified bodies. An antique clock with a finger lodged in it, the digit from a woman who went missing twenty years ago. A musty valise with half a foot locked inside, from a guy with a rap sheet who stopped causing trouble way too suddenly. An old garage sale-quality oil painting with streaks of dried blood mixed in with the red on the canvas, the last bit of DNA from a child who wandered into the guy's store and got permanently lost.

Enough woolgathering; it's time to clean up this mess and get out of here. Common sense would recommend I stand up slowly, but I don't. My knees straighten without any creaks or pops, and I charge into the bathroom to perform my ablutions. I don't have any food, but I'm not hungry. Instead, I chug water from a smudged glass, forcing myself to hydrate.

It's Tuesday, I think. It's 7:46 in the morning, and there's still no sound coming from upstairs. Come to think of it, I don't know what the girls upstairs do all day. Surely they must have summer jobs, but I also wouldn't be surprised if they fritter away their hours sleeping, eating junk, or slobbering all over their equally slovenly boyfriends.

I throw on some clothes, grab my bag, and head for the sidewalk. It's still pretty early, and I'm surprised to see Roger out on his lawn already. His shirt is on backwards, but he doesn't seem to care.

"Keely!" he calls out in that megaphone voice of his, as though I'm all the way down the block instead of passing right in front of him.

"Hey, Rog," I say.

He points at a squirrel climbing a tree across the street. "When I was a kid, squirrels were my favorite animals."

A bead of sweat runs down my back. "Well when I was a kid, I shoved Spencer Truitt down a flight of stairs because he cheated and his science fair project beat mine. His parents clearly helped him with it—I mean, the kid barely slid by in chemistry, and he wanted us all to believe he had bred microbes that could eat plastic, for God's sake. My project was better, and I did it all on my own. I deserved the win, not him. I wasn't going to let him go to the national science fair in California for a project he didn't even do. So, I waited until we were alone and he was at the top of the stairs, then I shoved him as hard as I could."

"Oh my goodness," Roger says, but his eyes are still focused on the squirrel across the street.

"Don't worry. He lived, but he was medically disqualified from attending the national science fair, and he had no memory of what happened. His spot went to me, not that it made any difference. Mother made sure I knew I'd always be second place."

I see a woman in hot pink athleisure rounding the corner a block away with half a dozen dogs. I'll have to finish up here quickly.

"I went to California once," Roger says, his expression dreamy.

"That afternoon, I dissected my first mouse. I wanted to see if its heart could still beat if it were broken. It couldn't. But how can that be true? Mine is broken, but it still beats."

Roger's not listening anymore; he looks like he's in a trance state. The dog walker is almost upon us now, and Roger's attention shifts to her.

"Good morning, doggies!" he says. Without saying goodbye, I slip past the mob of doodles and keep walking toward campus.

I stop at the crosswalk and wipe my nose on the inside of my shirt. The light turns green, and I cross the last street separating me from campus. I'm about to pass Darnall Hall on my left when a sharp-edged shoulder connects with my clavicle, throwing me off balance. I manage to catch myself before I fall, throwing a glare of volcanic hatred at the careless oaf who ran into me.

"Watch it, asshole," I breathe.

The asshole in question is, I register with amusement, none other than Scaphism Steve from the Tombs. What a small world!

When Steve recognizes me, his face turns the color of a death cap mushroom. He opens his mouth to say something, then closes it again.

I smirk, absently rubbing my clavicle, where a bruise is already starting to sprout. "I've got some honey in my bag, if you're interested," I say.

Steve doesn't reply. He stares at me for a few moments longer, as though his feet have forgotten how to move. Finally, a garbled, unintelligible "Gahh," exits his livery lips, and in a whoosh of fetid body odor, he's gone.

*　　*　　*

My armpits are sticky with sweat by the time I climb the short flight of stairs to the main doors of the first floor of Healy Hall. I push through them into the slightly less sticky air of the red-carpeted foyer. In front of me, the grand staircase that is always full of smiling parents and embarrassed-looking students cheesing for pictures during the school year is empty. A huge oil portrait of some long-dead Jesuit looks down from the landing with piggy, judgmental eyes. I glance around furtively, then raise a big middle finger to the portrait of the Jesuit, staring at me as if I'm less than him just because nobody calls me 'Father'.

"Keely?" Airhead Ani's voice makes me jump, and I stuff my outstretched hand in my pocket so fast I jam my fingers.

"What, Annie?" I say, more harshly than I intend. Usually I'm here before she is, and I'm annoyed that she's startled me. I always try to keep on an even keel around Airhead, as much as possible.

"Oh," she says, taken aback. "Um, it's Ani, remember? You know, rhymes with Donnie... I, uh, are you okay?"

"Fine," I say curtly. "Why?"

"Oh, nothing. It's just... your face is a little red."

"I'm fine," I say again, modulating my tone a bit better this time, I think.

"Okay. Well. I was just going to ask you if you'd gotten the envelopes from the second floor supply closet. I thought you said you were going to do that yesterday, but I can't find them anywhere."

I can't believe this sugar-sucking nitwit is accusing me of negligence. My cheeks start to burn, and I give Airhead a surreptitious evil eye. "I'll go get them now," I say. I can't remember if I got the damn envelopes or not, but either way, I already need to get away from her.

"Thanks," she calls out after me, but I pretend I don't hear her. I'm climbing the scarlet stairs two at a time, the air feeling hotter and hotter the higher I go. Healy is a painfully old building, and the AC isn't great. That's what I get for going to a three-hundred-year-old school, I suppose.

I reach the landing, give the black-cloaked, two-dimensional Jesuit another forceful middle finger, and start up the back half of the stairs, now taking them only one at a time. More portraits of dead priests line the mahogany-paneled walls, and my middle finger is starting to ache at the joint. I look down, and my face feels as red and hot as that crimson-colored carpet. My heart is pounding so hard I can hear it; hell, I bet Airhead can hear it downstairs in the relative cool of the office.

I reach the top of the staircase and take a few steps on the faded linoleum of the second floor. I manage to make it to the wall before I completely lose my balance, falling against the wood paneling and sliding to the dusty ground. My head is throbbing, my vision swimming. For a brief second, I swear I see red horns painted on the Jesuit hanging on the landing. I blink, and the horns disappear, but a faint halo like an afterthought remains. I think I might be sick.

Maybe I was still drunk when I woke up this morning, and it just took this long for all that alcohol from last night to finally dissipate enough to leave me feeling like total and complete horseshit. I probably should have risked that Advil with the water I chugged.

I take a few more breaths, trying not to gag on my own saliva, which tastes like sulfury rotten eggs. When I'm able to push myself up to a shaky standing position, I head off to get those damn envelopes before Airhead gets perturbed. The last thing I want is for her to come up here and find me like this. She'll just try to give me some sort of weird remedy from her enormous Louis Vuitton purse her parents got her because she begged—yes, I heard the whole ridiculous saga. I don't need her ginger oil or her lavender lozenges or her 'miracle cure for hangovers,' which is really just Pedialyte. What kind of infantile adult uses overpriced medicine for babies on herself instead of just drinking Gatorade to get the same electrolytes?

The force of my hatred for Airhead Ani gets me going again, but just those few steps down the hall leave me feeling drained, and the sunlight coming through the thin, slit-like windows is burning my eyes. I almost feel like I do after yet another failed sexual encounter, the kind where the guy, drunk and eager in the beginning, gets scared when I pull out my knife and starts pushing me away—not too strongly, of course, because I've tied him up—and ends up mewling like a lost kitten instead of taking it like he should. I never end up satisfied, and the guys always leave with tears in their eyes. They'll never tell a soul, that would emasculate them for sure, so it's not like my hunting ground really diminishes with each encounter. I think about Scaphism Steve; he would have been pliable enough, but the bone-deep revulsion I felt about him from the instant he invaded my space made him a no-go.

I feel like I'm sinking deeper and deeper into some sort of pit of despair so painful it feels physical instead of metaphorical. This is the worst hangover I've ever had.

The supply closet door looms in front of me, dark wood with a tarnished gold knob. I twist it hard enough to hurt the skin on my palm, and the door opens grudgingly. Inside, there's a single bare lightbulb, but I don't turn it on, knowing the light would be too bright and it would give me an instant migraine.

Feeling around in the gloom, my hand lands on a box with the lid ripped off. I shuffle my fingers through it and feel dozens of letter-size envelopes lined up like playing cards in a deck. I grab the box, which ends up being a poor choice, because somehow I lose my balance. When I fall to the floor, I feel the envelopes fly around me in a scene far too dramatic to be real, but it is. Then, because my life is one giant slip n' slide of agony, the door closes, leaving me in velvety darkness, my ass smarting from hitting the bare wood floor with more force than seems possible.

I'm alone in the dark, but it's not an unfamiliar place for me to be. As a kid, I spent a ton of time in my frilly cupcake room with the door shut and the lights off, trying to pretend I wasn't in a frilly cupcake room, wasn't Keely Rexroth at all. I pretended I was someone else—a girl with a mother who actually cared, who looked at her when she spoke, who saw her as she was instead of how she wanted her to be. A girl with a mother who thought she was good enough and a father who wasn't afraid to give her the comfort she needed.

I take a few deep breaths, trying not to choke on the stuffy air. I am okay in this supply closet, a familiar darkness caressing my sweaty skin. My head still hurts like it's been stabbed with an ice pick, but without all that searing light, I can finally focus my thoughts for a minute.

I'm in a safe place, but those thoughts go somewhere lonely and distant, so far away I can't even call them back. My mind is an anchor thrown out to sea, but the line has broken and it's drifting down to the bottomless depths, and there's nothing I can do about it.

I feel a wetness on my face, and I'm not sure if it's tears or blood from my lips, which I have a bad habit of chewing like they're gum. I run my tongue over my mouth, finding iron-tasting bitterness.

I suck my lips into the black hole of my mouth. I'm the kind of person who likes my steak as raw as possible, because the taste comforts me, centers me. I'm still adrift, but now I'm not rocking quite so much.

One of my hands is still clutching an envelope, and I crumple it ferociously. If it weren't for Airhead and her ridiculous need for envelopes right this very moment, I wouldn't be in this cramped closet feeling way too many emotions. Nobody really needs envelopes nowadays. Airhead Ani can just send an email like a normal person.

I know Airhead was put in that office with me specifically to torment me with her vapidity. I know I'm a 'ticking time bomb,' as my dear former roommate put it, someone who is difficult to handle safely and who might blow up at any second, and those self-righteous Jesuits put me with Airhead, just to see what would happen.

My other hand finds a fresh envelope on the floor, and before I fully understand what's happening, my fingers are gripping the paper like a violin bow and I'm using my opposite wrist as the violin strings, slicing, slicing,

slicing. If I were an instrument, the volume would be at *fortissimo*. My flesh burns where the paper runs across it, until the moment of sweet relief comes, the skin opens, the warm ichor starts trickling, and the hand clutching the envelope is still going up and down. I haven't done something like this to myself since I arrived at Georgetown; I've been channeling all my pain into the animals I dissect, allowing us both to be liberated by the flow of their blood. After such a long hiatus, the slicing feels even more euphoric, like a drug addict relapsing after a year of sobriety. Even if I wanted to make it stop, I don't think I could, because now the rest of me is in the bottomless depths with that anchor, and I don't even want to try to fight my way back to the surface.

CHAPTER ELEVEN
A First Aid Kit Won't Fix This

I have no idea how long I've been in this closet. I can't see, but I know my arms are criss-crossed with stinging, razor-thin paper cuts. Airhead's probably thinking I just left her in the office on her own, or maybe she's so absorbed in texting her Ken-doll boyfriend or reading *The Bachelor* fan blogs that she hasn't even realized how long I've been gone. Either way, when I get back, I'll just pull a sweater over my arms and tell her the line was long at Starbucks. That's something her tiny, caffeine- and sugar-fried brain can understand. It won't even matter that I won't have a Starbucks milkshake concoction clutched in my hand. Airhead isn't that observant.

My tailbone aches from the fall, and I shift slightly on the floor to take some pressure off my ass. My cheeks are wet again, and a slime-trail of snot is snaking down from my nostril to my upper lip. Sharp pains stab into my chest, but I welcome the pain because it helps ground me.

I should get up to leave, I really should, but I feel glued to the floor. If I wanted to stand up, I know I could, but a heaviness stronger than any bout of mild depression I've ever felt keeps me pinned. Moving feels both unnecessary and impossible. I could stay here for hours, days even. As a child, hunting for ways to earn Mother's attention, I often wondered how long it would take them to find me if I slit my wrists in the bath. Considering how long it took them to even notice I was gone after I hid under the couch cushions for the entirety of Thanksgiving Day when I was six, I always thought they wouldn't have found me in the bath, surrounded by cloudy pink water, before it was too late.

*　*　*

There's almost zero warning before I hear the handle of the supply closet door twisting, a screechy, rusty sound, and then the door is opening, light is tumbling in, and I'm shielding my eyes with my shredded arms like some sort of sickly vampire in a bad horror movie.

"Ah!" A deep male voice pops the bubble of silence I've been enjoying, and it takes a minute before my eyes adjust enough for me to open them wide and see who exactly has intruded on my private moment.

The man standing in the rectangle of light in the open doorway isn't totally unfamiliar, but I can't place his name. His black clothes give him away as a Jesuit, which isn't exactly surprising—this whole floor is full of offices for the Jesuits. His face is jowly, his head mostly bald, and his eyes are a blue so light they're almost white.

He holds out one slightly pudgy hand, the one not clutching a massive mug, to help me up. "Hello there," he says, evidently recovered from the surprise I gave him.

I ignore his hand and push myself up into a crouch, then to a standing position. When I look at his face again, his eyes are darting all over my figure like some sort of pervert. He is a priest, after all.

When he doesn't say anything, I follow his eyes down my body, feeling self-conscious about my arms. The cuts aren't as bad as I'd thought, but they're also impossible to ignore. Bright, angry-looking scratches line both of my forearms, as though I've gotten in a fight with a cat and lost (although, when I'm trapping the occasional stray cat foolish enough to get too close to my apartment, I never lose. I've found the easiest way to subdue a cat is to mix crushed-up Benadryl into a bowl of mashed-up Spam).

I expect the Jesuit to ask me what happened, but all he says, in a tone that's too forced and cheery, is, "And what would your name be?"

Well, asshole, if I could have picked my own name it would have been something darker and more androgynous, like Bryn or Clio or Dex, but my parents named me after Mother's mother, whom she idolized. Mother has never let me forget just how much I've failed to live up to the moniker. "Keely," I say, the name like sand, gritty and sharp, on my tongue.

"Keely," he repeats, rolling my name around in his too-wet mouth. He pulls a neatly folded white handkerchief from his pocket and hands it to me. "That's a lovely name. I'm Father O'Meara. I don't believe we've met before?"

He doesn't recognize me, but he looks familiar. Then again, I work in the Chaplains' Office. I'm sure I've seen him around, I've just been lucky enough until now never to have spoken to him. I wipe the handkerchief across my cheeks, then cup my nose and blow loudly. The square of immaculate cloth smells like peppermint. "I don't think so," I say. I refold the handkerchief, now laden with my snot and shame, and hold it back out to him.

"You can keep that," he says, obviously trying not to grimace. I stuff the dirty handkerchief into my pocket. Finally, he addresses the slashed-up elephant in the room. "Are your arms alright?"

I look down again, trying to act surprised at what I see there. "Oh, wow," I say. I'm normally a good liar but my voice sounds strange, even to me, as if the dark hole I've seemed to have fallen into since walking into the building this morning is sucking away my carefully crafted facade. "I was looking for envelopes, and then I slipped, and I guess it just sort of…" I trail off, trying to sound incredulous, but I can tell I don't quite pull it off.

"Mhmm," he says noncommittally. "I have a First Aid Kit in my office, and a lovely kettle of peppermint tea. Shall we?"

One pudgy hand gestures down the hallway as he steps out of the doorframe. His blue-white eyes are cold, calculating, sharper than his demeanor would make you believe. This is a man who misses nothing, and deep in my stomach, I feel a kindling of fear, a hot violet flame.

I don't want to go to his office just to sit through more of his intrusive questions, but I don't have much choice. I already look strange to this man; I can't afford to let him think there's something actually wrong with me.

He's walking down the hall now, and my traitorous feet are following along behind him. The ceilings are high, and our footsteps echo in the tubelike space. There's a rustling behind me, and my fingers find a stray envelope stuck to the back of my pants. I grip it and pull, letting it float away in my wake.

We reach the door of his office, which is open. This guy must be one of the top Jesuits or something, because his window overlooks Healy Square, surely one of the most coveted views. It's big, too—there's a dark wood desk in the middle, absolutely massive, and the left wall is covered in a floor-to-ceiling bookcase, complete with one of those brass library ladders that slides along the shelves. In front of the desk are two plump leather chairs, and to the right there's a humming mini-fridge and a worn couch covered in throw pillows. I want to laugh, because this is not what I pictured for a Jesuit who's taken a vow of poverty, but laughing would not be the right move at this particular moment. Plus, if I start laughing, I don't know if I'll be able to stop. Instead, I sit down in one of the chairs in front of his desk while he pours tea into a chipped ceramic mug. He hands it to me; I'm surprised at its weight. It wouldn't take much force to brain him with this thing.

"So, Keely," he says, rummaging through his drawers for the First Aid Kit. "What brought you to the supply closet?" His voice is so light and sunny, as though he's a kindly shopkeeper in a New England town asking me what brought me to his neck of the woods. I don't buy it, but I can't do anything besides answer.

"Like I said, I was looking for envelopes," I say. "I work in the Chaplains' Office downstairs."

O'Meara claps his hands together, the sound meaty and moist. "Oh, of course! That's where I've seen you before. I thought you looked familiar.

You've got those unmistakeable gray eyes, like Athena."

I don't know what to say to that, so I just stay silent. He's not the first man to comment on my eyes, and I'm sure he won't be the last, either. Men like to point out obvious things about your physical appearance as though you should be thanking them for discovering something secret about you. My eyes roam over his desktop, looking for a pair of scissors, just in case an opportunity presents itself to use them. They might be more convenient than the mug.

Finally, he finds what he's looking for in his drawers and sits up straight, putting the First Aid Kit on the desktop. "Now," he says, "let's have a look at those cuts."

The whole thing feels weirdly invasive, and in addition to the ball of fear burning in my abdomen, I start to feel a twin flame of anger somewhere in my throat. I can take care of myself, and I certainly don't need this pervy priest getting his nose all in my business.

I do the bare minimum to appease him, only slightly turning my elbow creases toward him so he can see the tic-tac-toe of cuts. In the bright light streaming through his windows, the cuts really don't look that bad. I try to tell myself they look accidental.

"Hmmm," he says, ripping the plastic envelope off an individually packaged antiseptic wipe. He unfolds the towelette and hands it to me. "Here you go, let's start with that."

The towelette is uncomfortably warm in my hands, but I swipe it quickly up and down both arms. It stings more than the cuts, and I narrowly avoid cursing. It wouldn't do to curse in front of a Jesuit.

"Good, good," O'Meara hums. He fans out a set of bandages between his hands, studies my cuts, which are all up and down the skin from my knobby wrists to my elbows, and then tuts. "You've got quite a few of those," he says, again stating the obvious. "They don't look too bad, though. Do you think any of them are deep enough for a Band-Aid?"

"No," I say, probably too quickly. "No, I don't think so. Like I said, they're just paper cuts. An accident."

"Mhmm," he says again, and I hate his patronizing tone. He doesn't believe me.

"Well," I say, eager to be out of his office and away from his penetrating gaze. "Thanks for the help, Father. I really should be getting back now." I push up from the chair and start to leave.

"Keely," he says. "Perhaps these would help?" From a drawer of his desk he pulls a stack of fresh white envelopes. "No need for you to go back to the supply closet, eh?"

I can't tell what his angle is, but I take the envelopes from his outstretched hand anyway. "Thank you," I say, but there's no warmth in my voice. I set the mug down on his desk, ignoring the coaster he's placed there for my convenience.

"You're very welcome," he says, holding eye contact for a beat too long, those blue-white irises scanning my face, making me feel like one of my own animals strapped to my table, about to be dissected.

"Well… bye," I say, turning and heading for the doorway.

"Have a blessed day!" he calls out behind me, but I'm far enough down the hall that it isn't weird for me to avoid responding.

As I walk down the hallway, the echoes of my footfalls sounding even louder than they did before, I can't help but feel that something has shifted in my universe. I've been alone for so long, operating on the edges of most peoples' awareness, and I've liked it that way. I've liked it very much.

Now, there's a rip in the dark fabric of my life that's been a shield from prying eyes. For the first time in a long time, somebody has turned. Somebody is looking right at me. Worst of all, somebody is seeing me.

CHAPTER TWELVE

What Is He Doing to You?

When I come back down from the second floor, hands stuffed with envelopes and forearms covered in paper cuts, not to mention at least an hour after leaving the Chaplains' Office, Airhead Ani doesn't so much as say, "Oh my God, what happened?" As I slip into the chair behind my desk, all she says is, "You know, I think I'm going to try eyelash extensions."

"What?" I grunt, hoping I've misheard her. Some people just want to give you reasons to hurt them, and apparently Airhead is one of them. It's less fun for me that way, but hey, I'm not going to say no to someone offering their fragile selves up on a silver platter.

She takes the envelopes from my hands. "Oh, I probably won't do it, I was just thinking—it's so annoying having to curl my lashes and put mascara on everyday, maybe if I just go for it and get the extensions, I can save some time in the morning."

My chair squeaks as I swivel, and I realize Airhead switched our chairs while I was gone. It is a well-known fact that of the two chairs in the Chaplains' Office, one is good—smooth, comfortable, ergonomic—and one is bad—squeaky, uncomfortable, stiff. She knew the good chair was mine, and yet she still switched them.

So I don't really feel bad—not that I ever do—about ruining her day.

"You know," I say, "I actually have this lash growing stuff one of my science friends gave me. It's from South Korea, where, as you know, beauty is, like, their number one thing. She swears by this stuff. I haven't tried it yet, but hey—I can get more. I'll give it to you, if you want? Friends get it for free." I smile, hoping it looks genuine, but not really caring if it doesn't. It's not like Airhead is sharp enough to notice.

"Oh my God," she says, squealing. "Yes, that would be amazing! Thank you!"

"You got it, girl," I say, winking.

A few hours later, it's almost time to head home, and Airhead has spent the rest of the day playing Candy Crush on her phone, with the exception of the brief interlude when Father Dancy came in to talk, trying to prove he can still carry on an intelligent conversation. She was all ears, heavy on the flattery, sucking up. Father Dancy is the oldest person I've ever seen in my entire life. I've heard he's only eighty-four, but he looks well over one hundred. In my personal opinion, he's mostly senile and shouldn't be teaching anymore. For God's sake, he called us 'gentle ladies' and, with a straight face, asked if it was 'uncomfortable wearing pantyhose in this heat.' I could easily slip something into a cupcake I bake just for him, something that wouldn't leave a trace. Or, I could follow him back to the Jesuit Residence one evening, wait for him to get to the top of a set of stairs—God knows Georgetown is full of them—and then stick out one foot. That's all it would take. His bones must be like glass. I'd like to hear them shatter.

Now, I'm using my phone to look up Korean skincare brands on Amazon, hoping to find a tube of something that looks like mascara but has zero English on it. I'll dump out most of the mascara and add just the tiniest bit of Nair or some other hair remover. Airhead's too stupid to realize what she'll actually be getting. I lick my lips, thinking about how she'll come to me, completely eyelash-less, crying, asking me what is this stuff? I'll just say that's how it works, you lose all your old growth eyelashes first to make room for the new, longer, stronger ones. It makes for a more permanent solution, Annie, you'll see. Just trust me.

She'll nod and smile and be grateful, maybe correct me on the pronunciation of her stupid name again, and just keep loading up her eyes with Nair until she goes blind. The whole situation is not unlike Regina George and her Kalteen bars in *Mean Girls*—how Regina gets fatter and fatter without having the tiniest inkling why it's happening. I love that scene; I must have watched it a thousand times on YouTube, minimizing the browser window in a flash if I ever heard Mother's footfalls outside my room.

Seriously, sometimes I wonder how people like Airhead get into Georgetown.

After an eternity, work is over, and I'm feeling pretty good—I've got a plan (I just ordered a tube of Korean 'mascara' on Amazon, it'll be here tomorrow), I'm feeling even-keeled again, and I bet there's a new animal in my trap tonight. I hope it's a squirrel; there's something soothing about petting an amputated squirrel tail. They're so soft, like a feather duster.

As I walk through campus back to my basement apartment, my hands start to cramp. At first, there's just a tiny tingle in the tips of my fingers, and I ignore it, thinking maybe it's an effect of the heat, making my hands swell. As I pass Reiss, the feeling gets worse—I try to bend my fingers, but they feel stiff and unyielding. When I do finally succeed in moving my knuckles, I can't unbend them, leaving my hands stuck in a claw-like rictus. Something is wrong.

Deep breaths, deep breaths. I'm a scientist, and I'm going to be a surgeon. I can figure this out.

I walk faster, past Darnall Hall, across the hospital parking lot, all the way to the intersection of 37ᵗʰ and Reservoir Road. The cuts along my arms are pulsing, and when I look down, I see thin rivulets of blood breaking through the razor-thin scabs.

Heat and humidity and maybe not enough water, that's all it is. I don't recall when I last had a drink of water. I also don't think I ate lunch today.

I don't remember any of it well, I only remember the day in flashes: being in O'Meara's office; Father Dancy's unwelcome visit; talking to Airhead about her ridiculous eyelash extensions—everything in between is a bit of a blur, and now I can feel the hot liquid pooling in the cups of my curled hands, and with each step droplets of scarlet fall to the pavement.

As I get closer to my apartment, I feel my fingernails digging into my palms, hard, harder, hardest, until the skin breaks open like the peel of an orange, more blood spilling out. My hands are soaked now, saturated, I can feel it, I'm leaving a crimson trail behind me. My eyes stay straight ahead as I walk—I don't want to see what's happening, it's enough to feel it—

"Keely!" comes Roger's voice from barely five feet away. I didn't even notice him standing in front of his dry flower beds.

"I can't—" I squeak, hoping he'll just go away, but he doesn't.

"There's a cardinal in that tree," Roger says, pointing behind me. Instead of turning to look, my eyes drop to my hands. I can't avoid it anymore.

I suck in air like a dying fish—there's nothing there.

"What's wrong, Keely?" Roger's voice sounds very far away now.

When I look down, my paper cuts are scabbed and dry, and my hands are smooth and unscathed, with no pools of scarlet, no whiplash of gore. My fingers unfurl like flower petals, and before I can make sense of everything, I'm running away from Roger, my hand is gripping my key, I'm unlocking the door, and then I'm descending the short flight of stairs into the basement.

The chair at my kitchen table is scarred and heavy, and I slump into it, my bruised tailbone hitting the wood with a painful thunk. No, whatever I think is happening isn't happening. I'm just overtired and dehydrated; I read a case study once about a man who got lost in the Sonoma Desert for fourteen hours without water, and by the time he stumbled onto some road somewhere and got rescued, he was having hallucinations. He thought he was walking through the gates of Heaven—ha, to think such a place exists!—so when he got in the good Samaritan's car, he tried to kiss the driver's feet as if she were God.

I just need some water, that's all, just some water and I'll be fine.

On shaky legs, I walk to the sink, grab a glass from the cupboard, and fill it with water. I drink greedily, only just now realizing how thirsty I am. When the glass is empty, I fill it again and, again, I empty it.

The glass goes into the sink and I stand there, heaving, panting, feeling the sharp pain in my chest like an undertow of blackness threatening to pull me away and out to the dark sea. Something isn't right with me, I know that, but this feels off in an entirely new way. It's not just poorly controlled costochondritis.

I'm back at the kitchen table, sitting, and the doctor's bag is cracked open in front of me. I don't remember seeing it on the table when I came in, but I was not lucid. I can't be sure I'm lucid now, either. I should know how long it takes for water in your stomach to enter your bloodstream, but I don't.

Then my fingers are inside the bag, flitting over the instruments that have the power to heal and harm in equal measure. It all depends on context and intent, right? I tip the bag over, letting the instruments clatter onto the table. I thought I did a better job cleaning them, but several are still stained with rat blood. The tableau reminds me of one of my favorite movies, *The Texas Chainsaw Massacre*. I should really rewatch that when I get a chance.

The cuts on my arms are pulsing, that familiar, dull pain that soon gives way to the tingling pleasure that makes the embarrassing need for bloodshed so worth it. The wave of depression recedes like the tide going out.

"What should I do?" I ask the silent basement, aware even as the words leave my lips that I'm speaking to no one.

"About what?" comes a barking voice from the direction of the stairs. I let out a breathy squeal, and I can't tell if that's anger or fear running through my veins.

"Keely?" another voice yells, and now I recognize them—it's a couple of the girls upstairs.

When I say nothing, hoping they'll just go away, the first one knocks loudly on the stairwell wall and then narrates what she's doing. "Knock, knock!" she says. "Anybody home?"

Footsteps start to descend, and like a gunshot I'm on my feet and standing at the base of the stairs. This is the biggest downside to my basement apartment—there's a door separating me from the upstairs, but the key is the same one that opens the front door, which means those girls can intrude on my privacy whenever they want. I've been a fool to find comfort in a false sense of security, thinking a twist of the lock from my side of the door would deter them if they really wanted to come down here.

"What is it?" I say.

"We just need to talk to you about something," one of them says. I level a penetrating stare at them, the same look I use to stymie inquisitive tourists who might ask me for directions to the Leavey Student Center or the Washington Monument. Two of my roommates stare back at me, seemingly unperturbed. I haven't seen them in awhile. Time has not been good to them; a fresh breakout of angry acne on one, a terrible haircut on the other. I stifle the urge to point these things out.

They reach the bottom of the stairs, and instead of getting the hint that I do not want them to invade my private space, they elbow themselves around me, heading toward my kitchen table.

Oh, no. My kitchen table is still strewn with dirty surgical equipment, something that is definitely for my eyes only. Trying to be as discreet as possible, I shove my way past them, blocking their view of the table with my body.

"What is it?" I repeat. Beads of sweat are popping out on my forehead so forcefully I can almost hear them. Whatever happens, I can't let them see my instruments. I try to make myself as big as possible to keep their view obscured.

"Maybe we should sit down?" one of them says, making a move for my table.

"No!" I say. "My kitchen is—uh—cluttered right now." I hate how flustered I sound, how weak and guilty.

"Dude, we don't care," the other one says.

Out of the corner of my eye, I spot my backpack dangling by one frayed strap from one of my kitchen chairs. With movements so quick I surprise myself, I grab the backpack and hoist it onto the table, covering the instruments. It will have to do.

Just in case it doesn't, I slip the smallest scalpel into my pocket—for insurance.

"Fine," I say, turning back to them. "Sit."

They make themselves far too comfortable, and I perch rigidly in my own seat. With terror, I wonder if they would have come into my private sanctuary even if I wasn't home.

"So, uh, Keely," one of them says. "Me and Carly wanted to talk to you, because, um, it's been a little loud down here."

I blink. How could they possibly hear me over their nightly ruckus?

"Tiff is just being nice. Miriam and Penny are pretty freaked out by the weird noises they keep hearing coming from here."

Ah. So those are their names—not that I care.

"Weird noises?" I repeat. Maybe if I play innocent, they'll think I am. It usually works.

"Yeah," the one called Tiff says. "I don't know, like, squeals? Animal-sounding stuff?"

Carly's eyes are roaming around my apartment. I need to get them out of here as soon as possible before they see something they shouldn't. I have my scalpel, but I don't want to clean up another mess.

I plaster on a fake smile. "Oh, my God," I say. "I'm so embarrassed. Yeah, um—that was me."

"That was you?" Carly says, raising a skeptical eyebrow.

I look down in a show of mock chagrin. "Well, I wasn't alone," I say.

Tiff's pimpled face breaks out in a too-big smile. "Oh, shit," she says. "So Keely's finally taking our advice after all!"

Carly isn't so easily convinced. I need to keep an eye on her from here on out, mostly because I think she'll be keeping one on me as well. "Really. You had a guy down here?" She pauses, considering me. "Or a girl?"

It's time to end this, now. "What can I say? Evan is really good with his hands." I smirk. "And tongue."

"I'm so proud of you," Tiff says, elbowing Carly.

"Still, though, those are some weird-ass sounds," Carly says. "Girl, what is he doing to you?"

"More like what isn't he doing to me," I say. "You name it, we've done it. You girls should really think about being more adventurous."

"Jesus," Carly mutters. "I don't want anything to do with a guy who would make me squeal like a dying animal."

For a second, my smiling mask shivers, but they don't catch it. Thank God for dim basement lighting.

"Well I certainly would," Tiff says. "I haven't had a good hookup in ages."

I pull my phone from my pocket, making a show of pretending to get a text. "Oh, that's actually Ethan right now," I say.

Carly's eyes snap back to me. "I thought you said his name was Evan?"

Carly, you're annoyingly sharper than I thought. "It is! We role-play, sometimes I'm Keely and sometimes I'm Kelly, you know how it is."

"Hm," Carly says. "Right."

"Come on, Carls, let's go," Tiff says. "Leave Keely to her sexting."

"Fine," Carly says, getting up slowly. "But yeah. You know. Keep it quiet."

Tiff leans in conspiratorially. "I don't care if you're loud. I can live vicariously through you." She stands and winks. I want to throw up.

"Have fun with Evan! Or Ethan! Whatever his name is," Carly says over her shoulder.

"Get it, girl," Tiff adds.

Their footsteps fade away as they climb the stairs, then the traitorous door shuts with a thud that no longer sounds as solid as it used to. I don't even bother to run up and lock it behind them—now that the barrier has been so brazenly breached, there's no way I can ever feel safe here again. I slump in my chair, the air whooshing out of my lungs in one long blow. My heart is jackhammering in my chest. That was too close.

This place, what should have been my secret, private haven, has been compromised. It's all too much, between Carly's beady eyes scrutinizing me at home and O'Meara's inopportune probing at work. There has to be somewhere else, because if I don't find a new place, I won't be able to experiment. I won't be able to advance my education, and that is absolutely unacceptable.

I push my backpack away, the surgical tools clattering underneath it, and press my forehead into the ugly wooden table. It still smells coppery and rancid. I sit there for a long time. When my eyes drift closed, I let myself slip away into precious oblivion—the only place I have that is truly safe.

*   *   *

I'm dreaming, I have to be. There's simply no other explanation. My feet are moving, I can see them, barefooted, slapping the sidewalk outside of Darnall Hall. A hot breath of night air flows over my face, and my cheeks feel so warm I must have a fever. Someone is coming from the other direction, another student, and my mouth opens and I say, "Hey there," and the boy gives me a strange look, a backwards nod, and keeps walking. My mouth is frozen in a rictus grin, and I desperately yearn for this to be sleep paralysis instead of something more dangerous. I've read about it, and maybe if I can wake myself up somehow, I'll be able to move for real, but something's wrong, because I can feel every chunk of gravel press up against the soles of my feet, every sticky droplet of humidity bead on my skin, every whoosh of fetid air as another person passes me by, the strange barefoot girl who can't stop smiling.

Something is wrong, very wrong. Darkness steals back over me, and I gratefully let it carry me away.

The next thing I know, there's a comforting warmth pressing against my breasts and stomach. In response, my body has molded itself around the source of this lovely heat. I want to stay in this liminal space between sleep and wakefulness, where I can feel the calming power of this connection without having to think too hard. A sense of relaxation I can't remember ever feeling before steals over me. This is what it's like not to have to be alone.

Wait. Sharp tingles of awareness pop my snug bubble. I should be alone right now. I haven't invited anyone into my apartment, into my bed. Evan/Ethan isn't real. This is bad; whoever—or whatever—is in my bed with me should not be here.

Panic evaporates my last vestiges of drowsiness like sunlight on morning fog. My breath is spurting out in shallow gasps, and I'm trying to be as still as possible as pain radiates through my sternum. The lump of warmth next to me snores and twitches, and I nearly scream, reflexively reaching for the scalpel I keep on my bedside table, my hand scrabbling in the empty air.

When my eyes finally adjust to the dark, I can barely make out the contours of the room I'm in. It looks like my old dorm room: a narrow rectangle walled in by white cinderblock, cheap wooden furniture crammed in like Tetris pieces. This is not my basement apartment. This is not my room. This is not my bed.

No, no. It's happening again. Mother isn't here to tie me to the bed anymore, the ropes leaving rashy marks I covered with long sleeves and tall socks.

The lump next to me snores again, deep and throaty. It's a boy. I'm in bed with some boy who lives in the dorms.

I slip my hand back behind me, feeling for the edge of the mattress. I need to get out of here, right now.

The boy is facing the wall, and he must feel the way my hand is grasping for escape, because he pushes back against me, snuggling. Still asleep, he belches softly, and it reeks of stale beer and sulfur. My lips curl in disgust, and I can't stay here for one more second.

As swiftly as possible, I pull back the sheets and slip to the floor. The boy flips over to face me, and I freeze, crouching low enough to smell the decades of foot sweat ground into the nubby carpet—now my own will be a part of the stench, too.

"Wait, come back," he says, but his voice is still thick with sleep, and it sounds more like 'Way, cun ba."

My heart is fluttering in my chest, my breath still coming in shockwave gasps. I can't waste any more time. I make a break for the door, ripping it open. The hallway lights are never off in the dorms, and for a brief moment, the boy's room is coated in a bilious yellow. It's brief, but it's enough.

The boy wakes up.

"Hey!" he calls out, more coherently, just as the door closes. "Who are you? What the fuck!"

I can tell from the arrangement of the floor that I'm in Darnall Hall, my old dorm. Muscle memory propels me to the stairwell, and I fly down, taking the steps two, three at a time. I don't stop until I'm on 37th street, nearly back to my apartment.

Just outside of a sphere of streetlight, I let myself collapse under a tree. Tears streak down my face, pooling in the hollow of my throat. I'm not wearing any shoes, and another bolt of panic shoots through me as I realize I may have left something behind in the boy's room. Please, no. I don't know how I'd explain away my shoes in his room, much less something more damning—my house key, or maybe my ID.

I can't stay here sprawled on the uneven sidewalk. There's the faintest hint of light peeking over the Burleith rooftops, and I'm not going to be accosted by some early morning jogger or overeager dog walker. The collar of my shirt is wet with tears, but at least I'm wearing a shirt. On bruised and blistered feet, I limp the few remaining blocks home, grateful to find the outside door to my apartment is unlocked.

My backpack and doctor's bag are still on top of the kitchen table, and I collapse in a chair, reaching for my scalpels. The tears won't stop coming, and I imagine sticking a surgical needle into my tear ducts to sew them up for good.

I can feel my face grimacing. My body still remembers the warmth of another person next to me, the way it made me feel less alone. A deep, shuddery breath whooshes from between my cracked lips, and I wonder, not for the first time, if I should finally get some help.

Mother's voice slithers through the air, the memory slapping me like a cold wind. "Absolutely not," she said when my father brought it up at dinner one night when I was eleven. "Keely does not need therapy." She spat out the word like it was dirty, and my father recoiled.

"Ellen," he said, his voice meek. "Keely told me she's been having some troublesome thoughts—"

Mother turned to me. "Keely," she said coolly, "are you having troublesome thoughts?"

There was only one way to respond when Mother was like this. "They're not that bad," I said, risking a glance at my father. That's not what I'd told him yesterday, when he'd found the neighbor's dead hamster in a shoebox under my bed, stiff from rigor mortis. I'd been studying its decomposition, taking notes in my diary. My father had sat me down and we had the only real and honest conversation I can ever remember us having—and I threw it away the moment Mother stared at me with those steely gray eyes, the same ones that are nestled into my own skull.

"See, Howard?" Mother hissed. "There's nothing wrong with Keely." She glanced over at me again, saw me picking at my peas. "She's certainly not perfect, but she doesn't need therapy. She just needs discipline. You and I both know, Howard, that psychiatry is the red-headed stepchild of medicine. It's ugly, unnecessary, and a complete waste of time. Not to mention a complete waste of money."

I didn't look up, but I could feel my father staring at me with his watery blue eyes. It had taken a lot for him to stand up to Mother even a little bit, and I had let him down. There was no rebuilding that shaky bridge, and I knew it.

"But, Ellen—" he tried, but she cut him off, as she always did. His weak chin, mirrored on my own face, wobbled.

"Enough, Howard. I know about the hamster, you don't need to go into it again. I'm eating, for God's sake. It's not a 'cry for help.' Don't be dramatic. What would Keely need help for? Do we not provide her with every damn thing she needs?"

My father remained silent, and Mother turned her wrath on me. "Keely. Do we not provide you with every damn thing you need?"

I speared a pea, then pushed it off my fork again. "I have everything I need, Mother," I said, staring at my plate.

"Look at me when you speak to me," she said.

My eyes rose to meet hers. "I have everything I need."

Instead of smiling, she sneered. "That's right, you do. Now from here on out, you need to do better, Keely. No more of this dead animal nonsense, and no more talk of ludicrous psychiatry."

We ate the rest of our dinner in silence, but the message was loud and clear. My loneliness, my brokenness, my occasional somnambulation starting from the age of seven when all I dreamt of was escape, all of the things that were wrong with me were my fault, and mine alone. It was my responsibility to fix them, otherwise Mother had no use for me, this weak, defective child.

That night was the first time I split my own flesh with a pair of nail scissors, right on the inside of my thigh where no one else would see. The relief was immediate, cleansing. That was also the last night my father really spoke to me. After that night, there was nothing beyond the superficial conversations one must have to get along in the world. The kinds of conversations that only make you feel more alone instead of less.

The tears have started to dry on my face, leaving sticky trails. I press the pad of my thumb into the point of my scalpel, not quite hard enough to pierce the skin. I'm so unbelievably pathetic—here I am, valedictorian of my high school (by default, Mother's voice chirps in my head, since the rightful valedictorian was pulled from school halfway through senior year after teachers found cocaine in his locker—which was surprisingly easy to plant, I found), rising sophomore at Georgetown, pre-med, and I'm still that deficient child Mother can't stand. I'm sleepwalking into random beds at night, for God's sake.

I move the scalpel to my bare inner thigh, tracing the tic tac toe of scars there. I let the scalpel slide into my skin, the relief immediate.

CHAPTER THIRTEEN

Mary, I Love Your Halo

I'm walking through campus toward the Chaplains' Office again, my hands shoved deep in my pockets. My index finger finds a hole in the left pocket, and I dig deeper, until I can feel my too-long nail against my wounded flesh, pressing hard. Last night's incident was no more than a blip, an unconscious accident spurred by stress. That's all. There's nothing 'wrong' with me—I was just upset over the invasion of privacy, like anyone would be. Those girls came down into my sanctuary without an invitation. If I hadn't acted quickly to shield my bloodstained scalpels, things might have ended very differently.

I press my feet gingerly into the sidewalk. My toes are blistered from my barefoot nocturnal escapades, but I'm trying to ignore the pain and think about other things. It couldn't be more clear that I can no longer operate in secrecy in my basement—not when the girls upstairs now think it's perfectly acceptable to pop down there whenever they feel like it. I need someplace where I can fully be myself, where I can experiment and learn and do the research I'm meant to do.

It's almost unbearably sunny outside, one of those hot Georgetown summer days where humidity hangs in the air like an impenetrable mist. Things rot faster in heat like this, which can be a good thing or a bad thing.

I'm walking past Copley Hall, bordering the main lawn, when I notice it: something both beautiful and deadly, not to mention nostalgic.

The petals are scarlet instead of white, but I'd know that flower anywhere. It's oleander. How strange that I've never before noticed the clutch of glossy green leaves and blooms redder than fresh pieces of gore. Maybe it's not so surprising, since the flowers only bloom in the summer. Also, the bush is wedged behind the statue of the Virgin Mary that watches over Healy lawn from its place against the wall separating Georgetown from the residential streets beyond the front gates. I certainly would never approach Mary to pray or whatever it is that good Catholics do, otherwise I would have at least noticed those distinctive green leaves. Now, the crimson blossoms surround Mary like a halo. I always thought of the Virgin Mary as a poison to the female psyche, an ideal real women can never live up to.

Poison. I first encountered the magical properties of oleander while home alone on a Saturday night in middle school. Channel surfing led me to a particular movie: *White Oleander*. Besides introducing me to a fascinating new way of hurting someone, I was entranced by the relationship between the mother and daughter. I couldn't help but envy the way the mother felt about her child—how she loved her so much, she never wanted to let her go. If *White Oleander* were my life story, I would more likely be a victim of Mother's oleander poisoning than her possessiveness.

Without realizing it, I've veered off the path and walked the few steps over to the Mary statue. I've heard a single oleander leaf can kill an adult. How simple it would be to pluck one now, stuff it between my lips, and chew through the bitterness to the darkness awaiting me on the other side.

I'm so preoccupied, I don't notice the group of Hughes students sauntering through the lawn toward Regents Hall until they pass behind me. I don't want to be seen right now, not with these thin lines of scab running up and down my arms, but it's far too hot for long sleeves and there's no time for me to hide.

Luckily, I don't have to. They're so absorbed in their conversation they don't even notice the girl a few yards away, crouching in the shadows in front of Mary, reaching for the oleander.

"Did you guys hear what happened to Lewis last night?" one of them asks.

"What?" That sounds like Erica. I freeze.

"Dude, he woke up in the middle of the night and there was this random chick in his bed, and she was, like, cuddling him."

My entire body goes cold, and my legs give out before I can regain control. Now I'm on my knees in front of Mary, probably looking like I'm praying. My fingers find the grass below me and start digging, scrabbling around to clutch anything solid. I had no idea I was with a Hughes kid last night.

"What!" Erica again. I'm not so distracted by my own panic that I can't make note of Erica's severely limited vocabulary. Maybe she's not as perfect as she seems.

"Yeah. Apparently she jumped out of his bed and ran away before he could get a good look at her. It was super fucking weird."

The whole group of them—maybe four or five, I can't tell without looking over my shoulder, and I don't want to call any attention to myself—is directly behind me now. I don't even want to breathe for fear of missing something.

"Lewis was so blackout last night, I wouldn't be surprised if he imagined the whole thing." Good. I didn't imagine the alcohol I smelled, then. The less he remembers, the better. I don't want to have to make him forget—but if I have to, I will.

"Seriously?" Well, at least that's a different word from Erica.

"I don't know. He said there was all this dirt and shit in his sheets when he woke up, but his feet were clean. So somebody else was obviously there."

"Or Lewis just hasn't washed his sheets in way too long."

More laughter. They sound like a cloud of buzzing flies. I wish I had a fly swatter.

"Have you guys considered that Lewis is just full of shit, like usual?"

Even more laughter. I don't think all normal human interactions involve this much guffawing, but I could be wrong.

"Or there's some seriously batshit girl running around, cuddling unsuspecting guys."

My face is clenched in a grimace, and I wait until they're completely out of earshot before I move again, pushing to a standing position on trembling legs. It sounds like I left nothing behind besides some dirt, at least—no trace evidence to lead back to my identity. Plus, they only half-believe his little story. With effort, I push my face back into a neutral expression.

When the shock and relief pass, the anger rolls in like a tsunami. How dare they talk about me like I'm some freak. It must be so easy to be them, ensconced in their cushy laboratory positions with stipends and free housing, protected from loneliness and fear by their camaraderie. It's not that simple for everyone. Some people have to snatch at warmth wherever they can get it, consciousness and consent be damned.

The Healy clocktower chimes—nine a.m. With one last, longing look at the oleander, I swivel around and walk toward the Chaplains' Office.

Glancing down, I notice my cuts are healing much faster than I would have expected. I guess shallow cuts heal quickly, deep cuts heal slowly, and the ones you can't see never heal at all.

CHAPTER FOURTEEN

What Do We Do with Taffy? We Stretch It, Of Course

For a moment, I feel whole, like the person I could have been if I'd had different parents. I feel like a person who is completely comfortable being herself, who doesn't know what it's like to stare into light-filled apartment windows at night and seethe with a toxic mixture of hatred and longing. In this space, the person I am doesn't want to vivisect small animals or stab Jesuits. Right now, I just want to love and be loved.

Good things don't last long, especially not for me. The pleasant warmth fades into a sticky, sweaty heat. My left arm has gone numb, pinned under my side. Something is pressing up against my chest, and my right arm is draped over the lump—

No, oh no.

I yank my arm away from whoever is in bed with me, then curse myself for the sudden movement. If I'm not careful, I'm going to wake the person up. Unfortunately, I'm not as lucky as I was last night. Instead of lying next to the edge of the bed and freedom, I'm wedged into the sliver between the inert person's body and the wall—which is not white cinderblock. It's drywall painted what could be a light blue or even purple.

I'm not in the dorms, that much is obvious. So where the hell am I?

"Hunhhhh," the lump next to me groans. Then, to my horror, the lump turns over in the narrow bed to face me, the movement dramatic and heavy, like a whale breaching. In the dim light coming through the cracks in the closed blinds, I can see my companion is male.

I recognize him. I don't know his name, but he's with the Hughes kids, too. My lips tighten into a thin line while his mouth opens in a yawn, and a wave of morning breath assaults my nostrils. It's rank, but there's no reek of alcohol, which means if this guy sees me, it won't get written off as a drunken hallucination. I need to get out of here.

I don't know what the right move is here. I could rush out like I did with the guy last night, or I could creep out as slowly and silently as possible. My palms start to itch with anxiety.

He shifts and yawns again. "Don't go, Gina," he says, or at least that's what I think he says. His words are sleep-addled, but he's starting to wake up. It looks like my decision has been made for me.

In one swift movement, I rip the covers off, launch myself over him, and run for the door.

I think I'm in the clear as the door handle turns underneath my fingers, but then he mumbles, "Hey! Who's there?" There's fumbling behind me, as though he's looking for the light switch.

By the time a lamp snaps on, I'm through the door and running across a tiled living room. Goddamnit, you'd think it would be easier to find a way out of a house this small. This must be a student townhouse, but no two are the same and besides a few random house parties I attended at the beginning of the year in the hopes that I could be someone different at Georgetown, I've never been in one. Grunts come from the guy's bedroom, and I know I only have a few seconds to make my escape.

I whip my head to the left. There: In the corner of the room, a small staircase leads up. My feet—bare again, of course—snag on empty beer cans, kicking them into the furniture with metallic clangs. I couldn't be louder if I tried. There better not be light sleepers in this house.

I finally make it to the staircase, which, thank the God I don't believe in, leads to a battered door that, with a swift twist of the knob, burps me out onto the Georgetown sidewalk, dimly illuminated by hazy moonlight.

"Hey!" I hear again behind me, as though I need another kick to get the hell out of here.

It takes me a second, but I know where I am. 36th Street, between O and P, the entire campus separating me from my apartment in Burleith.

I'm just rounding the corner onto O Street, heading for the University front gates, when I hear the townhouse door punch open behind me and a voice calls out, "Come back here!"

I don't stop running until I'm nearly in the lap of the John Carroll statue poised in front of Healy. I circle around to the statue's back, comfortably out of sight of the front gates should the guy pursue me this far. I collapse in a heap in the dry flower beds, the air hot and oppressive around me even without the sun blazing down.

My breath is coming fast, my rib cage feels as though it's about to crack open, and my heart is beating so hard I think it might tear apart my flesh and pop out into my hands. Honestly, I would welcome that at this point. If that were to happen, I'd finally get my name in a medical journal—as an incredible case study instead of as an author, but hey, we all work with what we've got.

I look down at myself and take stock. What I've got is two bare feet, four broken toenails, a pair of boxers—I grimace; they're definitely not mine— and my Georgetown Basketball t-shirt, sans bra.

I can't believe I managed to walk all the way from my apartment in Burleith, through campus, out the front gates, and into one of the Hughes townhouses without anyone seeing or stopping me. Jesus Christ, if I'm wearing the dude's boxers now, I must have been nearly naked. My breath catches. I better not have left my pants—or panties—in the dude's room.

Before I can stuff my emotions back into the dark hole in my mind where they belong, I'm curled up into a ball, my face buried in my arms, sobbing. With the adrenaline draining out of me fast, I can feel every cut, bruise, and blister on my feet. There's a searing pain where one of my pinky toenails was almost completely ripped off, only a jagged stump of cuticle remaining. This is not normal. Normal people don't end up like this, balled up in the fetal position next to the John Carroll statue in the middle of the night, wearing a random guy's boxers, sober as a judge.

I wish I could go back to that brief moment before I woke up and the nightmare began, when I was floating in warmth, happy to just drift, full of love for myself and those around me. There must be people who feel like that all the time: comfortable, content, cheerful. The tears start coming even harder, which I didn't think was possible until this moment. Erica is definitely one of those people, living her life with the confidence that every good thing coming to her is earned, and it will always be that way.

People like Erica have no idea what it's like to be me, not a goddamn inkling. If she did, I wonder if she'd have some empathy for me—stray, rabid dog that I am—or if she would press a gun to my head and put me out of my misery at the first opportunity.

I don't want to stop thinking about Erica, because thoughts of her stoke the anger inside of me, which, if I let it, will grow so big it burns away all the tears, all the sadness, all the weakness. The heat of anger is nothing like the warmth of another person, but it will keep my body and soul together—for now.

It's not fair for people like Erica and all the other privileged Hughes kids to swan about like they own the place, like life is as easy for everybody else as it is for them. They don't know what true pain feels like. They've never suffered like this.

My hands find the dirt beneath me, and I dig my nails into the earth, squeezing great clods of it like I wish I could squeeze Erica's throat. It isn't fair for me to hurt so much when others hurt so little, or not at all.

Without warning, a raspy snicker comes from somewhere in front of me, near the entrance to Healy Hall, startling me out of my thoughts. It can't be that guy—I would have heard him coming.

I scan the building's facade in the streaky moonlight. Nothing. Maybe

I imagined it—wouldn't be the first time.

Rasp-snicker. Shit—there it is again. Something's over there. I'm not imagining it.

"Hello," I call out, more demand than question.

Silence. Then—*rasp-snicker.* That's it. If someone wants to mess with me right now, when I'm bruised and broken and wearing someone else's underwear, then let's fucking go.

I pull myself up and stride on my blistered feet toward Healy, toward the source of the infuriating sound. "Get over here," I snarl. "Show me your face, dickhead."

I'm so focused on finding a fear-twisted face that I nearly trip over the real perpetrator, crouched in a corner between the Healy stairs and the wall.

It's a rat. It's just an especially repulsive rat, bloated with too much Dumpster pizza, its scaly tail whispering back and forth across the concrete. *Rasp-snicker.*

Without a plan in mind, I reach out to grab the little vermin, to pull it close to me, but he scampers away from my fingers at the last second. With a loud chitter, he runs toward the side of the building, heading for the path between Healy and Copley Halls.

No. He's not getting away from me—something has to go right tonight.

I sprint after him, ignoring the sharp edges of loose rocks digging into my feet. I reach out just as the rat rounds the corner of Healy, raking through his greasy fur with my long fingernails. The little bastard is slippery, oozing out of my grasp again. A groan of frustration barrels out of my throat. He'd be the perfect experimental specimen.

We're both around the side of the building now, and I don't even see the metal door until the rat draws my attention to it. The door is slightly ajar, and the rat has managed to squeeze himself through the crack just enough to get horribly stuck.

My lips curl into a grin. Perhaps this night won't be completely fucked, after all.

The rat's back legs are scrabbling fiercely, its tail swishing across the concrete like a frenzied metronome. *Rasp-snicker. Rasp-snicker.*

My hands are steady—future surgeon's hands, of course—as I reach for the plump body. My fingers close around the rat's abdomen, and I'm just about to pull him away from safety when, in his last burst of terrified energy, he manages to shoot through the crack in the door like a bullet. I want to scream, but then I hear it: the echo of the rat's body falling, falling, falling, hitting walls on the way down. Finally, after what feels like far too long, there's a wet, crunchy plop.

My anger evaporates, replaced by morbid curiosity.

The door is still ajar, as though it's been left invitingly open just for me. I reach out, slipping my hand into the crack, reveling in the cold of the metal on my hot skin.

I pull.

The hole behind the metal door is dark, but it doesn't scare me. Something inside me reaches out to touch the darkness, to feel it like a velvet curtain. It's soft, warm, seductive. All-enveloping.

A sliver of moonlight barely touches the inside of the open space, illuminating not the beginning of a hallway, but a ladder bolted to the wall— leading down, down, down. I turn around, grip the doorframe, and press my bleeding feet onto the first rung.

*   *   *

As I descend, I hear the door above me close with a barely audible click. I don't worry that somebody might have seen me. If the Hughes kid was going to chase me, he would have found me while I was still feeling sorry for myself behind the John Carroll statue.

My eyes adjust to the gloom, just like they always did when Mother would lock me in the hall closet for some infraction or another. I'm not sure if it's due to all the practice I got as a child, or if I was just born for the darkness.

The odor of stagnant water, something jungly, permeates the air. Somewhere deep under the bowels of Georgetown, machinery clunks away dutifully, punctuated by the hiss of steam. Absently, I wonder how successful my animal traps would be here, where there isn't the possibility of escape. Quite successful, I think.

My feet touch solid ground, and then I'm walking with confidence through the utter blackness. My bare feet echo on what feels like a concrete floor, occasionally littered with shallow puddles. At one point, I crouch over on instinct, practically crawling through a tight space I explore with my searching fingers. I hear the sound of water rushing through pipes around me, and drops of something warm splash on the top of my head. I've heard about the maintenance tunnels under campus, everyone has, but I've never been inclined to go looking for them. This seems like an easy place to get lost if you don't know where you're going.

On the other hand, it also seems like an excellent refuge for utter privacy. A thrill runs through me—I could be as loud as I want down here, and so could my experimental subjects.

My body continues to move through the darkness with unerring certainty, as though I've been here before. Before long, I see a faint glow ahead. I turn towards it, then the ceiling lifts and I can stand. I'm in a small concrete chamber, an offshoot of the main tunnel. A single bare bulb dangles in the darkness, penetrating it only so far as the borders of the room. The walls are not smooth; little nooks and crannies make the entire thing look like an Escher painting, and doltish kids have covered the walls in haphazard graffiti: *Viggy was here. Georgetown Basketball 2005. Julie sux cock in hell.*

Not the most creative bunch, but I'd expect nothing more.

My feet stop moving and, suddenly exhausted, I plop onto the floor. The cement is unexpectedly cold on my ass, a nice counterpoint to the stifling humidity of the rest of the tunnel atmosphere.

As I sit, my brain starts scrambling again. I'm losing the confidence I entered this room with. I can see the dark wave in the distance, coming toward me, threatening to pull me under for the final time. If I let myself get lost down here, I'd become like the minotaur in the labyrinth, pitied and hated in equal measure.

Experimentally, I call out, "Hello?"

My voice pings around the small chamber like a pinball, sending filaments of sound radiating through the connecting narrow tunnels. I know there's nobody else here. Despite the presence of the graffiti indicating students once scuttled through these claustrophobic halls, I feel safe.

Silence fills the room again like a noxious gas, and I worry some self-destructive part of me has brought me down here, deep in the tunnels, only to leave me to die, abandoning me like the wounded animal I know I am. It's what I would do with Airhead Ani, if I were bolder and more creative. I picture the nitwit sitting alone in this cramped room, sweat running into her eyes and mingling with her pointless tears. No one would be able to hear her scream, and she'd pound on the walls until her hands were raw and bloody, like hamburger meat. Oh, I'd bet she'd be wishing she'd done something more interesting with her time on earth than talk about eyelash extensions and suck down Frappuccino after Frappuccino.

I'm standing up now, and I realize it's because I heard a skittering in the corner, something big and furry and terrified. It's the rat, of course, the same big Georgetown Dumpster rat that led me here in the first place. I'd forgotten all about it; I hadn't even noted the lack of crunching bones under my feet when I reached the bottom of the ladder. Somehow, it survived the fall. Now, it's cowering in the corner, eyes like beads of oil, its tail a leathery rope, its fur a slimy tangle. When it sees me, it screams, and the sound is so wonderful my lungs contract in laughter. This is something I can handle: I can bring the animal's terror to a satisfying conclusion. I know what it's like to be wounded, shivering in the corner, and I can give the rat what no one ever gave me—an end to the dread, freedom from the pain. The thought fills me with so much joy; I'm still laughing as I kneel down close to the animal, who seems paralyzed with fear—or, maybe, I suppose, with injuries sustained during its free fall. I'm still laughing as my hands reach out for its grimy body; I'm still laughing as my fingers close around its neck and twist, the sound of the bones snapping making me laugh even harder, until I'm falling to the floor with elation, the limp rat clutched to my chest, its rank blood oozing onto my shirt and the Hughes kid's boxers.

I've never killed an animal for anything other than experimentation before, and the realization chokes off the laughter in my throat. I can't let this animal go to waste.

The light has gone out of the rat's eyes, leaving them dull, like the hard plastic beads I used to spend hours threading onto bits of stretchy string, Mother thinking I was making friendship bracelets for the friends I didn't have. I was actually making tiny nooses for the family of mice that had taken up residence in our basement because I wanted to study the biological effects of suffocation. I ended up keeping all of the bracelets on my wrists, ready to strangle a mouse at a moment's notice. Sometimes those other kids at school, who everyone thought were so cute and sweet, would hook their snotty little fingers through the strings and pull, sending little beads flying everywhere. They'd fake cry and pretend it was an accident, and the teacher would rush to comfort them, ignoring me, the girl whose bracelets were broken, who started picking up the beads on the floor without any prompting, because craft supplies are expensive and we aren't going to get anymore, Keely, because crafts are irrelevant to being a scientist. Most of the time, the teacher wouldn't even make the other kids apologize, she'd just tell them to go off and play, and she'd be the one crouching down with me, picking up little beads, but she'd throw her piles away in the trash, not realizing that mine were going straight back into my pockets. She didn't even ask.

I've been squeezing the rat's neck for too long now, and its head is floppy, stretched away from its body like rodent taffy.

Now it's time to do what everyone does with taffy: stretch it, of course. I've got one fist gripping the rat's body, the other one clenching its head, and I'm pulling, pulling, pulling, ready to test the tensile strength of a rat's cervical spine as if I am testing my own. That's an experiment worthy of me, surely. Soon there's a surprisingly loud rip and the body and the head are no longer connected. Still-pulsating gore and bits of matted fur drop to the floor and cover my palms, and now I know something I didn't know before. That's the point of research, after all.

I let the rat's body and head fall to the cement floor with a moist smack. I feel freer than I ever have in my entire life. Along with my experimental rat prey, it feels like I've killed, or at least severely injured, the prey inside me, too—its voice echoing everything Mother ever told me.

I wipe the blood on the Hughes kid's boxers, feeling exorcised.

CHAPTER FIFTEEN

You Can't Trust a Priest

When I come back to myself, I'm laying in my bed in my little basement apartment, the covers on the floor. My feet are coated in a thick layer of dark grime. I'm not sure, but I think I spent the rest of the weekend in the tunnels.

Thin slats of light shine through the narrow window above my bed. My best guess is that it's Monday, which means I've got to get my ass to the Chaplains' Office. The thought of another whole week with Airhead Ani doesn't rankle like it would have even a few days ago. I feel above her, somehow. She is too small to be a concern to me, even though she might still be an annoying, vapid pile of human garbage. She can't aggravate me if I don't let her. She can be like a bit of string dangled in front of my catlike paws.

A smile spreads across my face like a sore, and then I'm up and out of bed, yanking socks over my dirty feet. In the bathroom, I pull my ragged hair into a low bun, splash water on my face, and swipe some lip balm across my chapped lips. As I'm finishing up, a thirst so intense it's physically painful grips me, sending me barreling toward the kitchen sink, where I hold my head under the faucet, mouth open, gulping until the need goes away.

*　*　*

On the way to work, I watch a boy dressed from head to toe in Vineyard Vines madras plaid open a fresh paper bag from Uncommon Grounds, sniff at what's inside, scowl, and toss it in the trash can outside the Leavey Student Center without even taking a bite. He walks off, totally unperturbed. These pompous jerks just buy whatever they want with daddy's money, then throw things away instead of using them—or in this case, eating them. Anger at the kid's entitled wastefulness mingles with the low growl in my stomach, and I can't help but take a peek in the trash can to see just what disgusted the rich douchebag so much that he had to throw away fresh food.

It's an egg and cheese bagel, grease starting to lightly dot the outside of the paper bag. My stomach growls again. The bagel is still warm, the cheese dripping over the lightly crisped edges. The eggs are a little sour, but I'm not complaining. Scoring that bagel means I don't have to talk to anyone, and I can keep my hunger at bay.

I'm stuffing the last of my scavenged breakfast into my mouth when I round the corner from Red Square, only to find the inescapable Hughes kids again, sauntering together in a toxic bunch toward Regents Hall.

One of them guffaws, then says, "Did you guys hear? The Georgetown Cuddler struck again!"

"What?" Erica. Jesus Christ, again with the insipid monosyllabic questions.

"No way, man," one says. "Who did you hear that from?"

"You guys seriously didn't know about this? It was Jude! He woke up and thought it was Gina in bed with him, but it obviously wasn't, because the girl ran out of there so fast. He tried to chase her, but she basically disappeared out the front door."

"Shit," one of them says.

"What!" Erica adds. What a bright and incisive addition to the conversation.

"Wait, wait," the first one says. "That's not even the best part."

"What?" If there weren't witnesses, I swear I'd grab Erica by the throat right now and choke her so she'd never be able to say 'what' again. She doesn't deserve the privilege, quite frankly.

"Jude said he's pretty sure the girl was, like… wearing his boxers."

There's a moment of quiet shock, then they all burst out that inane guffaws yet again.

"No!" one says.

"What!" Erica again, of course.

"Are you sure Jude's not full of shit?"

"I'm sure. I mean, he doesn't even drink, dude. Jude was stone cold sober."

"Damn."

"That's kind of creepy," one says.

"Yeah," the first one agrees. "But it could have been worse. I mean, it's not like she did anything to him."

"I bet he wishes she did," one says, and high fives the first one.

"She did steal his boxers," the first one says. "Not cool. Those are like thirty bucks a pop."

They all laugh again, and I want to scream.

"I, for one, would happily welcome the Cuddler into my bed," the first one says. "I could use a little action."

"Who's gonna be next?"

The conversation continues in this vein as they clop through Red Square, not noticing me even though I'm staring right at them the entire time they're within view.

I burp, and a bit of stomach acid comes with it. I swallow it back down, clench my teeth against the rage begging to overtake me, and try to remind myself of the new sanctuary I've found, where regular rules do not apply, and I have free rein.

It doesn't completely work; I'm still incensed. I've been labeled: the Georgetown Cuddler. What a ridiculous moniker. What happened to me— waking up in random guy's beds, having no memory of how I got there, feeling terrified and so alone I want to die—is nothing to laugh about. In the tunnels, I felt like I was invincible. Now, I feel like I'm barely holding myself together and nobody is even trying to help. Instead, they're laughing.

Maybe next time I'll give them something to really laugh about, something really fucking hilarious.

I open the door to the Chaplains' Office, and my fingers are still good and greasy when I clap Airhead Ani on the back, leaving an oily handprint on her light pink cardigan right between her shoulder blades. If I can't hurt the Hughes kids right now, Airhead will have to do. When she takes that flimsy sweater off later, I'm sure she'll have no idea how she managed to ruin it. If I'm lucky, maybe she'll think she has some sort of sweating disorder, and she'll come in here tomorrow and talk to me about it, since I'm pre-med, and ask my advice. I'll tell her I saw a study about how OxyContin can stop unusual sweating patterns, but I suspect any opioid might do the trick. Then I'll sit back and see if she's vain enough to take the bait and ruin her life.

"Did you have a nice weekend?" she asks me, as though my comings and goings are any of her goddamn business.

I say, "No. Not really."

She looks flustered. Excellent. "Oh," she says. "I'm sorry to hear that. Everything okay?"

"Far from it, actually. My rat died."

Now she looks both disgusted and uncomfortable. "You… you have a pet rat?"

"Well, obviously not anymore," I say, letting her mistake the glimmer of malice in my eyes for tears.

"I'm, uh, I'm sorry to hear that." Now, she's looking around the room, hoping for any sort of distraction to get her out of this.

"I'm sorry to tell you that. I had to bury her with my own hands." For effect, I hold up my slick palms. She grimaces.

"Must have been a hard weekend," she says, too nonplussed to let the conversation lapse into complete awkward silence.

"It was," I say, my voice grave. "Beelzebub was a good rat."

"That's so interesting," Airhead says. "I, uh, I didn't know anybody around here had a pet."

I level a laser-focused gaze right into her eyeballs, projecting an air of condescension. "You didn't think anybody in the entire Georgetown neighborhood had a pet?"

"No, no," she says, "That's not what I meant. I just meant, like, I'm surprised a Georgetown student has a pet."

"Had a pet," I correct, letting my eyes sparkle with moisture again.

"Oof," she says eloquently, adding nothing more. She's finally decided perhaps silence is better after all. Good.

The rest of the morning is pleasant because she's not talking. She's playing Candy Crush or some other mindless game on her phone in between texts to her boyfriend. When I peep over her shoulder as sneakily as possible, I see my name and the words 'weird' and 'pet rat' in the blue text bubbles she sent. It would be insulting to see how little she thinks of me, if not for the fact she doesn't think much at all.

I spend my time ignoring her and cleaning up the shared drive on the office computer, something Airhead was asked to do weeks ago. When she brought it up to me, she said something along the lines of, "It just sounds so hard… like, how do I know what to delete and what to keep? Or how to organize what goes where?" The sound of her whining voice irritated me, and her laziness really cemented my loathing for her right then and there. Before that, I'd been on the fence—kind of. Too bad for her.

As soon as the clock hits eleven, Airhead stands up. "I'm going to lunch," she says. Normally, she'd halfheartedly invite me to join her, or offer to bring me something back from the food court, but not today. Today I've creeped her out, given her a reason to find me unpalatable. I'm not sorry about it, either.

"Have fun," I say. "Where are you going?"

She looks surprised at my desire to engage her in further conversation. "Oh, I don't know, I'll probably just grab something from Vittles."

"Would you mind getting me something, too?"

"Oh, uh, sure," she says, looking like she would actually very much mind that.

She's about to turn to leave when I say, acidly, "Don't you need to know what I want?"

"Right, right," she says, a pained smile on her too-rosy cheeks. I can see the dark line where her mismatched foundation meets the paleness of her neck.

"I'll have one of those little cans of Spam, a jar of dill pickles, some mayonnaise—the little packets are fine, but bring a lot—and Wonder Bread. Not regular white bread, Wonder Bread." I pause for gravity. "Wonder Bread," I repeat.

I make prolonged eye contact with her until she frowns and says, "Um, okay."

"I'll Venmo you," I call out as she starts to turn away. "Bring me the receipt."

"Sure," she says over her shoulder

"Thanks, Annie!" I call out as the door to the office slams closed behind her.

A giggle burbles up out of my throat once she's out of earshot. I've played this perfectly. Vital Vittles doesn't stock Wonder Bread—I know because I've asked in the past, as I actually do like Wonder Bread—and at this point, I don't think Airhead is going to want to ignore my very specific wishes. She's going to have to walk all the way down to the 7-11 on Wisconsin, or maybe the CVS even farther up, or the Safeway in Burleith. She's going to be gone a long time, which works out great for me. When she does return, sweaty and out of breath and annoyed, I'll make myself the world's most fragrant sandwich of jiggling Spam, pungent pickles, and heaps of mayonnaise, all smushed together between two pieces of the whitest white bread that is basically cake. While I eat, I'll face her and talk about my fake dead rat, telling her all the details about how it died while I chew with my mouth open. I can't wait.

The door to the Chaplains' Office opens again, and there's no way Airhead should be back yet. I turn, a scowl already forming on my face, and see that nosy bastard O'Meara standing in front of the desk. The fluorescent lights bounce off his bald head.

"Keely," he says with way too much cheeriness pressed into that one word. "I was hoping to find you here."

I summon back my mask, the one befitting a normal college girl who works in the campus's main religious office. "Father O'Meara! How nice to see you. What can I do for you?"

O'Meara looks around, jowls swinging, ensuring the office is empty, and then takes a seat opposite me. In one hand, he's got a large mug, probably full of that vile peppermint tea he's always chugging. "Well, Keely, this might not be the easiest conversation to have."

I arrange my features to some approximation of concern. "Oh? Is something wrong, Father?"

He sighs, and I can already tell this exchange is not one I want to have. I should have gone and bought my own damn Spam and pickles.

"Keely," he says again, as though saying my name will endear me to him in any way. "About last week."

Last week… last week feels so long ago. Between having my privacy invaded by my housemates, finding myself in bed with two different, unfamiliar men, and then discovering my sanctuary in the tunnels, I've had a lot going on. But, right, now I remember—the envelopes, the paper cuts, O'Meara finding me in the closet.

"What about it?" I say, my voice coming out a bit more roughly than I would have liked.

"Well…" he trails off, looking for the right words, but I can tell he's practiced this little speech already. It's all a farce, and it makes me angry. "Our conversation last week left me feeling a tad uneasy."

"Uneasy?" I cock my head, trying to look innocent.

"Yes," he says, more firmly, as though he's finding his footing. "I'm not saying you didn't tell the truth about what happened in that closet, that's not it at all. It's just… I spent the weekend praying, asking the Lord for some guidance in this matter."

"Did he answer you?" I ask, trying to keep the snide tone out of my voice and not completely succeeding.

Father O'Meara frowns. "He did, actually, and I think you should heed his advice, too."

When he doesn't elaborate, forcing me to feign interest just to keep the conversation from dying painfully like I wish he would, I ask, "And what's that?"

He clears his throat. "Well, I think you could benefit from a touch of counseling."

Hell, no. Counselor is just another word for therapist, and therapy is, as Mother says, the 'red-headed stepchild of medicine.' People should be strong enough to work through their own problems.

"Counseling?" I know I sound as dense as Erica, repeating the last word of each of his sentences, but I can't help it—it's either that or scream.

"Yes," he says again. "The student mental health center has some excellent counselors, who are trained to help students through whatever troubles they may be facing."

My mouth is twitching at the corners, and I try to force my features to fall into blankness instead. "And what troubles might I be facing?"

O'Meara chuckles. He actually chuckles, in this weird patronizing, avuncular way that makes my flesh want to crawl right off my sharp bones. "That's not for me to say, Keely. I just want to connect you with the right resources, to get any and all help you might be needing."

"And what if I'm not in need of any help?"

O'Meara's blue-white eyes twitch at the note of challenge in my voice. "I hope you can see how beneficial counseling might be, even if you don't necessarily think you need it." He leans in closer, and I can smell something sweet on his breath: that wretched peppermint tea. I want to gag. "If you're concerned about money, the student mental health center offers services completely free of charge."

His insinuation is insulting, but I'm able to control myself, keep my still-greasy fingers from slipping around his puffy pink throat. "Thank you for that information," I say, requiring all of my self-control to modulate my voice. "But I'm entirely fine. I just spilled some envelopes. That doesn't mean I'm crazy."

O'Meara puts his hands up, his red neck turkeying backward. "No, no, no," he says, "that's not what I'm saying at all." What a liar. "Hundreds of students benefit from talking to a counselor. I'm not suggesting there's any sort of mental illness at play—although if there were, there's nothing wrong with that, either—just that speaking with someone might make you feel better."

"I feel fine," I say, smiling in the same vapid way Airhead Ani does.

Apparently, the Airhead-smile doesn't work on pricks like O'Meara. He puts his hands down, and the I'm-just-your-friend facade crumbles. "Look, Keely," he says. "I'd hoped you would be interested of your own accord, but I can see that's not going to be the case." He sighs heavily, as though he's upset with me for making his job unnecessarily harder. "I'm concerned you may be hurting yourself. I need you to get help, otherwise I don't think you can continue to work in this office."

I can't believe he's serious. He's really threatening to terminate my on-campus job if I don't see some underpaid, unskilled student counselor who doesn't deserve to know a single thought that runs through my mind. Even if I were really sick—which I'm not—and refused treatment, he would actually rip away the one thing that's allowing me to pay my rent because Mother refuses to cover my housing if I'm not working in a lab during the summer. "Father" O'Meara my ass. This guy is the worst of the worst.

"I see," I say, and as the words leave my lips, I can tell I'm close to losing control.

"I'm sorry it's coming to this, Keely. But I couldn't live with myself if I ignored the signs." It's more like he couldn't live with the liability if I had some sort of break with reality and lashed out while working as a representative of the Chaplains' Office. What a fool he is; I know I can keep myself under control far better than any fifteen-dollar-an-hour 'therapist' with a few months of training and an IQ far below mine who couldn't even begin to understand me.

I take a deep breath. I can work my way out of this, I know I can. I'm not losing my work-study position, not like this. If I have to play his game, then I'll play—just not by his rules. The voice coming out of my mouth is sinuous, sibilant. "I understand completely. I'll stop by the mental health center and make an appointment on my way home."

O'Meara's entire body relaxes back into the chair. I hate the way he faked his little performance. He knew he had the upper hand all along. "I'm so happy to hear that, Keely."

My lips curve into a smile that is really a snarl underneath. "I'm just happy I've got someone looking out for me, Father." For a single second, I allow myself to think this might be true. It isn't, but even if it were, I don't know if I'd recognize what that feels like, to have somebody who actually cares.

The second passes, and his eyes twitch again, just a bit. He's seeing me, really seeing me again, and I hate it. My revulsion feels like venom in my capillaries.

"I'll make a call," he says, his voice full of phony concern. "To the mental health center. Make sure you can get an appointment as quickly as possible."

"Wow, thank you," I say, and I'm back to feeling like a clenched fist, mixed emotions swirling inside of me. I know something is wrong with me and has been for a long time. Maybe letting someone in wouldn't be the worst thing in the world.

"Anybody who is too interested in you just wants to take advantage of you," Mother told me the first time I asked if a friend could sleep over. "If someone wants to be your friend, you run the other way. If someone wants to hurt you, you hurt them first."

So—yes. It would be bad to let someone in, especially when there's no way of knowing if O'Meara is genuine. He might be a priest, but way too many people have been hurt because they trusted a priest.

O'Meara needs to leave, and right now. I'm coming unglued, and I can't let him see that. The bastard is going to phone the health center not so I can get an early appointment, I know that, but so he can be sure I really go to counseling. What a sneaky asshole.

"You're very welcome," he says. I'm angry with myself for thanking him for intruding into my life so insidiously, and I'm furious with him for truly thinking he deserves my thanks. "Well, you have a nice lunch, now."

I plaster the smile on my face as he leaves, giving a little wave instead of trusting my mouth to do any more talking. When the door to the Chaplains' Office finally closes again, leaving that sickly-sweet smell of peppermint dangling in the air, I pull the trash can out from under the desk and retch until I'm only dry heaving.

When I'm done, I cover the gunk with crumpled pieces of printer paper and shove it under Airhead's desk. I slump in my chair, breathing heavily, trying not to scream.

Some time later, Airhead barrels back in, a plastic Safeway bag digging into her pink forearm. I hope it's chafing her skin. She's sweaty and unkempt, her eyeliner starting to run down her face, turning her into a raccoon.

She thrusts the bag at me. "I got your lunch," she says.

"Mmm," I grunt. The thought of eating anything makes my stomach roil again, but I push down the nausea and take the bag, the plastic straps nearly slipping from my sweaty hands.

"You're welcome," she says, a bit too snottily for my liking. "You owe me—"

"Thank you again for buying me lunch," I say, cutting her off, trying to regain some sense of balance. "You didn't have to, but it means a lot. You know, after all I've been through."

"You can Venmo—"

"Mmm, yum," I say, lifting the can of Spam and jar of pickles out of the bag and swallowing back bile. "You're a good friend." I peel open the can of Spam, the gelatinous mass glistening under the fluorescent lights. I give it a little shake, watching it jiggle. It releases a meaty aroma that doesn't help my queasiness, but it does blot out the sickly sweet smell of O'Meara's peppermint tea. I let the Spaminess envelop me, chasing away all the weakness, all the pain, all the vulnerability no one can ever see.

CHAPTER SIXTEEN

There's No Place Like Home

Airhead Ani makes some sort of excuse to ditch work early and leaves after lunch, which doesn't bother me in the slightest. I need space to think—my mind keeps returning to O'Meara. I can't get a read on him; for all I know, maybe he's trying to throw me off my equilibrium, rattle my cage, mess me up so I'll fall far enough for someone else to take my place in the Chaplains' Office. I shake my head, scrambling the thoughts like a kaleidoscope, hoping a new, sensible picture will take shape. It doesn't.

Regardless, I need to get O'Meara to turn and look somewhere else, away from me—and that means keeping him happy, letting him think he has the power he's so desperate to exert over me. If he thinks I'm falling in line like a good little Catholic, maybe he'll stop looking at me so damn hard.

When I leave the Chaplains' Office that evening, my feet carry me briskly past Copley Hall, through Red Square, past Reiss, all the way to the student counseling center near Darnall Hall. No doubt O'Meara phoned them the minute he got back to his office, so I'm sure there will be an appointment waiting for me to claim. I push open the doors and see the receptionist half-standing over her desk while packing up her big quilted Vera Bradley bag, stuffing dirty Tupperware and a frayed wallet into its depths.

"Can I help you?" she asks, and I detect a trace of annoyance. I know it's close to closing, you shrew, but come on, this is the counseling center. Try to assemble a welcoming smile. I've had a hard day, and I'm not in the mood for this shit.

"Yes, actually," I say, drawing out my words, punishing her with my slowness. "I'm… in need of an… appointment."

"Alright," she says, sighing as she sits back down at her computer. "And what's your name?"

"Keely Rexroth."

Her eyebrows shoot up, no doubt recognizing my name from O'Meara's call, and she becomes more solicitous. "Ah, yes, of course. We can get you in at nine tomorrow morning, Keely. How does that sound?"

I appreciate the newfound unctuousness of her manner, but not the way it came about. I don't want favors from a meddling Jesus freak like O'Meara. "Hm," I say. "Let me check my schedule." I know I have nothing going on tomorrow except work, and that isn't a problem, thanks to O'Meara. I make a show of opening up my Calendar app anyway, scrolling through the day, hemming and hawing. The receptionist shifts in her chair, restless.

"Would that be okay?" she prompts again.

"Uhhh… yeah, I think so. I just have work, but that shouldn't be an issue. I mean, people are late to work all the time for important appointments, after all," I say.

"Right. Would you like an appointment reminder card?" she asks, clearly hoping I will say no and leave so she can waddle to the bus stop and get on the grimy city bus that will take her back to her sad, shabby apartment.

"What's an appointment reminder card?" I ask, knowing full well what an appointment reminder card is. I'm not a total dipshit.

"Oh, well, it's a card with your appointment date and time written on it, so you don't forget."

"Hm. Do most people get those?"

"No," she says, speaking quickly. She glances around as though she's lying, which she probably is. She's saying whatever she can to get me to leave faster—another person's attempt to control me. I don't like it, so now my goal is to make her miss her bus so she has to stand out for another twenty minutes in this wet heat, her armpit sweat soaking the handles of that stupid Vera Bradley bag.

"Well, I actually think I'd like one. Please," I say, channeling 'Madame Leila's' molasses-slow drawl.

"Alright," she says, sounding put out, even though it's her job to do things like this. Hurriedly, she grabs a little rectangular piece of paper and a pen and scribbles down my appointment information. She thrusts it at me over the desk, and I take the time to put my phone back in my pocket before reaching for the card in her plump, outstretched hand.

"Thank you," I say. "So, I'll see you tomorrow, then? How long have you been a student counselor?"

Now she looks really pained; she realizes she's definitely going to miss her bus. Excellent. That's what she gets for trying to mess with me. "Oh, I'm not a counselor," she says. "Just the receptionist."

"Oh, so you couldn't hack it as a counselor," I joke, putting a smile on my face that isn't really a smile.

"No, nothing like that," she says, flustered. "I just—look, I'm sorry, I really have to go, it's after five and I'm about to miss my bus—"

"Oh my goodness, I'm so sorry I've kept you at your job for"—I make a show of checking my watch—"two minutes and twenty seconds past five. To legitimately help a student in need, no less. I'm such a monster."

She closes her eyes and takes a deep breath. I've ruined her day, I can tell. "Look, I'm sorry, I didn't mean to rush you out. My apologies." She's now decided placating me is the fastest way to get me to leave. Boy, is she wrong.

"That's alright, I understand. I'm lucky I can just walk a couple blocks to my apartment in Burleith. Where do you live?"

Now she's really uncomfortable. She does not want to tell the weird girl in front of her where she lives, not at all. "Oh, closer to downtown," she says vaguely.

"Oh, cool," I say, "Where downtown? I'm pretty familiar with the area. I take a lot of long walks down there, mostly at night."

I think I can see tears welling in those piggy eyes. If so, I hope they're both frustration and fear. It's a heady combination. "The U Street area. Look, it's been lovely meeting you, Keely, but I'm afraid I really must go. My boyfriend is taking me to dinner tonight, and I can't be late for the reservation."

We both know she doesn't have a boyfriend, but I'm getting tired, too, and I'll save my deadly pounce for another time. I put my hands up in a backing-off gesture. "I get it, I get it," I say. "You have a nice evening with your boyfriend"—I put extra emphasis on the word we both know is a lie, then make a show of squinting at her nameplate—"Rachel Borrister."

"Good evening to you, too," she says, and I know she's shaken. I know her full name, I have a general idea of where she lives, and she knows something's not right about me.

I slap a blank grin on my face, the kind of smile you see on serial killers in their mug shots, the ones who have been caught in the act but will never, ever, tell you where the rest of the bodies are buried, and finally take my leave. When I peek back over my shoulder, I see Rachel Borrister slumped over her desk, her shoulders heaving. Nobody cries like that out of frustration alone; no, she's feeling that frustration and fear cocktail. Drink up, you insufferable nag.

As I walk home, I'm nearly giggling with giddiness. I have a new plaything now, so maybe counseling won't be so bad. I'll think of Rachel Borrister as the appetizer every time I walk into the office, the little amuse bouche I can use to whet my manipulation skills before the counselor main course. I mean, it can't be very hard to pull the wool over some university counselor's eyes. If they were actually any good, they'd be working in private practice, charging rich people exorbitant amounts to listen to their petty problems. They wouldn't be roughing it in a college counseling office for a laughably low wage. In no time, I'll get them to certify me with the 'A-OK' sticker and get O'Meara off my back. I need to blind him.

Metaphorically for sure but, in a perfect world, also literally.

"Hey, Keely," Roger says. Somehow, he always manages to startle me. Either he's dangerously quiet, or I'm far less aware of my surroundings than I like to think.

"Roger, do you think it would be so bad to hurt a Jesuit?" I ask.

"Why would you want to hurt a Jesuit?"

"Oh, I don't know, maybe just for the sheer audacity of his greediness. Rog, he threatened to take away my job, my financial aid, my undergraduate career, and therefore my entire life trajectory just because of a few paper cuts on my arms. I'm not the crazy one here. He clearly is."

"People sometimes think I'm crazy," he says. "But I'm not. I have a traumatic brain injury."

"You're sane as they come, Rog. The best part is, this guy calls himself a Jesuit. I don't think Jesus would blackmail a student like that, do you?"

"Nobody should blackmail you, Keely. That's not right."

"Damn straight. See you later."

I leave Roger sitting on his front porch, twirling a piece of grass between his fingers. I don't know when Roger became less of an experimental subject and more of a dumping ground for my thoughts, but I don't care. He will never tell a soul.

I get to the door of my apartment, but a new realization dawns on me. I won't be sleeping here tonight, maybe not again for a while.

My hands are quick unlocking the door, quicker still stuffing metal trays, towels, and the rest of the equipment I'll need into my backpack. I add a few changes of clothes for good measure, because it wouldn't be wise to give O'Meara any more reason to get involved in my business. Wearing the same set of clothes two days in a row might ring his alarm bells, and I'm not going to take that chance. My feet kick off the soiled ballet flats with the holes in the soles and shove themselves into a pair of old tennis shoes. Before long, I am sitting back at my rickety kitchen table, my bag packed, my shoes laced. The doctor's bag, my last necessary item, is in front of me, but my hands are at my sides, dangling like dead worms. I don't pray, but maybe this is what it feels like for people who do.

*　　*　　*

Peacefulness washes over me as I linger, still and quiet, in that small chamber I discovered off of the main tunnels. Down here, I've found a home, a place where I can do the sort of advanced experiments those other undergraduates never even dream of.

It's times like these I'm glad I don't have friends, the kind who want to know what you did last night and how your day is going and if you're nervous about that big exam coming up. It's none of their business. The girls who live above me were nosy enough before their intrusion, asking me when I was going to find a boyfriend and did I want to join them for spaghetti on Sunday night. I don't need some oafish boyfriend, and I hate spaghetti. Since their intrusion, I've shunned them like they're radioactive.

The single bare bulb dangles overhead, illuminating the squirrel splayed open on the metal tray before me. I've liberated a sturdy little table from Healy and lugged it down here, plus a thick blanket I've pinned up to obscure the entrance to this chamber. Along with a battery-powered camp light I found in a storage closet in the Yates gym, I've got everything I need.

Now I just have to get to work.

Vivisection still eludes me; the squirrel only lived for a few drugged out minutes after I wrenched open his ribcage, but I won't let myself be discouraged. In this hallowed space, where privacy is an expectation instead of a luxury, I'll get better—that's the whole point of experimentation, after all. I've been dissecting the squirrel for a while now, exploring how his body works. I'm still learning new things, even though he's dead. This isn't the vivisection I wanted, but I was still so excited when I realized how well things were going that I almost drooled right into the squirrel's open chest cavity.

My mind drifts as I run my tongue along my teeth. If I did have people close to me, I'd have to account for certain uncomfortable realities, like, say, the way I've noticed my gums bleed when I chew, and my teeth have started yellowing just the tiniest bit, with the addition of a nervy sponginess each time I bite my lips. To be fair, I can't remember the last time I brushed them. I certainly didn't pack toothpaste or a toothbrush for relocating to the tunnels. That would be silly; after all, there's no running water down here. I've repurposed an old chemical drum for a toilet. The stench doesn't bother me; I'm too focused on my work, on the heady atmosphere of opportunity.

After a few more minutes, I believe I've learned everything I can from the squirrel—which was quite a bit more than I expected.

I will become a surgeon, one way or another. I've been on the right track, I just need to push harder, farther—something I couldn't do with the girls upstairs sticking their blackhead-peppered noses into my business.

I pick up the squirrel's body in my sure, steady hands. With a quick movement, I slice the squirrel's tiny neck, decanting the rest of its blood onto the surgical tray. It pools slowly, the heart having stopped pumping a while ago. I give the body a few squeezes and shakes, and when it's dry, I hold the limp form in one hand while I root through my doctor's bag with the other. When my fingers close around the surgical pins, I pull them out.

Mother never let me decorate my room the way I wanted to—it was always pink and frilly, the opposite of what I would have liked. A grin spreads across my face, because down here, I can put whatever I want on the walls. Everybody likes a bit of decoration.

Part of the wall near the back of the chamber is made of a sort of soft plywood that is easily pierced, which is convenient. I wedge the pins between my lips, then hold the squirrel's body against the wall. Carefully, I push the pins through his flesh in strategic locations until my mouth is empty and the squirrel is stuck on the plywood, looking like one of those anatomy books that shows every layer of tissue.

I step back to admire my handiwork. My groan of contentment echoes around the chamber. I'm honing my skills, sharpening them like knives.

This is the first step to the future I deserve. Who knows, maybe if I play everything just right, I can still get into the Hughes program. From what I've seen, those kids aren't as bright as that dimwitted medical school recruiter seemed to think. I mean, any program that would willingly accept Erica, with her limited vocabulary and overall vapid dullness, over me clearly has been misled at some point.

I'm going to set the record straight.

CHAPTER SEVENTEEN

I Came Into Your Bed, But I'm Not Looking for Anything

The floor in my tunnel chamber is cold and hard when I fall asleep, but it doesn't stay that way.

Horror floods me when I awaken later and recognize, again, the pleasant warmth, the comfortable connection, and the alien togetherness of another person next to me.

Fuck. I've done it again. I can't keep letting this happen. I need to lock myself into the tunnels at night, bind my ankles with rope like Mother used to, set alarms to go off every five minutes to keep me awake and where I'm supposed to be—something, anything to stop this dangerous game my subconscious is playing.

A snore goes off like a bomb right behind my ear, blowing up the last vestiges of sleep. I'm lying on my side, and dim light from the hall trickles through the open doorway to illuminate a tiny one-person bedroom with little more than this bed and a Munchkin-sized dresser. There's no way this space has been zoned as an actual bedroom; it's not even half the size of Mother's walk-in closet.

An arm plops over me like an overfed python, squeezing me against my strange bedfellow. A crotch with a noticeable bulge presses against my ass, and the guy lets out a little moan. Jesus Christ, this is the third time I've done this, and not one guy has jumped out of bed the minute he feels a strange body next to his. These guys just latch on to me like what's happening is totally normal, as though they're expecting random women to hop into bed with them at any hour of the night. That's some patriarchal entitlement right there.

The bulge at my backside is getting more insistent, and I'm getting more annoyed. Time to go.

I'm not as scared as I was the first two times this happened, mostly because anything can become routine if you do it enough—even terrible, confusing things. I'll just slip out as quietly as possible and go back to the tunnels where I belong.

There's an immediate snag in my plan, though: this horny prick's arm is around me. For the first time, I'm the little spoon instead of the big one, and that presents some complications. I'm going to have to move him so I can get out.

"Mmm, Erica, can't leave yet," he mumbles.

I freeze. For some reason, this dude thinks I'm Erica.

It's hard not to chuckle at the irony; 'Madame Leila' told me to learn from Erica, and here I am, ass pressed against what must be her boyfriend's crotch. I half-consider giving this guy something to dream about, but then decide firmly against it. I don't want Erica's sloppy seconds; I just want her spot in the Hughes program.

I'm not one for gentleness, unless I'm performing a delicate dissection, of course, but I muster up every ounce of tenderness I have to pluck this guy's arm up and off of me, trying to keep him unconscious for as long as possible. My fingertips are pressed against his wrist, lifting, lifting—

He slams his arm back down, squeezing me tighter than before, tighter than anyone would consider appropriate. Air shoots out of my lungs in an audible whoosh, and I tense, waiting for him to wake. I don't blame Mother for shackling me to the bed as a child; in her way, she was protecting me from situations like this.

He grunts again, but doesn't scream, or yell, or throw off the covers. The reek of morning breath envelops my nostrils like a noxious cloud. It's hard to believe Erica hooks up with this oaf voluntarily.

Okay, if I'm going to get out of here quickly, I'm going to have to eschew any gentleness. That's fine, I like things better rough anyway.

When his grip loosens the tiniest iota, I move fast. I squeeze his wrist and pull as hard as I can, yanking his arm up and wriggling my body to the floor. There's a surprised grunt that quickly turns to an angry growl, and before I can regain my balance and make a run for it, his meaty fingers are entwined in my hair, pulling me back toward him.

"Oh, no you don't," he says. His voice is much deeper than I would have expected; most of the college guys around Georgetown are still in the throes of pimpled teenagedom, with voices that crack when they throw out lovely overtures like "Nice ass" or "Are those double D's?" Somehow, those guys— guys like Scaphism Steve—still think they can find girls who will respond positively to that sort of immature crap.

I don't have time to think about things like that, though—not when those thick fingers are digging into my scalp, yanking my head back onto the bed.

"You came into my bed, babe. I know you're not Erica, but this is what she gets for being busy tonight," he says. "You, on the other hand, are clearly looking for something."

I say nothing, trying to turn my face away. I know I can see better in the dark than most people, and even though the light is probably too dim for him to see much, I can't risk the chance that he might recognize me one day. If I had my doctor's bag with me, I'd plunge a scalpel into his eye sockets, blinding him forever.

Instead, I snake my right hand up to meet his fist and rake my fingernails through his flesh, pushing as hard as I possibly can.

"Ah! Fucking bitch!" he yells, but he doesn't let go. Goddamnit, that was loud. He better not wake his roommates. He must be really different with Erica, or else she's more of a glutton for punishment than I would have ever expected. With a surgical needle and some thread, I would sew those lips closed so he'd never make another nasty, misogynistic comment again.

His bed is on risers, and as he pulls my head back, my feet—bare again, for God's sake—start to scrabble to touch the rough carpet on the floor. I'm still turned away from him, but if he keeps pulling, I might be forced to face him.

"You're going to get it now, bitch," he breathes into my ear, the morning breath assaulting my nostrils once again.

I'm nervous about getting out of this, but I'm not scared. You see, most people have hangups about hurting another person, so even in a hurt-or-be-hurt situation, those sorts of people hesitate when they have a window of opportunity. I am not one of those people. If I had my trepan, I'd bore a hole not into his empty skull, but into that bulge he's clearly far too eager to use, letting his manhood drain uselessly all over his sweaty sheets.

I don't have any real weapons, so when my scrabbling fingers connect with what feels like a water glass perched on that tiny dresser, I don't waste any time. I grab the glass and bring it down hard behind my head, right where his face should be. There's a satisfying crunch—I think it's his nose—and a nasally "Unh!"

Those fingers in my hair don't let go, though. Next to my ribs, his legs kick just enough to knock the air out of my lungs.

I'm still gripping the glass, panting furiously, desperately trying to inhale some oxygen. Time is running out, so instead of going for his face again, I swing the glass against the bed frame, shattering it. Shards of glass fly out into the air like a firework, leaving a sizable piece still in my hand. In one swift movement, I bring that sharp edge right into the closest part of him I can reach with enough force to break the skin, which happens to be the fleshy part of his calf. For a second, I imagine it's my own, and vicarious relief at the bloodletting floods through me.

"Fuck!" he screams. My shoulders tense; if there's anybody else in this house, it won't be long before they come running. I feel his fingers loosen in my hair, and I lurch forward off the bed. I manage to escape his grasp, but not without leaving a decent-sized chunk of hair clutched in his fist. Whatever, it's not like I'm planning on donating to Locks of Love or anything.

Wait, though. There's the inescapable problem of DNA. I'm not going to kill the guy, and I haven't done anything besides defend myself, but entitled rich guys tend to get what they want. If he wants me right now, and I'm emasculating him instead by fighting back, there's no telling what lengths he'll go to to punish me. He could give the cops my chunk of hair, the follicles full of DNA, and sit back, waiting for them to find a match.

Calm down, I tell myself. My DNA isn't in the system, but I'm not going to take any risks, not with my future medical career on the line.

The guy is writhing on the bed, yelling, and the rusty scent of fresh blood is overtaking the cloud of morning breath in the hot, close space. I don't waste any more time; I pry open his sausage fingers and pluck my missing lock of hair right out of his palm, stuffing it into the cup of my bra, which I thank my sleepwalking self for wearing. Last time, I was just in the guy's boxers and a t-shirt—not nearly as convenient. Then, in a flash, I whip open the door, dart out into the hallway, and find, to my sheer and utter relief, the front door directly ahead. Two seconds later and I'm out in the muggy night air, the guy's screams dying behind me. Without taking stock of where I am, I start running down the street. I don't stop until I reach the *Exorcist* stairs, finally getting my bearings. I'm at 36th and Prospect, not too far from the entrance to the tunnels on the side of Healy Hall.

I scramble down the first stretch of the ridiculously steep stairs toward M Street before collapsing, my chest heaving, my scalp burning where the asshole ripped out my hair at the roots. The adrenaline is starting to fade, and exhaustion is taking its place, along with a heady, painful cocktail of fear, panic, and desperation.

I can't keep doing this. Slipping into random guys' beds was bad enough, now, I've actually fucking stabbed someone. It doesn't matter that he deserved it, because that's not the story everyone will hear. I'm sure he'll tell the police he woke up with some strange girl in his bed, and when he tried to confront her, she broke his nose and stabbed him in the leg. Then he'll sit back, cloaked in his entitlement, and let the police find and humiliate the girl he tried to rape.

Don't get the wrong impression. I mean, I'm into knife play during sex, but only with consent. I'm not a monster.

At least he doesn't have a big chunk of my DNA, and I tried my hardest to make sure he didn't get a good look at me. That's all I can do.

A harsh laugh erupts from my throat, almost like a cough. I still can't believe I ended up in bed with Erica's boyfriend. She really knows how to pick them, I see. There are pieces of her life I want, just a few, but that bastard with a superiority complex certainly isn't one of them.

I rub my now-bare patch of scalp. It's above my right ear and smaller than I expected, about the size of a nickel. I should be able to hide it, no problem.

I have got to stop this. I might not be so lucky next time. I might not get away.

As loath as I am to admit it, I might actually be in need of some help.

My luck hasn't run out yet, because my very first therapy appointment is coming up in just a few hours. I don't expect the under-qualified quack at the student counseling center to provide the sort of assistance I need, but having someone new to toy with always helps me feel more in control.

Pushing up with some serious effort, I climb the stairs and limp away from M Street and back toward campus, careful to stick to the shadows wherever possible. For just a second, I'm tempted to let myself fall back into the precipitous drop in homage to my favorite childhood movie, *The Exorcist*. I'd topple down those steep stairs into oblivion like that loser in the movie, Father Karras—but, of course, I don't. That would be admitting defeat, something my father made into a habit. I may have his weak chin, but that is where our similarities end. I'm far from defeated.

CHAPTER EIGHTEEN

That Philosophy Degree Is Really Going to Get You Places

It was a long, blistering walk back to my apartment from the *Exorcist* stairs at 6 a.m. I didn't want to go back to Burleith, especially sans shoes, but I couldn't go to my therapy appointment with bare, bruised feet, in clothes stiff with dried sweat and gore, having my hair in a rat's nest, complete with an obvious bald patch. You can't show up to therapy like that and try to convince the counselor there's nothing wrong with you. Even the miserable excuse for a counselor I'll surely be seeing won't fall for that.

After changing my clothes, running a brush through my hair and arranging it to hide the spot of bare scalp that still smarts, and using handiwipes to cleanse the grossest parts of me, I head back out. On the way, I ditch my stained clothes in a large Dumpster behind Darnall Hall. I'm never going to wear those again anyway—they still reek of that guy's sweat and my own primal fear.

Ugh. If the 'Georgetown Cuddler' wasn't big news before, it will be now. There's been an assault. A nose has probably been broken. A leg has been sliced like a Christmas ham. That's the story everybody will hear, how the unsuspecting, innocent young man suffered a vicious, unprovoked attack while he was peacefully sleeping. There's no way he'll sacrifice his masculinity and tell the police the truth, that it was a skinny girl who did that to him. He'll tell the police it was somebody big, who got the jump on him before he even knew what was happening. He never had a chance to fight back, which is too bad, because he would have decked the intruder. Blah, blah, blah.

I open the door to the counseling office and try not to touch my bald patch with my free hand, but I fail. It's like pressing a bruise: hypnotic, pleasantly painful.

I shake my head, attempting to banish the cloud of dread and confusion that settles around me now that I finally have a chance to stop and think about everything. This incident will make it to the police; if it doesn't, it'll make the news in some way, at the very least. That guy, the one with no compunction about raping a stranger, will want to spin this in whatever way he can to still come out on top. That's how people like that work.

Now, here I am, sitting in the waiting room of the student counseling center at 8:45 in the morning, my hair unwashed but at least pulled back, my body clad in a set of clingy clothes that smells bad only if you stick your nose right against the fabric. My feet are dirty, but I'm wearing shoes. You can barely see the scum ground into my skin that the handiwipes couldn't remove. I absently try to suck a clot of something bitter out from between my molars as I wait for the counselor to call me into the back room. I just need to get through this farce.

Rachel Borrister is not at the reception desk, which is too bad. I enjoyed sparring with her last night. Instead, a small man with pale, spidery hands sits in her spot, the light from the computer bouncing off of his glasses, betraying that he's looking at a lingerie website right now. Not that I really care; I'm the only one in here this early. I do wonder what this guy thinks is going to happen, though, with him getting himself all excited right in the middle of the office. I bet if I peeked over the desk, I'd see his hand furiously kneading his own crotch.

I stand up and approach the desk. "Hey," I call out, hoping to startle the little perv out of his thong-induced trance.

His cheeks flush bright red, and both of his silly little hands fly up to his face to adjust his glasses, as if to say, *Look, I wasn't doing what you think I was doing.* "Yes?" he says.

"When do you think the counselor will be in?"

"Oh," he says, relaxing a bit, "probably closer to nine. That's your appointment time, right?"

"It sure is," I say, giving him a sweet smile with too much teeth. I wonder if he'll notice how yellow they are. "So, you're new here?"

He glances around, as though hoping the counselor will pop in right at this moment and save him from any further conversation. "I'm just filling in today, usually I work behind the desk at Leavey."

"Ah," I say, placing my elbows on the top of the desk. "What happened to Rachel?"

"Rachel who?"

"The real receptionist. She was here last night. That's her name on the name plate."

"Oh. I'm not sure. She must have called in sick or something."

"And what's your name, then?"

He shifts uncomfortably—probably trying to hide the inconvenient bulge in his pants. "Spence," he says, his cheeks burning bright again.

"Is that short for something?"

"Spencer," he says. He turns his head slightly, and I can see from the reflection of his glasses that he's minimized or completely closed the lingerie website.

"Are you a student?"

"Yeah. Rising senior."

"What's your major?"

"Philosophy."

That's a stupid major. "That's rather impractical," I say, keeping that discomforting, toothy grin on my face. People aren't mean to you when you're smiling, especially when your eyes go blank and you're not really there at all. I'm starting to feel better, more myself.

"Wow," he says, those little hands fluttering nervously around his shirt collar. "I mean, I don't really think so. You can do a lot with philosophy."

"Like what?"

"Like, I don't know, go to law school."

"Are you going to go to law school?"

"No," he says in a tiny voice that matches his hands.

"Then what are you going to do with your life after you graduate?"

"I don't know, okay?" he says, that pathetic voice shimmering with a spiky panic he's clearly experienced before. I've struck a nerve.

"Better figure that out soon," I say. "You don't have much time left."

"I know!" he nearly shouts at me, and his loudness is still echoing around the room when the door to the back office opens and a thin woman steps through.

"Everything alright in here?" the woman, presumably the counselor, asks.

"Oh, everything's wonderful," I say, and I see Spencer nodding in my peripheral vision.

"Okay, well, Keely, right? Here for your nine a.m.?"

"That's me!" I say cheerily, hoping to pound her over the head with my absolute okay-ness, with how much I don't need her ridiculous attempts at therapy. Mother always hated psychiatry, but she said there was a special place in hell for therapists. Even my father would agree, both of them scoffing about people like this woman, who've gone to school for six months, maybe online, just to learn how to ask, "And how does that make you feel?" If she asks me that, I'll probably start laughing. That wouldn't be a good look.

I drum my fingers on the desk as a goodbye to Spencer, then follow the woman through a warren of hallways to a small room completely dwarfed by two large armchairs. I'm sure there are crumbs in the cracks between the cushions, and I try not to grimace as I sit.

"I'm Christina," she says, taking her seat and pulling a yellow legal pad onto her lap. From behind her ear, she pulls a pen. I hate people who keep writing utensils tucked behind their ears, as though they're so studious and thinking such profound thoughts that they might need to write them down at a moment's notice.

"Nice to meet you," I say, even though it really isn't.

"So, Keely, what brings you here today?" As if she doesn't know. I'm sure she's in cahoots with O'Meara.

I don't tell her the real reason, which is that an invasive asshole threatened me with work-study termination if I didn't. I also don't tell her about any of the dark thoughts and feelings I'm constantly pushing away because they're too terrifying to think about, or how I've started sleepwalking again and waking up in strangers' beds, or how cutting flesh makes me feel alive, or that I've been dissecting small animals in the tunnels and pinning their corpses to the walls as educational decorations. Instead, I say, "I've just been feeling a bit blue, and some of my friends recommended I come here to talk things out." I almost laugh, because I've never had a friend in my life—Roger doesn't count, he would stay far away if he knew the real me—much less more than one.

Christina writes something down. "A bit blue. About what, in particular?"

"Oh, nothing in particular, actually, just feeling sort of overwhelmed with school work. Not right now, obviously, because it's summer, but I'm thinking ahead to next semester, and it's a little scary."

"Scary how?" She cocks her head in a way she probably thinks looks inviting, but instead she looks like a dimwitted cocker spaniel.

Ugh, this woman with her repetitive questions and relentless prodding. I glance at the clock on the wall. It's only been three minutes.

"You know, lots of schoolwork, and I'm pre-med, so I'm thinking about starting to study for the MCAT."

"Ah," she says and writes something else down. "So it's mostly stress-related."

"Yes," I say.

"What coping strategies are you using?"

Just dissecting small animals in the tunnels under the school and pressing myself against sleeping strangers. You know, normal stuff. I absently scratch my bald patch, and for a second, I feel the press of tears behind my eyes. No one will ever hear the whole truth, about how a tormented girl was so lonely she had to resort to sleepwalking into peoples' beds just to feel the warmth of human touch. I rein in my emotions and try to sound upbeat. "Yeah, you know, the usual. Talking to friends, going for walks, watching movies."

"And those things aren't helping?" If they were helping, I wouldn't be here, Christina.

"They are, but not as much as they used to. I guess I just want to make sure I'm ready for next semester, you know, mentally."

Christina looks me over, taking in my clumpy hair and the dark bags under my eyes. She swallows, nodding her head sympathetically, then smiles. She has gaps between her teeth that make her look like an anorexic jack-o-lantern. "That makes complete sense, Keely. I'm so glad you came in. I can definitely help you with some stress relief strategies."

Most of the next hour is consumed by Christina offering banal suggestions I could have Googled—take a warm bath (no student at Georgetown has a bathtub, Christina), read before bed, don't watch too much TV, avoid excessive screen time, try exercising, eat a healthy and balanced diet, get plenty of sleep. She also recommends I visit a dentist, because somehow, dental hygiene affects mental health, and if I want to feel better, I should take care of my whole body. I want to calmly reply that she should be taking her own advice because I could drive a car between the gaps in those teeth, but I keep quiet. No wonder she's stuck as a student counselor; her advice really sucks. Now, if she'd said, 'Keely, what you really need to do is vivisect two animals at the same time and try to sew them back together to make a living hybrid,' well, then, I would have listened more closely—but she doesn't really know who she's dealing with, after all.

Five minutes before our time is up, I make my move. "You know, Christina, I feel so much better already, like a weight's been lifted. Just knowing I have a plan in place is so comforting."

"I'm so glad you feel that way, Keely. I'm happy I can help. Let's go ahead and set up weekly appointments so I can monitor your progress." She smiles that sickly jack-o-lantern grin again, and I wonder if she even has to floss, those gaps are so wide. Floss probably wouldn't do a damn thing.

"So…" I say, trying to sound unsure. "I don't really think I need something like a weekly appointment, plus I want to try those strategies we talked about and see what works for me. Can I just call if I feel I need some maintenance or something?"

Christina is nodding in the way that says *I hear you, but I don't agree.* "Well, Keely, while I'm really happy you're feeling energized to make some changes, I think everything will stick best if we start with a weekly schedule, at least for now. We can always taper off later, but I find that students who only come for one appointment don't always thrive later, and just end up coming back in a worse state than if they'd kept up regular 'maintenance', as we like to call it, from the start."

"Oh." I'm so annoyed, my mask is starting to slip. My voice sounds like a dead thing rolling around in my mouth.

Christina's smile falters. "Is that alright with you, Keely?" No, it's not. I don't have time for this. Plus, if there was even the tiniest part of me that wondered whether Mother was wrong, that maybe therapy would help me feel less alone, less damaged, Christina has killed it. No wonder Mother refused to put me in therapy—this shit is worse than useless. Maybe saving me from a counselor like Christina was one of her rare attempts at expressing something less than complete hatred for me.

"I thought I didn't need that much help, just some encouragement for the most part. Plus, I have an on-campus job, so it's a bit difficult to fit in appointments and still get all my work hours in."

The smile returns, and I imagine a candle burning the roof of her mouth, lighting up everything from inside, the flickering flame visible between those horrible gap teeth until the fire melts her sinuses and her entire face caves in. "Don't worry about that at all, Keely. I'm sure Father O'Meara will understand. He'll work something out with you."

Ah, there it is. I knew it. Christina is no Roger—for all his limitations, that man can protect my goddamn privacy, unlike this shrew.

"Oh, okay," I say, and I hate how weak my voice sounds. I've been outplayed. I can't let O'Meara think I'm not complying fully with his blackmail demand. I'll have to endure these sufferingly long hours with Christina and try to look like I'm making rapid progress until this junior league harpy finally cuts me loose.

"I'm so glad you understand, Keely," she says. "This really is for your own good."

I almost laugh, because the only one who knows what's for my own good is me. I want nothing more than to take the pen lodged once again behind Christina's ear and stab it right through her left eyeball. She'd have to live the rest of her life with an eyepatch, if, that is, she lived long enough to need one and I didn't decide to push the pen just far enough to scramble her brain like eggs.

"Well, it was lovely speaking with you," I say, my voice so saccharine it almost burns my tongue.

"And with you," Christina says. "Just work with Spencer at the front desk to get your next appointment scheduled. Next week, we can talk through what stress relief strategies you've tried, and maybe hone in on what's working the best."

I just smile and nod, instead of pointing out that the phrase is actually 'home in,' like a homing pigeon. Of course someone like Christina would get that wrong. She may work at Georgetown, but she's not exactly the cream of the academic crop.

I let myself out to the sound of Christina scribbling notes on her legal pad, no doubt writing up a report to send to O'Meara, even though everything is supposed to be confidential. I wouldn't be surprised if Christina has never heard of HIPAA or patient privacy laws. Perhaps all therapists would be better if they had traumatic brain injuries like Roger.

The philosophy guy with the small hands, Spencer, books me an appointment for next week without saying a single word, then writes everything down on an appointment reminder card and shoves it roughly across the desk.

"Thanks so much, Spence," I say, my voice dripping with poisoned honey. "And keep on working hard on that philosophy degree, bud. I've heard there's a huge demand for baristas who can quote Socrates."

The corners of his mouth tremble, and I feel better than I have all day. When I walk outside, heading toward the Chaplains' Office, I start thinking about the stress relief strategies that will actually work for me: manipulating Airhead Ani, performing surgery on Dumpster rats, slinking through the tunnels. None of those things are strategies Christina could understand— and that's why she's stuck asking trifling questions to oversexed, drunk college kids who just need Adderall or Valium to really get by.

I would thank God for saving me from that fate, but we all know God isn't really there.

CHAPTER NINETEEN

I'm Front Page News

As I walk through the hot morning toward the Chaplains' Office, the smattering of people milling about on campus barely gives me a second glance, but I do notice a subtle shift in the air. People wrinkle their noses, take half steps backwards. Hell, it's probably me. My jeans smell stale, my shirt has a small rust-colored stain near the bottom hemline, and my shoes are mismatched, but at least they're both black.

I spent last night in the tunnels again, where it's safe. I've got the ideal setup and all my tools: my doctor's bag, my metal trays, my barbicide, my cages, and my traps, of course.

I keep moving, and my hair feels slick as I pull it back with an elastic. Last night's experimental subject was a mouse with a massive testicular tumor. I tried vivisection, but the mouse bled out almost immediately. That tumor was something else; there were tiny chunks of tooth in it, making it a genuine teratoma. Teratomas are very rare in wild mice, a tidbit I learned in biology class. Testicular teratomas, however, can be quite common among inbred mice, which means my little test subject probably escaped from a lab somehow. I wouldn't be at all surprised if the mouse's great escape was a result of Erica's shoddy laboratory etiquette. She probably left a cage open when she was texting her brute of a boyfriend.

Anyway, the mouse and its testicular teratoma now adorn the wall next to my other experimental subjects.

I climb the few steps up to the front doors of Healy and let myself inside. The entrance hallway, meant to be impressive and imposing, smells musty. There's a light on in the Chaplains' Office, but I must be the first one here, because Airhead Ani never gets to work on time.

I'm wrong. As I turn the knob to go into the office, I see the outline of a self-righteous head perched atop a wormlike body sitting nonchalantly in one of the reception chairs. When I open the door, O'Meara turns to face me with an unctuous grin on his face. He's oilier than I am.

"Keely!" he says. "Good morning."

"Morning," I mumble, trying to keep the rage out of my voice.

"I was hoping to catch you before things got too busy for the day."

"Oh?" I sidestep him and come around to my chair behind the desk. I don't want him seeing my outfit, much less my mismatched shoes. He might get the wrong idea.

He leans in closer, and I can smell rancid peppermint on his breath. I hope he can't smell the sourness coming off of me.

"Well, Keely—" He stops, sniffs the air. Dammit. "Um. Actually, could I first have a cup of tea, if you would be so kind?"

Airhead usually gets O'Meara his ever-present cup of peppermint tea, and I'm happy to let her do it. The smell of peppermint has begun to nauseate me, associated as it is with O'Meara and his holier-than-thou aura of invincibility.

"Sure," I say through gritted teeth. I swivel over to the electric kettle and turn it on. In seconds, it's hot, and I pull a clean mug from the stack on a shelf above my head. I pour the boiling water into the mug, wishing I could throw it in O'Meara's face instead.

As I'm plunging the tea bag into the mug, he says, "I wanted to ask how your meeting with the counselor went."

Ah, of course that's why he's here. I should have known he'd be nosy—

like that's any of his goddamn business. Counselor-patient confidentiality clearly means nothing to him.

I don't say any of that, though. I just smile—no teeth, I don't want him to see how yellow they are—and say, "Oh, it was good."

"Did Christina help you work through what you needed to work through?"

I think about messing with him for a second, testing the limits of his knowledge by telling him I saw a different counselor, or that Christina told me O'Meara would make her life uncomfortable if she didn't make time for me, but I don't want to give him a reason to look at me harder. He's already too focused on me as it is.

"She sure did," I say, and then, because he's still studying me, I add, "We talked about some stress relief strategies."

"Good, good," he says, nodding. "Well, I hope regular appointments with her will keep you feeling good."

There it is, the next installment of the blackmail. Not only did I have to meet with a counselor once, but now O'Meara is insisting I go back on a 'regular' cadence, just like Christina recommended. This is some serious horseshit. For a second, I imagine slicing into his chest and cracking open the rib cage like I do with my experimental subjects, except his surgery would be completely unmedicated. I'd keep him alive long enough so he could see himself being disemboweled, then I'd rip his still-beating heart right out of his body and squeeze until it exploded.

I force myself back into the present moment, and from the way O'Meara is studying me, I wonder if he caught my true feelings flitting across my face.

"Sure," I say. "She was helpful."

"Excellent. Well, I'm glad to hear it. I was really worried about you, Keely."

As though anyone has ever been worried about me.

"Don't be worried," I say. "I'm just fine."

His eyes flick to my hair. I wonder if he can he see the grease shining in the fluorescent light. "Sure you are," O'Meara says, but his voice is doubtful, and I think he wants me to hear that tinge of disbelief. "Um, I don't mean to be indelicate, but when was the last time you had a good night's sleep? Or a hot bath?"

He did not just say that to me. I may not be the most ladylike person out there, but come on. All men should know never to say things like that to a woman. I don't really know how to respond, so I just splutter, "I'm fine. I'm fine."

He keeps eyeing me warily. "Of course. I just… your appearance has changed, Keely. I've seen many people in the throes of clinical depression, and failure to keep up on personal hygiene is one of the first signs that something is wrong."

I know everything he's said is true, and the word 'failure' keeps echoing in my head like a drumbeat. An unwelcome weakness creeps through my limbs. Mother would be appalled by my hair, my clothes, my teeth, my everything. I look nothing like the picture of female perfection she raised me to be. In Mother's eyes, women are only worthy if they have the look of a supermodel, like Airhead Ani or Erica, but the brain of a Nobel laureate. It's exhausting and impossible to try to be both, yet Mother never has any trouble—she is always dressed to the nines, happy discoursing about everything from Nietzsche to neurosurgery.

Not for the first time, I wonder what it would feel like to simply let myself fall, let myself stop trying so hard. I've always imagined falling would hurt, but maybe it would be easier if there was someone there to catch me.

Across the desk from me, my would-be savior slurps his tea far too loudly, and I push down my feelings of vulnerability as savagely as I possibly can.

"Thanks for checking on me," I say, the words like acid, burning my tongue. "But I'm fine. Really. My hot water hasn't been working lately, and my landlord is ordering new laundry machines. That's all." Neither of those things are true, but who cares. O'Meara can't fact-check me, not this time.

"Of course," he says, but he doesn't make a move to get up yet. It's like he's waiting for my mask to slip again, to confirm what he thinks he knows about me.

He stares at me; I stare back at him. For almost any other pair of people, this would probably be unbearably awkward, but I think we both know one flinch can betray a lot about a person. O'Meara doesn't want to miss a thing, and I refuse to let him see who I really am.

Finally, he says, "Well, I'll let you get to it," and starts the laborious process of pushing himself up from the chair.

Luck is not on my side today, because some ponytail-ed ignoramus comes bouncing into the Chaplains' Office just as I'm about to get rid of O'Meara. I don't know her name, but she looks vaguely familiar in a way that makes me want to bare my yellow teeth. Who is she?

"Father O'Meara?" she asks, giving me a cursory glance before turning back to the Jesuit.

"Yes?" he says, rising to his feet.

"I'm Kat Saunders, and I was hoping to ask you a quick question?"

O'Meara looks at me, probably calculating whether or not he should talk to Kat Saunders in his office, and then decides to stay where he is. His mouth is speaking to her, but his mind is still on me.

"Sure," he says. "What can I do for you, Kat?"

The girl is practically bouncing on her tiptoes. "Well, Father, I heard from my roommate—Jess Flatley, I'm not sure if you remember her—that you gave an awesome talk last year about your experiences with ghosts and exorcisms?"

O'Meara looks taken aback for a second, and I relish the moment. So he's not unflappable, after all. "Oh, yes, of course," he says. "And I do remember Jess." Yeah, right. It's like teachers telling helicopter parents how amazing and individual their children are, when in reality, every student is an indistinguishable snot-nosed brat.

Kat's eyes are shining with eagerness; it's disgusting. "I'm with the Hughes research program, and we were hoping you'd be willing to give a small group of us the same presentation?"

Now I know why Kat Saunders makes me want to projectile vomit across the room—she's one of the Hughes kids. They're supposed to be investigating legitimate natural phenomena with established scientific methods, not wasting the privilege they've been given on made-up ghosts and demons.

O'Meara's eyebrows shoot up, as though this were the last thing he was expecting this morning. He was probably thinking he'd crack me like a walnut shell and feast on the bitter meat inside, but instead he got handed this. I'm pleased. He needs something else to focus on, something that will divert his attention away from people like me who want to see him pushed down a dry well.

"Well, sure," he says, recovering his composure. "I'd be happy to."

"Yay!" Kat squeals, and the sound hurts my ears.

"But you should know, I can't go into the particulars of the exorcism rites," O'Meara says.

"That's okay," Kat says. "Anything you can tell us will be helpful."

"Helpful? This seems a bit out of your scientific realm, as I understand it. Are you all working on a project or something? "

"Oh, sort of," Kat says. "We're interested in the true story behind *The Exorcist*."

"That movie? Why?"

"Well, as scientists, we should look into both the things we can see and observe and the things we can't, right?"

I barely suppress a scoff. Once again, how is this bumbling, superstitious idiot worthy of the Hughes program?

Kat continues, "We've done some early research and we heard the story is based on something that really happened, and that the boy in question had his first exorcism right here at Georgetown."

Something in O'Meara's face darkens, and I feel immensely satisfied at getting a glimpse behind his mask, at even knowing he's wearing one at all. Some people walk around so unapologetically barefaced, as though there's nothing worth hiding—people like Airhead Ani, like Kat Saunders, probably like Erica, too. There's nothing to hide because there's nothing deeper than what you can see.

O'Meara clears his throat. He's uncomfortable. I lean forward hungrily, not wanting to miss a word.

"Well, I don't know too much about that," he hedges.

"That's okay. We heard you were, like, one of the foremost experts on exorcism in the world."

I choke back a laugh, picturing the whole Hughes group exploring campus with flashlights and too much false bravado, Scooby-Doo-style. This whole conversation keeps getting stranger and stranger, which is really saying something considering how high my tolerance is for the bizarre.

O'Meara flicks his eyes over to me, but I manage to look absorbed in my computer just in time. "I did consult for the Vatican," he says reluctantly.

"Awesome!" Kat squeals again. "Is it alright if I email you to work out a time? We'll have devil's food cupcakes!"

O'Meara laughs, but I can tell it's not a real laugh. Kat doesn't seem to notice. "Sure," he says. "Looking forward to it."

"Thank you so much!" Kat says. "I'll email you," she repeats, and then, in a haze of what smells like too-sweet coconuts, she twirls around and moves toward the door.

"Wait," O'Meara says, taking a quick step toward the retreating girl. Kat pauses and pivots, looking back at him.

"Yes, Father?"

He leans in, pitching his voice low, but of course I can still hear him. This is a small office.

"I heard what happened to Lewis Romero and Jude Baxter, plus Tom Carlson—that poor boy," O'Meara says. "How are you kids holding up?"

Kat looks down and away, the cheeriness evaporating like rain on sizzling pavement. "I mean, we're all pretty freaked out," she says. "With Tom getting hurt, it feels way scarier."

My entire body goes rigid, a taut bowstring. Panic boils in my stomach, ulcerating the thin tissue lining. They're talking about me and about those boys who found me in their beds in the middle of the night.

"Of course, of course," O'Meara murmurs. "How is Tom?"

Kat sniffles. I can't believe she's actually crying over a bag of dicks like Tom. "He'll be okay," she says. "It wasn't a very deep cut, and his parents are consulting with a plastic surgeon about his nose." She smiles wanly. "He'll probably end up getting a movie star nose out of all of this, so it's not all bad."

My heart is beating so fast, I worry they can hear it.

"I'm glad. I know campus security will be adding a few more officers on night patrol. Will Tom press charges if they identify his attacker?"

"I don't know," Kat says. "He says he didn't get a good look at whoever did this. But I'm so happy to hear we'll have a bit more protection, especially at night. Thank you, Father."

"Sure. Please contact me if there's anything else I can do for you, or for the other Hughes students."

Kat smiles. "Just the exorcism talk, that's all. I'll email you."

"Right, right." O'Meara pats her on the shoulder. "Well, stay safe out there, Miss Saunders."

"Sure I will," she says, and finally, she's out the door.

O'Meara stands motionless for a moment, staring after her. His eyes shift toward me one last time, but he says nothing. With a barely audible sigh, he walks toward the door and makes his own exit.

I barely have time to recover, the goosebumps on my skin just receding, my heart returning to something of a normal rhythm, when the door opens yet again, and Airhead says, "Morning!"

Louis Vuitton bag in the crook of her arm, she's got a newspaper clutched in the hand not holding a giant Starbucks cup. That's odd. I wasn't entirely sure she knew how to read anything longer than a Tweet.

"Dude," she says, dropping the paper on my desk. "Have you seen this?"

It's today's edition of *The Georgetowner*, and it feels like it's still warm from the printer. "What is it?" I ask.

Airhead sets her Frappuccino down on the wood of the desk—sans coaster, because she was clearly raised in a barn—and drops her bag to the floor. "Read the article on the front page! There's someone out there getting into random kids' beds and, like, cuddling them. Everybody's calling this person the Georgetown Cuddler, which sounds cute and all, but the other night some guy got stabbed."

My eyebrows squeeze together so hard I feel like they could pop the pimple brewing between my eyes. I knew there would be some sort of media coverage, but I didn't expect it to be front-page news. I grab the paper and unfold it, my eyes flying across the typed page.

*   *   *

Break-ins and Assault Targeting Georgetown
Students
By Cynthia Vauxhall

Within the past week, a spate of troubling break-ins have kept the Georgetown University community on edge. Two students, Lewis Romero and Jude Baxter, were awakened in the middle of the night by a stranger in their beds. In both cases, the intruder escaped before either young man could make any sort of identification. Baxter tried to give chase, but failed to catch the intruder. Both young men were unnerved by the incident, but were not physically harmed, and their valuables were untouched, ruling out burglary as a possible motive. Students have dubbed the unknown offender the 'Georgetown Cuddler.'

Two nights ago, the perpetrator graduated from

cuddling to violence, prompting both Romero and Baxter to inform the authorities about their own incidents. Tom Carlson's experience began the same as the other men's: he woke up to a stranger in his bed. However, when Carlson tried to restrain the intruder, he was punched in the face, breaking his nose. The intruder then proceeded to shatter a water glass and stab Carlson in the calf with a large shard.

"I'm not going to press charges," Carlson said. "I just want whoever this person is to be caught so they don't hurt anybody else."

Carlson is expected to make a full and complete recovery. When asked for a physical description of the intruder, Carlson said, "I mean, I'm a big guy, and this person still managed to get a few good shots in on me. I hope this doesn't happen to someone who can't defend themselves as well."

Police have little to go on regarding a description of the 'Georgetown Cuddler,' but they are urging the Georgetown community to come forward with any information that might be helpful in bringing this series of terrifying and escalating incidents to an end.

*   *   *

I drop the paper and shake my head. Jesus Christ, Tom didn't even tell the police I'm a woman! I'm surprised enough that Lewis and Jude either didn't catch or purposely left out that major detail, but Tom knows without a doubt that I am female. His masculinity must be even more bruised than

I thought, if he's willing to hold back essential information from the police just to protect his fragile ego. Sucks for him, but this whole thing has worked out rather well for me. I managed to break his nose after all, and the police are more likely to look for another guy, one big enough to hurt someone like Tom, instead of little old me. I do love being underestimated.

"… would totally want to help." Airhead has been prattling on this whole time, but I only catch the end of it.

"What?" I say, trying to keep the irritation out of my voice and only partially succeeding.

"I was just saying, like, I feel bad for whoever is doing this, I mean, kind of."

For a single, solitary second, Airhead seems less repulsive than usual.

She takes a big slurp from her Frappuccino, then says, "Maybe not, though. Like, you'd have to be a super messed-up freak to go around cuddling people like that."

Well, she ruined it. That's what I get for thinking she may not be a complete waste of oxygen.

"Yeah, I bet that person needs some serious professional help," I say, grinning. My yellow teeth feel like needles I want to plunge directly into Airhead's neck, ripping out her carotid. "At least you live on campus. Maybe it's safer."

"I don't live on campus," she says. "I'm at 3618 Prospect. One of the student townhouses."

It's laughable how nonchalantly she reveals her address. Anything that happens after this, she's asking for it, as far as I'm concerned.

"Oh, well, at least you have roommates."

"I don't, actually. I've got a one-bedroom all to myself."

I try to hide my glee. Just when I think Airhead can't get any less intelligent, she spills that little gem. She's the kind of girl who would tell a sketchy door-to-door salesman that her parents aren't home.

"Yikes. Well, you know one of the assaults happened, like, right next door to you," I lie, widening my eyes in mock horror.

She takes the bait, because of course she does. "Seriously? Oh God, I didn't realize that. But, like… doesn't the Cuddler only go after guys?"

"So far," I say. But it would be all too easy to change that.

CHAPTER TWENTY

Being on the Cutting Edge Is Almost Better than Being Perfect

All week, I can practically feel O'Meara breathing down my neck, hear the crunch of police-issue boots on the pavement behind me, smell the excitement of that stupid reporter Cynthia Vauxhall as she chases after a scoop as big as the Cuddler. Everything is pushing me farther and farther underground, where it's safe. With all that's been going on, I've barely been sleeping at all, which solves one of my problems, at least.

I've outfitted my subterranean operating theater more extensively, filling it with extra metal trays, surgical scissors, medical-grade thread, rubber gloves, and a bucket of antiseptic. It's honestly amazing to me what some neglectful professors left behind in their labs in the Reiss Science Building, once they made the move to the shiny new Regents Hall. Shockingly but conveniently, the doors of the now mostly abandoned old science building are always unlocked for enterprising students like me to take what I need. Long before I scored my doctor's bag, that's how I got my first set of instruments, which left something to be desired, sure, but at least the rest of my equipment is good quality. I had to hop over a homeless man sleeping in one of the Reiss hallways on the fifth floor to find everything I needed.

I'm so focused on my upcoming experiment and staying inconspicuous that I forget about the 'eyelash enhancer' I ordered for Airhead Ani until she pesters me about it. On Thursday, I put the little tube in her grasping fingers, just to shut her up so I can have some space to think. There's not even much joy in the subterfuge; I have bigger and better things to concern myself with.

When the day is finally over, I hustle back to Burleith to pick up a box of Cheerios and a bottle of water. I'll need fuel for tonight. I'm nearly set for one of my most significant experiments.

The Cheerios and water are in a bag slung over my shoulder, and I'm almost running back to the tunnels when I hear Roger's voice.

"Hiya, Keely!" he says. I slow to a stop, my breath coming in short bursts. Roger is wearing a mismatched sweatsuit despite the heat and munching on a stick of jerky.

"Hey, Roger," I say, still trying to stop panting.

Roger takes a massive bite of the withered meat and chews with his mouth open. "Look at that yellow bird over there!" he says, pointing to my left. I turn to see a red cardinal.

"Right, yellow. Good find," I say.

"What are you doing tonight, Keely?" he asks.

My face grows hot with excitement at the chance to share my brilliant plans with the one person who won't judge me—or remember a damn thing I'm saying.

"I'm glad you asked," I say. "I've got quite the experiment planned."

"What sort of experiment?" He takes another huge bite of jerky.

"Well, if I'm going to get into the Hughes program, not to mention medical school, I need to get ahead in any way I can. If people don't believe how brilliant I am from my transcripts alone, I'll have to show them."

"How?" He swallows, and I can see the beefy bolus slide down past his Adam's apple.

"You see, it's clear I've mastered the art of dissection. Give me an animal model and I will turn it into an anatomical diagram worthy of da Vinci. I'm not as steady with vivisection, but I'm starting to think that's a failure of the malnourished experimental subjects I'm using, not my surgical skills, of course."

"Of course," Roger parrots.

"I've learned enough, and frankly, attempting vivisection over and over is starting to get boring. It's time for something new, and that something is parabiosis." The word slithers off of my tongue like a soft, purring cat. I'm almost drooling.

"What's paralybis?" Roger asks, crumpling the empty wrapper of his jerky in his fist.

"Parabiosis, Rog. I learned about it in my first biology course, and when Professor Sliffert introduced the concept, all the other students made these silly horrified gasping sounds. Can you believe it? They'll never be able to hack it as real doctors if a picture of two mice joined together bothers them that much."

"Joined together in matrimony," Roger says, his voice flat. I can tell I'm losing him, but I don't care. Discussing my plans is giving me the burst of energy I need to counteract the fatigue fighting to take me over.

"Allow me to explain. In parabiosis, one animal's circulatory system— you know, their blood—is joined to that of another animal of the same species. This type of experiment has helped scientists explore everything from metabolism to aging, if you can believe it. Because of parabiosis, researchers discovered the hormone leptin, which regulates hunger, studied the effects of X-ray radiation on cancerous tumors, and investigated the role of the hypothalamus in obesity."

"My mother has obesity," Roger says. I resist the urge to remind him he should be speaking about his mother in the past tense.

"There is no limit to the breakthroughs I can make when I master parabiosis. I'll have medical schools eating out of the palm of my hand, and Professor Demetri will come begging me to join the Hughes program. You want to know something else? Maybe I'll even bring my conjoined friend home during Christmas break, just so Mother can see with her own eyes how talented I am. That would show her. See, Rog? I just have to focus on the positive." I will myself not to think about O'Meara, or the police, or the newspapers, or the sleepwalking.

"Christmas is next week," Roger says, clearly oblivious to the heat of summer. "I asked for a new computer."

"I love talking to you, Roger," I say. I can tell Roger things I could never tell Christina, that joke of a therapist.

"I like you, Keely," he says.

I know most of what comes out of his mouth is senseless, but his words make me freeze. I literally cannot think of a single person in my entire life who has ever said those words to me. My eyes prickle.

"I like you too, Rog," I say. I've never said that to anyone before, either. Maybe it's possible for me to make a friend, after all.

Roger's face goes blank, and the moment ends. "Look!" he shouts. "A bluebird!"

I look over my shoulder, and, for once, the bird hopping along the sidewalk is actually blue. Roger's damaged brain is endlessly fascinating.

"Right-o," I say. "I've got to go now. You have a good night."

"Merry Christmas, Keely!" he says as I resume my trot back to campus.

*　*　*

"Excuse me, miss?" It's barely fifty feet between the main doors of Healy and the entrance to my tunnel sanctuary, but I guess I didn't move fast enough to avoid whoever is accosting me now. I look up in the direction of the voice and find a paunchy man with a leathery tan wearing a Georgetown University Campus Security uniform.

My heart starts racing, and I try to plaster a neutral expression on my face. "Yes?" I say.

"Would you like an escort back to your apartment?" he asks. There's a wedding ring clamped around one fleshy finger, and I resist the urge to ask him if his wife knows he's in the business of being an escort. I don't want to call any extra attention to myself, not tonight—not when I'm about to perform the most cutting-edge surgery I've ever done. Parabiosis is what matters, not some overgrown mall cop imbued with a speck of authority.

"No, thank you," I say. This is strange. I've never been offered a security escort before.

It dawns on me as he says, "With the recent… ah, assaults, we're adding a few extra patrols around here. There aren't a ton of you on campus this summer, so we hope we can keep everyone safe." Of course, of course— O'Meara mentioned those extra patrols. Very inconvenient for me, but that just means I'll have to be even more careful. I'm used to hiding in the dark, and from the look of it, Mr. Leatherface spends every possible minute in the sun. This won't be hard, just annoying. Not unlike Tom Carlson's entitled bulge.

"Thank you, officer," I say, knowing full well this guy is not an officer, probably just a police academy dropout. He doesn't look fit enough to chase me even a single block. One blow to the knees would level him, I'm sure. "But I'll be fine. I'm not going far." That, at least, is the truth.

"Alright, miss," he says. "Well, if you need anything or feel unsafe, give us a call. Anytime."

"Of course," I say. Then, because he's still staring at me, I add, "Things have been a little scary, but I'm sure the excellent Campus Security officers will catch whoever is responsible for these malicious attacks."

With my tiny bit of praise, Mr. Leatherface straightens up, throwing his shoulders back. "We sure will, miss," he says. He nods at me, his wrinkled skin swaying with the motion. "You have a nice evening, now. Be sure to lock your doors."

"Always," I say, smiling sweetly, careful not to show my yellowing teeth or bleeding gums. If this is Georgetown's lukewarm response to a perpetrator like me, I shudder to think how inept they'd be if somebody really dangerous were stalking students.

Mr. Leatherface doffs his hat and ambles on his merry way. I sink back into the shadows of Healy and wait until he rounds the corner of Copley

Hall and disappears into Red Square. I keep waiting until stillness settles over the campus and the trickle of students, professors, and other personnel leaking out of the buildings ceases.

When things finally feel safe and quiet, I emerge from the Healy shadows and head for the tunnels. Today may have been tedious, but it's all worth it when I go to check one of my traps and find the largest rat I've ever seen. It's a nasty thing, covered in fleas and three particularly obese ticks, with sharp yellow teeth nearly as long as my big toes. When the rat sees me, beady eyes like chunks of obsidian glaring at me from the small wire cage, it snarls and hisses like something possessed. If I can't get it to work with me, maybe I'll leave it in O'Meara's office. It'd be like a gift—an opportunity for him to practice his ridiculous exorcism "skills." I can't imagine he gets to use them much around here, and I bet it's like any language: use it or lose it, even if the whole premise is a complete farce.

All of that won't be necessary, though, because I can get this rat, whom I've dubbed Harvey Weinstein, under control. It's being a jerk right up until I show it the rat I sacrificed earlier after dissecting its heart. I wanted to take apart the lungs, too, but time got away from me and I had to get a move on before I was late for work. I shove the carcass in front of Harvey, then rip off the head, throw it on the floor, and step on it. It's important to assert your dominance if you want to be obeyed—something Mother regularly demonstrated with my father.

Harvey immediately slumps into a dejected silence. Now and then, he makes little chittering noises, but mostly he paces around his cage, taking careful steps, looking for a way out. He won't find one. They never do.

A contented sigh slips from my lips, which look like discarded pieces of bubble gum since I've been chewing them so much. Harvey is absolutely perfect. Combined with the other rat I caught yesterday—which I've kept alive but sedated with some crushed Klonopin I bought off the same guy who sells me weed—I now have everything I need.

Speaking of Klonopin, I briefly consider using it on myself, as a way to keep my body out of strange beds, but I quickly dismiss it. Besides being wildly addictive, Klonopin turns people into zombies. I can't do my important work with unsteady hands and a brain clouded in pharmaceutical fog. The weed wouldn't be much better. Now, if I had an Adderall, that would be helpful. I make a mental note to poke around in the medicine cabinets at the townhouse back in Burleith to see if Carly or one of those other girls has something that can actually be of use to me. In the meantime, I've got some thick rope I can use to bind my ankles. It's worked before; it will work again.

Now, it's time to bring Harvey down yet another notch. I don't want him struggling while I'm performing my very delicate work. Without further ado, I mix some more crushed Klonopin into a scoop of Jif and push it through the bars of Harvey's cage. He takes a single second to eye me with distrust before hoovering up the drugged peanut butter. It won't be long before everything is perfect.

Tonight, I'll be using the modification of the Bunster and Meyer technique described by Kamran et al. in the *Journal of Visualized Experiments*. Kamran and the rest of the team linked two mice at the knee and elbow joints, then sutured the skin around the connections. This technique supposedly offers fewer postoperative complications and better survival. I need these mice to survive long enough to show everybody exactly what I'm capable of.

Harvey stops pacing and lies supine in the middle of his cage, pawing idly at the air.

I anticipate success tonight, even though this can't be more than a preliminary practice session. Although I can cut and suture, connect and stitch down here, there are some things I just can't do without a lab. If the conjoined rats live, it will confirm what I already know: that I have excellent sterile surgical techniques. The problem is I can't necessarily tell if the surgical procedure is successful at linking the two circulatory systems without some sort of marker. Kamran and colleagues linked one wild type mouse to one expressing a fluorescent protein called GFP. After the surgery, the researchers could detect GFP in the wild type mouse's blood, indicating the successful connection of the two circulatory systems.

It's just so elegant, so goddamn beautiful. That is what I'm missing, being barred unfairly from a lab. Don't get me wrong, the tunnels have been a gift, but I don't have special laboratory-bred mice with altered genetics. I'm relying on Georgetown Dumpster rats. I don't have blood testing equipment or imaging software than can identify the pinpricks of green light produced by GFP.

Given the limitations, this will have to be a practice run, a proof of concept. This is my application essay for getting into the Hughes program, into medical school. I need to show everybody who doubted me what I can do sans all of that fancy equipment, how impressive I can be even without grant money. Once they see what I can do, they'll have to give me everything I need to really make an impact—that is, if there's any justice in the world at all.

Harvey squeaks softly, the sound like a deflating balloon.

I cross the room and grab my other cage, which contains my second drugged specimen, whom I've named Kevin Spacey. I bring Kevin to sit alongside Harvey, to let them get acquainted. Soon they're going to be really close. Parabiosis: it's happening tonight. I can tell I'm salivating as I prepare my surgical instruments, and I wipe the drool on the inside of my shirt, which smells of mildew.

The Klonopin has now taken full effect on Harvey, and Kevin is still blissed out. One by one, I pull both rats out of their cages and set them down on my prepared metal tray. Using Velcro straps, I secure both rats' arms and legs, so they're firmly on their backs, their knee and elbow joints as close as I can get them.

The time, at last, has come, and my hands are moving swiftly, as though they've done this work a thousand, a million times before. My fingers grab for scalpels, syringes, tape, scissors, like the tentacles of an eager octopus. I feel more like myself than ever, and I inhabit my body in a way I never thought possible—my blood isn't mere liquid anymore, it's an electric current. My eyes are burning, but in a good way, a way that helps me see everything without having to stop and blink. My skin prickles, the small hairs rising on end, sensing even the minutest changes in the environment. This is what I was born to do.

Even sedated, Harvey never loses that wild sharpness. His greasy eyes follow me everywhere I go, as if he's trying to strike some last-minute bargain. Too late.

The bright light I stole from the photography department shines on the rats' oil-drop eyes. A smile distorts my lips, and I know that one day, I won't have to content myself with just animals. One day, I'll have real people on my operating table, people with problems I can fix, instead of problems I create just for the sake of learning. These hurt, broken people will come from all over just for the privilege of experiencing me work, even if I can't fit them into my surgical schedule. They'll consider themselves lucky to have seen me raise my scalpel, make incisions, excise lesions, biopsy cancers, remove faulty organs, and sew up what's left. Mother will hang my picture on her office wall, proud to tell everyone exactly who her daughter is. A feeling like sexual arousal courses through me, so strong and sudden it's almost painful. My mouth opens and a cackle spews out like projectile vomit.

The rats continue to stare up at me. Harvey is a beast of an experimental specimen, powerful and plucky. Kevin is smaller, more resigned to his fate, weaker. How lucky the small rat is to be joining a comrade who is so large, who has the spirit and vigor the small one lacks. I write a few observations in my lab notebook, trying to be as specific as possible, like any great scientist.

Mother will never expect something this impressive. Most people don't do parabiosis because it's too difficult. Not for me, though, not for me—I am doing this precisely because it is difficult. It can't be ignored. Being on the cutting edge is almost better than being perfect.

As I make the first incisions along the knee joints, I can't help but think about my own secret core of weakness, the dark place inside where Mother's voice echoes, perpetually insisting on my inferiority. Maybe one day, I'll be able to rip out my own veins and connect them to someone who doesn't feel so much pain, who can fill in all the gaps in my soul Mother ate away, piece by piece—the gaps that still keep me from being a complete person.

CHAPTER TWENTY-ONE

The Tunnels Were Built to Trap Demons

Something's wrong—not with the surgery, that's going swimmingly, better even than I expected. I hope it's not just beginner's luck.

No, something is wrong with the atmosphere. I've gotten used to the quiet of the tunnels, undercut by the low-grade hum of heavy machinery and the occasional drip of condensation from the pipes.

This is different. There's a disturbance in the air, an inconsistent flurry of sound just at the edge of my hearing. On the tray in front of me, I've connected the rats at every point except for one last elbow joint. This is not the time to get distracted.

My senses hyperaware, I return to my work. An incision here, a stitch there, and—wait. There it is again. That fizz of noise. It sounds like it could be laughter.

It echoes around the small space. There's no denying it: there are other people down here. Jesus Christ, this is like the situation with the girls upstairs all over again. For God's sake, I deserve at least a modicum of privacy somewhere.

The rats need a few more stitches before I can declare the parabiosis operation complete, but the voices are getting closer. I can't afford to be interrupted, not at this very delicate stage.

I freeze in place. There's nowhere for me to go, not if they're coming this way. The best thing I can do is hold my breath and hope none of those hapless interlopers enter my makeshift operating theater.

They're close enough now that I can hear their inane conversation.

"You guys are gonna shit your pants when you hear this," a male voice says. Gross. Men can be so crude.

"Good thing I'm wearing my adult diaper," another boy says. There's the unmistakable crack and whoosh of a can being opened. The slur in the boy's voice means that can is probably beer. Great. I'm dealing with a gaggle of drunken buffoons down here looking for some sort of adventure. That's either going to be easier because they won't remember much if they happen to see something I don't want them to, or harder because they'll be too blackout to find their way out.

"Okay, so, I was talking to this girl on Tinder—" the first boy starts.

"Tinder? Bro, seriously?" Another male.

"Yeah, dude, seriously," the first one says. "Anyway, I was talking to this girl on Tinder, she's a junior or something, and she was telling me about her plans for the weekend and shit, and then she asked me mine—"

"…And you sent her a dick pic," the beer opener says.

"Fuck you, dude. No. At least, not yet." More laughter. "Anyway, I told her I was going to go in the tunnels—I know, I know, we're supposed to keep it to ourselves, but c'mon guys, it was for a good cause—and she was all, 'No, don't do it, Brian, there's weird shit down there.' So I asked her what she meant, and she said she heard from her friend who had a class with one of the Jesuits that the original purpose of the tunnels was to trap all the demons looking for innocent souls, to keep them from possessing people."

There's a beat of precious silence, then they all start laughing—big, sloppy guffaws that confirm everything I already thought about their lack of sobriety. To be fair, though, they should be laughing. Everybody, except for maybe that self-righteous O'Meara with his Vatican consulting gig, knows demons aren't real. Which, of course, begs the question: Why are these kids wasting their time on this foolishness?

"What?" Tinder boy, whose name is apparently Brian, says.

"Trap demons? How's that supposed to work? Like, if you think you're about to get possessed, you go down there and run around until you lose the demon or something?" Ah, okay, there it is: a female voice. She has a point.

"It's like some weird version of the labyrinth with the Minotaur," says a different woman, her words echoing. There's a loud slurp. Their voices are getting louder, and my entire body goes rigid. Just keep walking right on out of here, please.

"Okay, okay," Brian says. "I admit, it sounds farfetched. But I, like a gentleman, feigned belief so I wouldn't make this chick feel weird."

"And how did that work out for you?" one of the other boys asks.

"Well, jerk-off, I've got a date with her next Wednesday."

"You're going on a date on a Wednesday?" a girl asks.

"Yeah dude, that's kind of a weird day for a date," a boy says.

"Whatever, guys, you're just jealous," says Brian.

"Well, I put on these diapers for nothing," the beer opener says. "That shit doesn't scare me."

"Good for you, bro," Brian says. "Then looks like we're all in agreement. The rumors about the tunnels are bullshit and have nothing to do with *The Exorcist*."

There's more laughter, and it's even louder now. This group of inebriates is as intrusive as a freight train in my sacred space. My silence has been shattered. I don't know what else I can do—the blanket prevents most of the light from leaking out of my operating theater, but it won't withstand anything but a cursory inspection. Thinking the chamber's remote location was security enough, I didn't do the best job hanging that blanket. My brightly lit, safe space doesn't feel concealed sufficiently from the dark passageway that, currently, is being used by a horde of dimwits who shouldn't be down here at all. Goddamnit. They're going to be outside my chamber any second. I hold my breath and clench my teeth, letting the pain in my dental nerves ground me. I really should start brushing my teeth again if I want to keep myself from looking like Christina, she of the jack-o-lantern teeth.

If only it were just a single person. That I could handle; one person wouldn't be missed, but instead there's a whole group of them traipsing around where they don't belong—and they're heading straight in my direction.

I can't really run anywhere in this cramped space, and hiding is the coward's way out. Plus, I can't just leave my rats, who need to be stitched immediately lest they bleed out. Speed is of the essence, otherwise all of this will have been for nothing, and I'll have to start over with new traps, new specimens, new timelines.

There's nothing for it but to keep working and hope I remain undiscovered. Even if they do stumble into my safe space, whatever I do, I can't let them see my face.

I bow my head and resume my work, hoping the few moments I spent focused on the commotion didn't destroy the integrity of the entire experiment.

My back to the chamber's entrance, I'm so intent on finishing what I started as quickly as possible that I miss the wooly flap of the blanket being pushed aside. It's not until I hear footsteps getting closer that I realize I've been discovered. I think it's just one person, and they're mostly silent so far. The rest of the group's clamor out in the hallway sounds as though it's receding. A surprising calmness descends over me, and I wonder absently if whoever is behind me has a death wish. I'm no genie, but that is one wish I could certainly grant—with pleasure.

Blood is filling the metal tray, soaking into the fur of both rats. Oh, no. I may have waited too long to finish this. There are just a few more stitches to make, and I can't stop now.

Those cautious footsteps are coming closer, and it both amuses and outrages me to think whoever is back there probably thinks they're being quiet, that I'm too stupid to notice them, that they've outsmarted me.

The footsteps stop, and I can feel the presence at my back, slightly to the right. The person is standing behind one of the concrete pillars. No doubt they can see what I'm doing, but they can't get a good look at me.

I want to see this mysterious intruder, though. Surgeons are notoriously competitive; if someone knows I've got the edge, that I've found the perfect operating theater, that I'm miles ahead of where they are, that could spell doom for me. Being the best means separating from the pack, not allowing the pack to catch up to you. Plus, if somebody figures out who I am and sees my work in progress, they'll probably get the wrong idea. I can't have that. Nobody is going to take the future I deserve away from me.

I've had enough. The intruder behind me needs to leave, right this second.

As if hearing my thoughts, there's an audible intake of breath, and a female voice I could identify even in my dreams hisses, "Oh my God." All the distortion in the tunnels disguised that voice before. Without another word, Erica's feet are scrabbling away on the dirt-dusted concrete, sending her stumbling back the way she came to rejoin the others.

Fucking Erica. If she's here, then the group out there must be the rest of the Hughes kids. The conversation between O'Meara and that Kat Saunders girl comes back to me—exorcisms, of course. The Hughes kids are looking for the "true story" behind *The Exorcist*, and they thought they'd find something in the tunnels.

I guess Erica got far more than she bargained for.

With that thought, cold sweat erupts from my pores. I'm fairly certain Erica didn't see my face, since I was turned away from her and most of the light was focused on my specimens, but she probably did see the full glory of my operating theater, and I must assume she saw my experiment in progress. Goddammit, she'll probably tell the rest of those Hughes kids. In fact, she's likely spilling her guts right now. What if they come back to have a look for themselves?

There's a faint rumble of drunken laughter from the others back in the hall before the cacophony starts receding even further. I walk over to the chamber entrance and yank the blanket closed so hard it rips right down the middle.

I know how these kinds of groups work; the Hughes kids are a pack, and soon they'll all know my secrets. There's another burst of faint, inebriated howling before the tunnels are quiet again; maybe I'll get lucky and they won't believe Erica or they're all so wasted they won't remember anything. I get one deep, shaky breath into my lungs before another thought occurs to me.

What if Erica tells the police?

I can't help it; I let loose a low, hiccuping laugh that sounds deranged even to my own ears. It threatens to go on and on until I choke and suffocate on my own panic. Without my conscious approval, my own glove-encased palm slaps over my lips, stifling the sound. I think the Hughes kids are far enough away by now that they didn't hear me.

There's a raspy squeak from the metal tray, and I rush over to find the cherry on top of what has turned out to be a shit sundae of a night. In the center of my tray, both of the rats are filmy-eyed, their fur beginning to congeal in the sticky puddle that surrounds them. I stick a finger under each of their noses and feel nothing—no whoosh of air, no intake of breath.

I am a failure.

Before I fully know what I'm doing, I grab the tray with both hands and hurl it across the room, sending spatters of blood and stray scalpels flying through the air. The tray lands with a clatter, and the partially conjoined rats flop to the floor with a wet squelch.

I drop to my knees and crawl over to the connected carcasses, cradling them in my sticky palms. They're still warm, and I press them to my chest. "I'm sorry, I'm sorry," I wail, knowing the rats will never hear my apology. They would have been my triumph, and now, because of Erica, they are my sacrifice.

I rock back and forth on the ground, holding the rats, until they go stiff and cold in my arms.

CHAPTER TWENTY-TWO

I Need a Security Solution

I had to retreat to my apartment in Burleith last night after my conjoined rats went into rigor mortis and I finally got up off the filthy floor. My encounter with Erica and the rest of her brainless gang made me feel vulnerable and exposed, like my security was firebombed. That's just one more thing Erica has taken away from me—and how much more will she take? Hundreds of scenarios run through my mind, none of them welcome: Erica bringing the authorities into my private space; Erica spying on me to steal more of my surgical secrets; the Hughes kids bumbling back to my operating theater to explore; my identity being exposed. All I can hope for at this point is that Erica doesn't believe her own eyes and that all the others were too blackout or too incredulous to put any stock in her story.

It's early, barely light out. I roll over and press my dirty face into the pillow, suffocating my moans of desperation. I nearly choke when I inhale flakes of dandruff that must have come from my tangle of greasy hair. I don't know what to do; everything, once again, feels like an overwhelming tidal wave. O'Meara, the Cuddler bullshit, and now this. I could leave the tunnels entirely and find somewhere else, but that seems untenable. The tunnels are—or should be—about as private as it gets in the middle of Washington, D.C. I've never been caught before, but maybe my luck is finally running out.

I moan again, letting every single molecule of carbon dioxide whoosh out of my lungs until I feel like a crumpled tissue. After another ragged, choking inhale, I finally pull myself up to a sitting position with my back against the wall. I've never felt this violated before, and I hate it. Even when that prick Tom Carlson tried to forcibly keep me in his bed, I didn't feel scared. On the contrary, since I knew I could handle him, I was buzzing with energy, ready to inflict pain.

Now, I just feel defeated.

I throw the covers off and dress hastily in something that smells merely stale instead of downright grotesque. Grabbing my keys, I go outside for a walk in the soupy morning.

I don't get far before I hear Roger's familiar trumpet call, "Keely!"

Roger is sitting on the very edge of his lawn, right next to the sidewalk. His feet are almost touching mine when I come to a stop.

"Hey, Roger. I was hoping I'd run into you."

"The sky looks so purple today," he says.

I look up, my eyes nearly burning from the almost violent blueness. "Sure," I say. At least purple is closer to blue than green is to red. Maybe that's progress.

"Why are you crying, Keely?" he says.

"I'm not crying," I say, but then I feel wetness pooling at the base of my throat. All these bouts of tears are getting ridiculous.

"That looks like crying to me," Roger says. "But I don't always know what's really there and what's not."

You and me both, Roger, I want to say. Instead something else comes out of my mouth, unbidden and unexpected. "What would Mother say about all of this? Me standing here, a failure, crying in the middle of the sidewalk?"

"You're not a failure," he says quietly, picking at a scab on his knee.

"Oh, I know exactly what she'd say, probably something like 'Keely, if you're not going to be the best, then you're doomed to be the worst.' Then my father would add some meaningless drivel like, 'Keely, honey, just try your best and that's all we can ask of you.'"

"All you can do is your best," Roger cuts in. "That's what my mom always says."

"That wouldn't matter to Mother. She'd just look at my father and say, 'Close your mouth, Howard, your stupidity is showing.'"

"Your mother doesn't sound very nice, Keely," Roger says, liberating the scab from the raw pink circle on his knee at last.

"Not all mothers are nice. Mine certainly isn't. She's always told me it means nothing to her for me to try my best. No, I have to be the best—or else she says it wasn't worth having a child at all."

"I wonder if I'll be a father one day," Roger says. Something about the hopelessness in his tone makes the tears come faster.

I let myself fall into an imaginary life, one where I'm a girl like Erica. I have a mother who thinks I'm wonderful just the way I am. I have a father who doesn't step back and let people hurt me. Maybe I even have a brother or sister—someone like Roger—who holds me up when I feel too weak or scared to stand on my own.

When I look back at Roger, a smile is plastered back on his face. "A beautiful day, huh, Keely?"

"So beautiful I think I'm getting a sunburn," I say, shaking away all thoughts of a different life. Daydreaming will get me nowhere. "I know I can't just become someone else, Rog. I have to work with what I've got."

"And what's that?" Roger asks, nudging my foot with his bare toe.

"Well, Rog, what I've got is the perfect subterranean laboratory with a privacy problem. What I need is a foolproof security solution."

A plan is already forming in my mind. I give Roger a little wave and continue on my way.

CHAPTER TWENTY-THREE

The Viet Cong Knew What They Were Doing

It's nearly six in the morning on a Saturday, and the authorities still haven't come for me. Either Erica kept her mouth shut or convinced herself what she saw in the tunnels was all a figment of her imagination. Perhaps my luck hasn't run out, after all—but I can't afford to get complacent.

Campus is about as empty as it's ever going to get. Despite how early it is, the humidity is already making me sweat. When I get to the Copley Dumpster, I'm elated because the bed frame I noticed last week is still there, sticking out from the pile of garbage like a chipped gravestone.

All of that wood is going to become the new door to my operating theater. Copley is right next to Healy and therefore about as close to the tunnels as I can get. I don't need anybody seeing me dragging splintered boards from a place like Darnall, on the opposite side of campus, all the way here.

It takes the better part of an hour for me to get the bed into the tunnels, and by the end I'm more sweaty from stress over the possibility of someone seeing me in the bright light of day than from exertion. When I've tossed all the pieces of the bed frame I need into the dark, I wipe my moist palms on my pants, pull the door shut, and head down the ladder myself.

My academic interest in ancient torture practices is really coming in handy right now, because everything I need for my new security system is both creative and torture-adjacent. The next looky-loo who comes into the tunnels is going to get a very unpleasant surprise.

The best booby traps are simple, effective, and meant to hurt, not kill. Just ask the Viet Cong. While the rest of my ninth grade history class was learning about draft dodgers and war protests, I was conducting my own independent study of all the hidden dangers the Viet Cong concealed for the American soldiers. History really can be fascinating, especially if you research what interests you the most.

Taking several trips, I carry the wood, piece by awkwardly shaped piece, to my laboratory's entrance. Using nails and a rusted hammer I found in a dark tunnel alcove, I patch the wood together until it resembles something like a door. Then, with a stiff brush and paint I found in a gallon bucket by the water heater, I transform the barrier into the same flavorless gray as the rest of the tunnels.

I take a small step back—that's all the tight space will allow—and admire my work. The door looks pretty decent; in the dim light, it's difficult to tell there's anything beyond the barrier. It wouldn't hold up to intense scrutiny, but the door is a last resort, anyway. Once I'm done with the rest of my security system, nobody is going to make it far enough into the tunnels to find me in the first place.

On to step two. The Viet Cong had it figured out. I don't need to reinvent the wheel here, I just need to adapt some of their more clever traps for my own use. Let's see, there were the ever-popular Punji sticks, which were sharpened lengths of bamboo or metal that stuck up from the bottom of hidden pits. When an American stepped on top of one, he would fall through, impaling himself. To make things even more gruesome, the Viet Cong often covered the sticks with excrement or poison to add infection to injury. Now that's what I call creativity.

Considering the tunnels have concrete floors, Punji sticks unfortunately aren't possible, and other things like grenades and cartridge traps are also out. Explosions underground, especially beneath an old building like Healy, are not an option—but there are still several other wonderful, effective traps I can lay.

The walls of the tunnels are coated with pipes of all sizes, which make them perfect for setting tripwires. There's also the added bonus that the tunnels are dark, so whoever tries to intrude on my privacy will never see their punishment coming. The Viet Cong used tripwires for all kinds of traps, namely the mace (a fabulous spiked ball), the tiger (a spike-encrusted board), and the bamboo whip (a spiked length of bamboo pulled back like a mousetrap). The Viet Cong were really into their spikes, it seems—and so am I.

Science isn't the only important subject. History can be fun, too.

I spend the rest of the day fashioning spikes from extra pieces of the bed frame. The sharpness of several scalpels has to be sacrificed for my booby traps, but it's all worth it. I can always get more scalpels if I need to. What I can't get is more privacy.

By the time I've assembled a couple of tiger boards, having foregone the other options because I couldn't find a ball large and sturdy enough to hold spikes and because there's not exactly an abundance of bamboo in Georgetown, I have no idea what time it is. Being underground can really impair your circadian rhythms, not that mine are that great to begin with. Now, my body is saying it might be nighttime, but it could just as easily be noon.

Time doesn't matter down here, though, especially since it's the weekend and nobody is expecting to see me until nine on Monday. I'm beholden to no one, which is very convenient.

I've selected three strategic locations for my spike studded boards. The first location is the fork in the tunnels where lucky people can choose to go one way and unlucky people can choose to come toward my laboratory. The unlucky ones will have about five feet to change their minds before they stumble across the tripwire made of heavy duty suture thread and get a face full of weaponized dorm bed frame. The second location is on the other side of the tunnel offshoot containing my laboratory. I'm covering all my bases in case someone manages to come all the way around and sneak up on me from the other side. Except, of course, they'll find that second tripwire before they even come close to my makeshift door, and boom: impaled. The third location takes some thinking. I don't want to put a trap right near the tunnel entrance, which might be an easier spot, on the off chance someone official actually needs to come into the tunnels for maintenance reasons.

In the end, I decide it's always good to have a little extra insurance, so the final tripwire is right in front of my laboratory door, connected to the walls at a diagonal to deter intruders coming from either direction. If somebody manages to see the first tripwire, or if there's more than one person and they don't immediately flee when their friend gets spiked, this backup system should protect me and my work from those pesky prying eyes. With a smile, I imagine Erica creeping through the dark, her ankle knocking against a wire, the whistle as the board whips into place to impale her.

I'm setting the final tripwire, the tiger board already in place, when my fingers stumble and drop the suture thread. With a menacing whistle, the board flies down, the spikes smashing against my new door with a wooden thump, gouging small holes in the fresh paint. A breathy little scream rips out of my throat.

I've nearly been impaled by my own fucking booby trap.

It's not until I've reset the board and firmly attached the tripwire—without messing it up this time—that I notice the blood dripping down my wrist.

I retreat into the brighter light of my laboratory to examine myself. I wipe the wound with a square of only slightly used gauze and find a two-inch gash on my arm. It's not very deep, but it sure is bleeding like there's no tomorrow.

A length of rubber tubing can serve as a makeshift tourniquet just to get the blood to stop flowing. For a moment, I feel myself drift out of my body and hover in the air above, looking down on the dirty girl crouching on the cold cement floor in a slowly growing pool of scarlet. Her hair is so stiff with grease and dirt that it looks like straw. Her shirt is torn, her jeans are dusty, and the shoes on her feet are riddled with holes. Around her, a scatter of surgical tools lie in the dust, a testament to her ineptitude. On the walls, splayed animal carcasses spill their insides to the floor as they rot. The stench is overpowering, but the girl on the floor doesn't notice it anymore.

The moment ends and I'm snapped back into my body like a rubber band. The bleeding has slowed enough that I can remove the tubing and attend to my arm with some hydrogen peroxide and a bandage. The peroxide doesn't hurt as much as I expect, maybe because seeing myself as I really am, even for just a second, was much more painful.

I had plans to do some experimental work down here this weekend, but I can't do anything until I've changed clothes. My soaked shirt is sticking to my torso, and suddenly I can't stand feeling like I'm a snake that needs to shed its too-small skin.

If only it were that simple: just change your clothes, and you'll become an entirely different person.

I can't walk across campus looking like this, with my sleeve ripped, my arm bandaged, and everything soaked in gore. I'm going to have to bring a goddamned suitcase full of clothes next time, because this is not going to happen to me again.

Careful not to set off my booby trap for the second time, I clamber out of my laboratory, step over the other tripwire, and head for the exit. If it's not already dark out, I'm going to have to wait until it is. If I can stick to the shadows, hopefully I can make it back to Burleith without anybody noticing me. I certainly don't want Roger calling out to me with his bullhorn voice.

The rungs of the ladder leading to the gray storm door are sticky—or that could just be the blood drying on my hands. It's hard to tell.

When I get to the top, I push the door open the tiniest crack, just enough to see it's dusk. I don't have to wait long, but I still have to wait.

I wedge myself into the ladder, hooking my arms through the rungs. My tricep aches where the spike bit into it. If the spike had gone through my chest, or stomach, or my fucking skull, I'd be looking like the animal decorations on my operating theater walls long before somebody found me.

The saddest thing is, the first person to sound the alarm about my disappearance would most likely be Airhead Ani or O'Meara, not Mother. It would take at least a few weeks, maybe even a month, until she realized she hadn't berated me in awhile. Then, when she couldn't get me on the phone, she probably wouldn't think much of it until a few more weeks had passed. Then, she'd be getting itchy to wound me, like an addict without access to their drug of choice. Only when she couldn't stand it anymore would she call the school, or the police, or someone to check up on me. When—if—they found me dead in the tunnels, she'd probably be flush with schadenfreude and triumph at being right: her daughter was, in fact, the failure she believed her to be.

I dig my arms tighter into the ladder, relishing the pain.

The bleakest part about it all is that if I really died down there, Mother probably wouldn't shed a single genuine tear for her only daughter, but I bet O'Meara would. He'd no longer have someone to harass with his 'holier-than-thou' act.

Below, I hear the echo of one of my cage traps snapping closed, then the long, low wail of an animal realizing its days of freedom are now behind it.

CHAPTER TWENTY-FOUR

Beware the Large Dog

When it's dark enough for me to make a run for it back to Burleith, I half-expect to feel a tap on my shoulder and the reedy voice of a security guard, but nothing happens. Campus is quiet, and the few people I do pass are engrossed in their phones. Normally I despise that sort of behavior—we're going to have a whole generation of people with kyphosis from constantly looking down—but tonight, I'm grateful for it.

I get lucky again when I reach my apartment. The lights are all off, meaning the girls upstairs are out for the night. In a rush, I rip off my shirt, stiff with dried blood and almost surely biohazardous by now, and throw it in the trash can. I'll transfer it to a Dumpster on my way back to the tunnels. I don't need any nosy roommates accidentally finding it.

I go to my tiny bathroom to wash the grime off my hands, and in the process, I catch sight of myself in the mirror and cringe. My mousy brown hair is nearly black with oil, dirt, and, most likely, some bodily fluids. My gray eyes are threaded through with fine lines of red, my normally pale face is so sallow it looks like an egg yolk, and when I grimace at myself, I see the yellowy hue of my teeth.

The shower groans when I turn it on, accustomed as it is to rare usage. I strip and hop in the tiny stall, the water running in freezing rivulets down my filthy body. My hair alone turns the water a sludgy gray color. I use the single bar of soap available to wash my face, hair, and skin. The chemical scent makes me gag lightly.

When the water starts to run clear, I turn it off and grab the ratty towel hanging on a hook on the wall. It smells of mildew, but it'll get the job done.

Five minutes later, I'm back in front of the mirror, dressed in clothes that may not be strictly clean, but are at least free of biological waste. There's a toothbrush in my hand, adorned with crusty toothpaste, and I'm trying to psych myself up to put the brush in my mouth. I hate having my teeth touched, even when I'm the one doing the touching.

When the brush finally hits my teeth, I yelp. The nervy sensitivity I've been feeling is far worse now, sending shooting pains through my jaw. I swear I can even feel it all the way to the soles of my feet. In comparison, the pain in my arm is negligible, even pleasant, not unlike the self-inflicted cuts criss-crossing other parts of my body.

As I brush, drawing blood and willingly subjecting myself to torture for the sake of appearances—and, I suppose, health—I take note of just how much pain can come from teeth. It could be useful in the future.

The last piece of the puzzle is my hair, which I tug a comb through and then call it a day. I don't look great, but I no longer look like the subterranean tunnel-dweller I really am. I'm going to consider that a win.

Into my backpack go a garbage bag of my soiled clothes, several sets of cleanish clothes, and, reluctantly, that toothbrush, a necessary evil. It might be awhile before I'm back here.

On my way out, I pop an Adderall I nicked from one of the girls upstairs—a welcome score. I have lots of work to do, and with the extra security on campus, I can't afford to wake up in someone else's bed again. It's simple. If I don't sleep, I can't cuddle.

Outside, the moonlight turns the trees into silver filigree. As I pass Darnall Hall, I toss the bag of bloody clothes into the Dumpster, crossing that off my mental to-do list. A light breeze knocks tendrils of my still-wet hair into my face, but I tuck it behind my ears instead of ripping it out. I've got restraint.

I'm about to pass Reiss when I see her, making her way down the Leavey Student Center steps, coming straight for me.

It's Erica.

I haven't thought about her that much today, given how absorbed I've been in my tasks. Seeing her now, I'm nearly drowned in a confusing tidal wave of rage, fear, envy, and something that could be longing. Without thinking, I pull back into the shadows at the entranceway to the old science building and make myself small. Erica is alone, and, like all the other zombies, staring down at her phone. There's a silly little smile on her face, which I find preposterous, because if she was really that affected by seeing me in the tunnels, you think she'd she look just a bit more traumatized. I can't help feeling the tiniest bit offended. Her encounter with me should have left a deep scar, but I'm still glad she's seemingly chosen to do nothing about what she saw.

Erica walks right past me, still engrossed in her phone. Before I know what I'm doing, my feet are tiptoeing behind her, careful to stay far enough back to have plausible deniability if she turns around. Past Red Square, Copley Hall, the John Carroll statue, the riot of red oleander around the Virgin Mary, through the front gates, and onto O Street, I follow her. She takes a right on 35th Street, and I'm about to call it quits—I don't want to get too far away from my tunnels—when she stops in front of a mint green townhouse and pulls a key from her pocket.

Ah. So this is where Erica lives. That's certainly useful information.

She opens the door and goes inside, briefly casting a rectangle of butter-yellow light on the sidewalk. I glance around, pleased to find I'm still very much alone. The pull to see what Erica does at night—besides invade other peoples' privacy—is irresistible. In a few short steps, I'm at one of the townhouse's front windows, ensconced in the shadow of the small alley between this house and its neighbor. If anyone walks by, I can either disappear down the alley, or turn around and keep going, as though

I'm just another normal student.

The first floor of the townhouse appears to be one big room: couches in the front, closest to where I'm peering in, then a dining table next to a fireplace, and a surprisingly roomy kitchen at the back. The bedrooms must all be upstairs. That's also good information to have.

There are four girls sitting at the dining table. Two I don't recognize, one is that bouncy Hughes girl who asked O'Meara to talk about exorcisms—Kat Saunders—and the fourth is, of course, Erica. Even though it's after nine o'clock, far too late for dinner, all four of them are laughing over bowls of something steamy and hot, looking like a goddamned commercial. There's a platter of garlic bread in the middle of the table, along with a wooden bowl full of salad. I can't remember the last time I ate a vegetable.

I can't hear what they're saying, but it doesn't matter. Their facial expressions and gestures are enough. They're smiling, talking animatedly, shoving forkfuls of what I can now see is pasta into their mouths. I look for traces of discomfort or disturbance in Erica's face, but find none. She certainly doesn't look like a girl who's been traumatized.

One of the girls I don't recognize says something, and they burst into laughter so loud I can hear it out on the street. They're all hunched over, giggling like children. Even when I was a child, I didn't laugh like that.

I can't help but wonder what it would be like to have a seat at that table, instead of standing here on the sidewalk looking in. I imagine biting into a warm hunk of garlic bread—in this fantasy, my teeth don't hurt—and piling my plate high with salad. Maybe I'd find whatever they're talking about funny enough to make me laugh like that, too. Maybe I'd feel like I belonged.

Maybe I'd matter to someone.

Stop it. Just stop it. I press the wound on my arm, invigorated by the fresh pain, which provides a boost better than any cup of coffee. It's bad enough that I'm staring at those girls, but it's even worse that I want to be inside that house with them at all. People only laugh and smile like that when they've got nothing interesting going on in their heads. Mother always said people who laugh out loud might as well wear a sign around their necks that says, 'I have a low IQ.'

Ugh. I need to get my mind straight. What I need to do is turn around, walk back to campus, and return to my tunnels. If I'm lucky, I'll have caught another rat in one of my traps and I can try parabiosis again tonight with no interruptions.

I want to pull away from the window. I know I should, but my feet won't move. There's something so intoxicating about watching these four girls have dinner. There's an ease to their movements, a lightness I find both enviable and alluring.

I'm so engrossed in my own thoughts, I don't realize until it's almost too late that Kat has gotten up from the table and is coming toward the door. For a split second, I imagine they've spotted me looking in and are coming outside to invite me to join them, to laugh and eat carbs and overdressed salad in the cozy glow of this townhouse they've made into a home.

The second passes and I've retreated to the narrow alley between Erica's house and its neighbor just as Kat opens the door with a creak. The smell of slow-cooked tomatoes and roasted garlic wafts into the night air, along with that ever-present laughter. "Did Amazon say the package was delivered?" Kat calls back into the house. "I don't see anything out here." One of the girls says something I can't hear, then Kat says, "Oh well, it's not like we need that crepe maker tonight anyway." There's another shotgun blast of giggles and the door closes, sealing all the warmth and comfortable smells back inside.

A crepe maker—of all the pretentious bullshit, I mean really. Wedged into the crevice, I feel the fire-hot blanket of my hatred descend on my shoulders once more. It may not be the snug glow of camaraderie, but it keeps me from freezing, all the same.

Since I'm already in the alley, I decide to keep going to try to exit this way. Towards the back of the houses, high wooden fences preserve the privacy of tiny yards—a real luxury in a neighborhood as cramped as Georgetown.

On the fence that isn't connected to Erica's house, there's a rusted 'Beware: Large Dog' sign that's seen better days. If the sign is any indication, that large dog is probably far too old and decrepit to need a warning.

At the edge of the fences, there's another alley, this one wide enough for a single car to weave its way around the residents' trash cans. I almost turn around to come back the way I came when something glints at the edge of my vision. When my eyes find the object, the corners of my mouth turn up in what I would consider a smile, but somebody looking at me might mistake for a snarl.

Next to the trash cans belonging to the owners of the Large Dog, there's a flattened, black-latticed rectangle that's bigger than the kitchen table in my apartment. Checking to make sure I'm still alone in the alley—I am—I bend down and grip the corners of the object with both hands, relishing the ache in my arm. When I lift it up, it's clear what it is.

A collapsed metal cage befitting a Large Dog who, I'm guessing, bit the dust not that long ago.

It's not heavy, and once I find the handle on the top, it's not particularly awkward to carry, either—which is convenient, because this is coming back to the tunnels with me. It's amazing what these Georgetown assholes will throw away.

Erica's face floats in front of me as I sneak back to campus as invisibly as possible. In my vision, she's sneering at me, her green eyes narrowed, which is just fine. Go ahead and stoke my rage, Erica. Dog cages don't have to be for dogs only.

CHAPTER TWENTY-FIVE
Of Course I Read Korean

The lights are off in the Chaplains' Office when I first arrive on Monday morning, just the way I like it. I sit behind my computer, relishing the darkness and working the kinks out of my neck from sleeping in the tunnels. I bend over and absently scratch the rope burns on my ankles. I don't even notice the wound on my arm anymore; it was only a shallow cut, after all.

I pull a pack of gum out of Airhead Ani's drawer and stuff a minty piece in my mouth. I chew it fast and hard until it's sticky even though it makes my spongy teeth hurt and my gums bleed, then squish it into the seat of Airhead's chair—it's the good one, of course, but it's a sacrifice I'm happy to make. As I'm pressing the gum into the black fabric, I remember Airhead called in sick on Friday. If I hadn't been so shaken from the Hughes kids' violation of my privacy the night before, I would have enjoyed her absence more.

Hopefully she'll be here today, if only so she can be the beneficiary of my little scheme. If she's still sick—or malingering, more likely—and somebody sees the gum, I'll just blame it on her. Some people can be so careless.

The bright blue of the gum sticks out, but assuming Airhead comes to work today, she won't even notice. She'll just plop herself in the chair like always, as though the good chair is her birthright. Later, she won't understand how she got gum all over her ass, ruining her expensive pants.

I'm so absorbed in my own thoughts, I don't notice the figure approaching the office until the door opens and Airhead walks in. "Why is it dark in here?" she asks. That's it—no good morning, Keely, or how was your weekend, Keely, just that nattering little question. There's nothing wrong with sitting in the dark.

"Because the lights are off," I say.

"Oh," she says. I expect her to flip the switch and flood the room with fluorescent light, but instead, she lingers by the door. "Maybe it's better this way," she says, her voice thick with tears.

"Why do you say that?" I ask.

A sob escapes her throat. It's delectable. "That eyelash stuff you gave me didn't work, Keely!"

"What do you mean?" I say, keeping my tone steady and even. To be honest, with everything else going on, I'd forgotten about my little prank. Right now, this is the perfect distraction.

With what she probably assumes is a dramatic flourish, she flips on the lights. "Just look at me! Look at my eyes! I thought you knew about this stuff since you're pre-med!"

It doesn't take long to realize the girl is completely lashless. Her big blue eyes look alien without their frame of dark fringe. It really does look terrible. This is even better than I expected.

I let out a patronizing laugh, and Airhead glares at me with those bare eyes. Without lashes, the effect is not nearly as menacing as she'd hoped. "That's just how it works!" I assure her, flashing a smile.

Confusion scuttles across her face like a crab. "Huh?"

"Girl, did you even read the label?"

"It's in, like, Chinese or something!"

"Korean, actually," I say. "The instructions clearly state that the formula works by first removing all of your old growth lashes so when the new ones grow in, they'll be even fuller and longer."

The righteous indignation drains fully from her expression, replaced by a weary look of relief. "Oh. You read Korean?"

"Sure. I lived in Korea until I was twelve, so I've been fluent all my life." That's not true at all, but she'll never know.

"That's cool," she says, sniffling back the dregs of her tears. "Well, thank God this is what's supposed to happen. I was so freaked out on Friday I called in sick so nobody would have to see me."

Ah, so it was malingering after all. "Don't worry," I say, even though she has absolutely every reason to worry. "Everything will turn out great."

Airhead makes her way behind the desk to join me and drops her bag on the floor. She doesn't even look down at her chair before collapsing into it, just as I planned. This is turning out to be an excellent day so far. "Thanks, Keely," she says. "So, how long is it supposed to take for the new lashes to grow in?"

"A few days, maybe a week and a half at most," I say. "It'll fly by, really."

"Ugh," she says. "I'm not sure I would have tried this if I'd known that."

"It pays to speak Korean," I say, and turn to my computer. I've wrung all the tasty juice out of this conversation.

"So—" she begins, but she's cut off by a cheery voice that instantly turns my mood sour.

"Good morning, girls," O'Meara says, breaking the atmosphere of the room more harshly than if he'd fired a shotgun straight into Airhead's lashless face.

"Good morning," I respond.

"Good morning, Father O'Meara," Airhead adds. "Is there anything I can help you with today?"

O'Meara sits heavily in one of the chairs in front of my desk. "If you wouldn't mind, just a cup of the usual tea, please."

"Of course," Airhead says. She stands up, flashing the sticky blue glob on her ass, and turns away to prepare the peppermint bilge water O'Meara loves so much. I catch a confused look on his face. If he noticed the gum or her distinct lack of eyelashes, he decides not to say anything.

Perhaps he's wiser than I thought. At the same time, that would have been a fun conversation to witness.

With Airhead occupied on the far side of the small room, O'Meara leans in toward me.

"I just wanted to check in on you, Keely. See how things are going." He wrinkles his nose slightly, and I can't help but wonder if sleeping in the tunnels last night undid all the good of yesterday's shower.

"On me? Why?" I ask, all wide-eyed innocence. Without her eyelashes, that's the only expression Airhead is capable of wearing. I almost laugh, because I know something he doesn't, and the feeling is so wonderful it's almost painful, like being held down and tickled until you scream.

"Well, I just wanted to see how you were holding up. How you've been finding those stress relief strategies you spoke about with Christina."

I can't believe he wants to do this with the world's most obvious eavesdropper standing right behind us. Nobody at this school is capable of respecting individual privacy.

"They're working like a charm," I say. "Can't you tell?" I cock my head, daring him to contradict me. Jesus Christ, at least I've showered and changed my clothes. There's no way he'll comment on my personal appearance again.

O'Meara smiles, but it doesn't reach his eyes. "Of course, of course."

"Here you go, Father," Airhead cuts in, handing O'Meara a steaming mug.

"Thank you," he says. Airhead goes back to her seat, which is just inches from mine.

"Anyway," O'Meara says, lowering his voice as though that will do any good, "please know that you can come talk to me at any time. You do have a support system here at this university, Keely. Don't forget that."

My eyes meet his, and as hard as I search for disingenuousness, malice, and deception, I find only a raw honesty that startles me. For a brief moment, I let myself slip back into my fantasy life, where I have friends who cook and eat dinner together.

As it always does, Mother's voice crowds out all pleasant thoughts. "Girls who are going to succeed don't have friends, Keely."

O'Meara must have seen all of this simmering emotion pass across my face, because he whispers, "You're not alone, Keely."

Ah. There's the lie, after all.

With effort, he hoists himself up and ambles to the door. "Have a blessed day, girls."

When he's gone, leaving me feeling far worse than I did before our encounter—which has become standard practice—Airhead Ani decides to add insult to injury.

"Something in here reeks. God, Keely—is that coming from you?"

CHAPTER TWENTY-SIX

Yeah, I'm a Fan of Wisey's

Airhead Ani leaves for an appointment at three o'clock, still griping about the stench in the office. The smell may be coming from me, but she's the one making a fool of herself. It's funny how she thinks she's got us all tricked by being vague and not specifying what type of appointment she's got, hoping we'll think it's a doctor's visit. The effect is ruined by looking under the table and seeing where she's stored her gym bag and yoga mat. Plus, I heard her talking on the phone to one of her vapid friends about how Lululemon is offering a free yoga class at 4pm today. I'm not that stupid. That 'appointment' is obviously a free yoga class, but whatever. When she walks out of the office, there's a blob of bright blue the size of a quarter positioned right on her butt crack. It's impossible to miss. Between that and the lack of eyelashes, she's certainly going to get a lot of stares.

I'm relieved to have the office to myself for the remainder of the afternoon. I need time and space to think. With O'Meara riding my ass about therapy, I can't afford to let him see me slip up or get sloppy. Then there's Erica—she's a wild card. She certainly didn't look upset when I spied on her the other night and saw her laughing it up and stuffing her face with her roommates. At the same time, I know better than anybody how easy it is to pull a mask on and hide what you really are.

My heart starts to beat faster thinking about Erica, drowning out the sound of the clock ticking toward five. I don't think anybody would believe her even if she squealed about what she saw in the tunnels. It sounds farfetched, that's for sure—"Please, help, I saw a girl in the tunnels dissecting a rat"—I mean, come on. Even I wouldn't believe her, and I'm the girl who was dissecting the rat.

That's what makes her the wild card. I still don't know how much she knows, or what she's going to do with the information she has. A dull pain blooms in my chest, but I try my best to ignore it.

I don't have to spend long wondering, because at 4:55 on the dot, my wild card comes walking into the Chaplains' Office, the door thudding shut behind her.

I'm able to arrange my features into something resembling normal by the time she reaches my desk, but I can feel my eyes still wide with shock and trepidation. If she talks to me like I'm a normal person, I'll have some peace of mind. If, on the other hand, she takes one look at me and runs screaming out of the building, I'll need to clean out my subterranean lab—booby traps and all—pronto, then wait for Erica to lead university authorities on an underground investigation that will yield absolutely nothing, tarnishing her credibility. When I think about Erica, crying and begging the investigators to take another look because she's sure of what she saw, I smile. Perhaps the latter option wouldn't be so bad. Erica would probably wind up in therapy right alongside me, except she'd actually need it.

There's a heart-stopping moment where our gazes connect, her piercing green eyes boring into my gray ones. I maintain a polite smile while my hand moves under the desk to find the letter opener with the sharpest point, just in case. My fingers grip the handle so hard they start to shake as Erica seems to search my face. The room is so silent I can hear a toilet flush all the way down the hall.

After what feels like an eternity, she finally speaks.

"Hi," she says.

No screaming. I guess I have my answer—or at least a piece of it. The pain in my chest starts to recede, and my fingers uncurl from the letter opener.

"Can I help you?" I ask.

"Yes, um, I was hoping to make an appointment to speak with a Jesuit," she says, and I can hear a slight tremor in her voice.

"Sure. Any Jesuit in particular?" If she doesn't know one, it's dealer's choice—and I know exactly the right one. There's a middle-aged Jesuit named Finnahy with a, shall we say, touchy reputation. Word around here is he'll be transferred within the year, but for now, he's still teaching, and, more importantly, taking private student appointments.

Damn, though. She has someone in mind, I can tell. "There's an older Jesuit, I'm sorry I don't know his name. He's got to be about eighty, walks with a wooden cane?"

I know exactly who she's talking about, which means I can really unnerve her now—if she's as stupid as Airhead Ani, that is. I twist my face into a mask of confusion. "You must be talking about Father Skapka," I say. Who, I don't add, does not exist.

"Oh, okay."

"Are you messing with me?" My voice is a cauldron of suspicion.

"Excuse me?" Her innocent eyes go wide.

Time to go in for the kill—metaphorically, for now. "Father Skapka has been dead for a year," I say. "I had to help clean out his office."

"What? That can't be true. I just saw him in Red Square!" I want her to be sputtering, shocked, but instead she's almost laughing, as though I'm the ridiculous one.

This certainly isn't the reaction I expected; Airhead would have been in hysterics by now. Why isn't she crying?

"I don't know what to tell you." There's a hard edge to my words I can't completely control. "You must've seen someone else. Although there aren't any other Jesuits that old on campus right now." There is no Father Skapka; she definitely saw Father Dancy out there, but I want her to think she's seen some sort of phantom. That should terrify people like her who buy into all that supernatural bullshit, right?

"Hm. Alright, then. I must have seen a ghost, I guess!" She's smiling at me, and the sensation is so strange, I start to feel dizzy. If this reaction is anything to go off of, she's nothing like Airhead.

When I don't say anything, she rushes to fill the silence. "I've heard weirder things. My parents are anthropologists, so I'm no stranger to stuff I can't explain. I really hope I did see a ghost, that would be so cool!"

I want to tell her that no self-respecting scientist believes in ghosts, that she's no better than O'Meara with all his exorcism and demon nonsense—but then an idea hits me. O'Meara, of course. I'll hook her up with him. He needs somebody to bother who isn't me. Foisting Erica on him will be the perfect distraction; I'm tired of being under his magnifying glass.

"Look. I can schedule you with Father O'Meara, how about that? He's a good one," I say, proud of myself for faking sincerity so well.

Erica smiles, all perfect white teeth. "Father O'Meara? Yeah, yeah, that would be great."

I click around on my computer for far longer than it takes to pull up his schedule. Finally, I say, "Father O'Meara could see you on Thursday at noon, if that works."

"Yes, that would be great."

"Cool. What's your name?" I ask, even though I already know it.

"Erica Harris," she says. "And you're…" She looks for a nameplate on my desk, but I don't have one.

"Keely," I say. She still doesn't show any sign of recognition, which is fine with me. Clearly she doesn't remember seeing me come out of Professor Demetri's office the day she stole my Hughes spot, or the time she buzzed me into the lab with her GOCard not that long ago when I went to see Dr. Gunderson.

"Nice to meet you," she says. I almost laugh, because she's going to eat those words one day, even if I will have to work harder to unnerve her than I do with Airhead.

She's about to say her goodbyes and turn to leave when I blurt out, "You're one of the Hughes students, aren't you?" I'm not exactly sure what I'm doing, but I don't want to let her leave, not yet—not until I'm one hundred per cent sure I've tamed this wild card, that she's not playing with me to gain some sort of advantage. I need to be certain of what she knows, what she thinks she saw, and who she told about her night in the tunnels.

She looks surprised and says, "Yeah, I am."

"I applied for that program, actually. I wasn't accepted, though. They'd filled all the spots by the time I had my interview with Professor Demetri. Too bad there's a limited number of positions. I guess they don't make exceptions, either."

"Ah," she says. For a second, her face twists into something that could be guilt. "Yeah, that's kind of an annoying restriction." She looks nervous, as though she might apologize, but then her face smooths out again. She's not going to come clean about the exception that was made for her, of all people.

"Yeah, it really sucks. That's why I'm working here, actually. The Chaplains' Office pays a pretty decent stipend, and I get some work experience for my résumé, I guess." That's total crap. Med schools don't care about useless office busywork.

"Are you living on campus?" she asks.

"Not really," I say, then catch myself, because that's a weird answer. I don't feel like I live only in my basement apartment, especially when I've been spending so much time in the tunnels. "I've got an apartment in Burleith."

"Ah, gotcha. I'm in one of the townhouses near the front gates," she says, as if I don't know exactly where those privileged Hughes kids get to live, much less the exact mint green townhouse where Erica eats big Italian dinners with her roommates.

"Yeah, I've seen you Hughes students walking around."

She pipes up, "Did we have a class together or something? You look familiar."

My mask goes rigid for a split second and then relaxes again—if she recognized me from down there, that would have been the first thing she said after she screamed. She must finally remember our encounter outside of Demetri's office, or maybe the one in Dr. Gunderson's hallway.

"It's possible. I assume we're both biology majors, right?"

"Yeah," she says, placated. "That must be it."

"Whose lab are you working in?"

"Dr. Gunderson's. I'm enjoying it so far." This feels like a canned response, but I need more. I have to know if she's just playing with me.

"Good, good. I'd love to hear more about it." Like how often you're there, and whether or not you're alone, and if there are any scalpels stocked in the lab drawers.

"Sure, I'm working on—"

I cut her off, because a brilliant plan has come to me. "Want to grab lunch sometime?" I say. No better way to rip her heart out than to befriend her first. Get close, figure out her weaknesses, then hit her where it will hurt the most. Teach her a lesson about snooping, a lesson she'll never unlearn, no matter how many years of therapy she pays a fortune for. If she even makes it that far, of course.

"Yeah, that'd be great," she says.

"Does tomorrow work?"

"Yeah," she says again. "Are you a fan of Wisey's?"

I vehemently hate Wisey's, that 'student favorite' deli right outside the gates. Of course Erica would 'be a fan,' but whatever. I can choke it down. "Love it," I say, the lie slipping easily from between my chapped lips.

"I'll see you tomorrow in front of Healy at eleven-thirty," I say, and she responds with an upbeat "See you then!"

She's gone in a swirl of some type of perfume that's strangely enticing and makes me feel giddy, like pheromones. I'm even more befuddled now than I was before I officially met Erica. I shake my head, attempting to clear it. I need to figure out who she really is, and, more importantly, what she really wants.

CHAPTER TWENTY-SEVEN

Hot Chick or Hot Mess?

Sweat is beading on my lower back as I stand in front of Healy Hall, waiting for Erica so we can go get some disgusting food at Wisey's. I slept in the tunnels again last night, once again wrapping a thick rope around my ankles and tying it to a water pipe to prevent somnambulation. Erica's slippery, and I knew I'd need a clear head to stand up to her scrutiny at such close range. I didn't want to wake up in yet another filthy boy's bed, pressed against a warm creature stinking of alcohol and body odor. When I awoke this morning, there were a few troubling clues that I'd tried to escape my bonds anyway: frayed hacks into the rope and a clumsy yet almost successful attempt at untying the knot. Maybe I should start sleeping in that giant dog cage if this continues. I'd rather do that than develop a dependence on Adderall.

It's 11:34, and I'm starting to get antsy. I don't have her phone number, so I can't text and ask where the hell she is. Of course she would keep me waiting; people like Erica feel entitled to everything, including another person's time.

In preparation for our lunch, I ran back to Burleith at dawn to splash water on my face and change into the cleanest pair of clothes I own—in this case, jeans with one torn belt loop and a dull gray t-shirt that used to be white—and run a brush through my hair. A large chunk of it came off in the bristles, but I don't really care. I always pull my hair back, anyway, especially after that prick Tom Carlson ripped some of it out.

Now, I'm nearly vibrating with a mixture of excitement, anticipation, fury, and a strange sort of arousal that isn't sexual but still feels salacious. There's an almost painful grin plastered on my face that proudly shows as many of my yellow teeth and inflamed gums as possible. It's a smile that is meant to both comfort and unnerve.

My ragged fingernails are digging into my palms, and I'm about to turn around and go back into the Chaplains' Office when I spot a long brown ponytail bobbing toward me. The ponytail is connected to a tanned girl with a bouncy stride—Erica. It's 11:42.

"Hey!" she calls when she gets as far as the edge of Copley Hall. When she pulls even with me, she says, "Oh my God, I'm so sorry. I had an RNA extraction that took way longer than I expected. I would have texted to tell you I was running late, but I don't have your number."

If she had an RNA extraction that took that long, she clearly doesn't know what she's doing and shouldn't be allowed in a lab at all.

I just look at her, my masklike grin still in place, and say, "No worries. Glad you could make it!" The words are so fake they taste like Splenda in my mouth.

She smiles back. "Shall we?" Ugh. I've always hated people who say stilted phrases like that as though it's a completely natural thing to do. I resist the urge to mock her.

"I'm so glad you suggested Wisey's. I just love the Hot Chick sandwich." The words sound weird coming out of my mouth, but she doesn't seem to notice.

"No way! That's my fave, too." Of course she would say that. If you just Google 'What is Wisey's most popular menu item?' the Hot Chick pops up. I don't have quite enough information to conclude that Erica doesn't have a single original thought in her empty head, but I'm getting closer.

As we start to walk, I glance at her face. She's wearing an expression of consternation, and I'm going to poke and prod until I understand its source. Maybe she's still upset about seeing me the other night, down in the tunnels. I wonder if she can tell how bitter and ferocious I am underneath all of this.

I almost laugh because this whole situation is preposterous, and Erica can't even see it. She's too wrapped up in her own life, in whatever small, insignificant things are happening to her, to realize she's about to have lunch with the same person who probably put that look of consternation on her face.

We start walking, and Erica talks pretty much nonstop, about her anthropologist parents, her favorite restaurants, her roommates. The whole way over there, she says just one interesting thing, something I should have guessed but didn't: she's going to O'Meara's exorcism talk tonight. Of course she is—that Kat Saunders girl came in last week to make the appointment, and she's in the Hughes program, too. Who cares about the *The Exorcist* beyond its cinematic value? Are they really so bored with the opportunities they've been granted that they have to go searching for ridiculous bullshit like demons?

I cut in to ask, "Do you actually believe in that stuff?" I try to keep the derision out of my voice, and I'm not sure I succeed.

Erica shrugs. "Like I told you before, my parents have exposed me to some weird things through their research. I'm open to the possibility of another world out there."

"But aren't you busy with all your research?"

She shrugs again. "Sure, but that's only a nine-to-five job. Don't get me wrong, I love the work, but it's not my whole identity. It's fun to do something totally different once I leave the lab."

I'm so flabbergasted that I lose my ability to form words. How does she expect to succeed at anything if she doesn't make it her 'whole identity?'

I'm saved from having to say anything else because we've finally reached Wisey's. Erica tells the pimpled guy behind the counter she wants a Hot Chick, a large Coke, and an Oreo cookie. Somebody's feeling like a glutton today.

It's my turn now, and luckily, the power of speech comes back to me. I know I've talked myself into a corner, so I have to order that stupid sandwich. I compromise, though, and only order half, plus water to help wash down what is sure to be an awful taste. I can smell it from here.

I'm reaching into my pocket for my wallet when Erica turns to me and says, "I've got this, it's on me."

"You don't have to," I say, trying to keep the anger out of my voice. I can tell from the way she's looking at me she thinks she's doing a good deed, buying lunch for the poor work-study girl. She bulldozes over my protests and shoves her credit card at the cashier.

We find a spot on a bench in the shadow of Healy Hall, and Erica immediately rips into her sandwich as though she's been starving for months. If I weren't so disgusted, I'd be a little impressed. Maybe there's something interesting in her, after all. Hunger like that can't be satisfied by food alone. I know from experience.

I start off the game by prodding her, asking her to tell me what's wrong. "So, Erica," I say, swallowing a minuscule bite that's just as rancid as I expected. The parmesan pepper dressing is so sharp it sends a bolt of pain through my molars. "I can't help noticing you seem a little, well… off today."

She acts surprised, as though she really doesn't think all of her emotions are so obvious. She has a dangling piece of chicken stuck between her front teeth and a smudge of that vile parmesan dressing on the corner of her mouth like some hot mess, but she wipes it away so quickly it's as though she read my thoughts.

She puts down her sandwich and sucks on her Coke. Her slurp is so loud it feels as though it echoes around the quad. "Off? What do you mean?"

I put my sandwich down, too, happy to have a break from its reek. "It's just… is something bothering you? I have a sense about these things."

She slurps again, twice as loudly. "I guess I'm not very good at concealing my feelings," she says, and I nod with fake solemnity.

A heavy sigh slips out of her lips. "Some weird stuff has been happening lately, that's for sure."

I cock my head. "Weird stuff? Like what?"

"Okay, so… this didn't happen to me personally, but it's still strange. You've heard of the Georgetown Cuddler, right?"

My entire body goes cold and rigid like a slab of frozen bacon. "Yes," I say slowly.

If Erica notices my change in demeanor, she doesn't react. She's too wrapped up in her own petty drama. "Well, the last person who got… I feel so weird saying 'cuddled,' because this wasn't cute at all… I'll say 'assaulted,' even though that doesn't feel right either. Anyway, that person was my boyfriend, Tom."

The few bites of Hot Chick I managed to swallow start to creep back up my throat.

Erica takes another bite of her sandwich. "It was so freaky. He said he woke up with this person pressed against him, and at first he thought it was me, so he tried to, like, spoon the person. Can you believe it? How creepy is that? That he was, like, spooning a random person?"

The bolus of Hot Chick in my throat starts crawling back down my esophagus in relief. Tom clearly spun the story to Erica the same way he did to the press, meaning she knows nothing about what really happened. I gesture for her to continue.

"Then, when he realized what was happening, he got upset, as you can imagine. When he tried to get the person out of his bed, he got punched in the nose."

Damn right he did.

"I thought that would be the end of it, but then the person smashed this water glass Tom had on his dresser and freaking stabbed him in the leg with one of the pieces of broken glass. How twisted is that?"

I'd say it sounds more like self defense, but that's just me. "Damn," I say, widening my eyes in mock horror.

"Right?" Erica takes another bite of her sandwich. She's really powering through that thing. "Yeah, so, Tom was pretty disturbed by what happened, mostly because he was thinking about what could have happened if the person had assaulted someone like me instead of him. He's a strong guy, so he was able to defend himself and all."

No, he really wasn't.

"Yeah, that's pretty scary," I say. "Are you worried something is going to happen to you?"

Erica shrugs. "I mean, not really. It seems like the Cuddler only goes after guys. Plus, there's more security guards out on patrol at night now, and the police are aware of everything, so I feel pretty safe. Maybe I should be more worried, but it all just seems so… out there."

"Yeah," I say, surprised at her nonchalance. A plan is already forming in my mind—a plan to take advantage of Erica's false sense of security the same way she took advantage of mine in the tunnels. "I'm sure you've got nothing to worry about."

Erica slurps her Coke and blurts out, "Oh yeah, and then I saw 'Father Skapka' coming out of Lauinger yesterday." She wiggles her fingers as though she's trying to play up the drama.

"You mean… the ghost of Father Skapka?" I say, trying to leach the humor from her voice.

"Yeah, right," she says. The corners of her mouth lift up in a smile, and I still don't know what she really believes.

Her face grows pensive. "I mean, if he really is a ghost, I feel bad for him. Ghosts only linger if they're not ready to move on. I wonder what Father Skapka needs so he can, you know, stop being a ghost."

Hm. This is still not what I was expecting. I wanted tears, goosebumps, and panic—not sympathy. For some strange reason, my eyes start to prickle with tears.

Erica goes on, "He must be so lonely, stuck here, mostly invisible, hoping somebody notices him and helps him move on. It can't be easy."

It's not easy, Erica. It really is lonely to be invisible, working underground, hoping somebody notices you and gives you everything you deserve.

"I wish I knew how to help him," she says, her tone indecipherable. "Although, in other cultures, ghosts are protectors of the living, so maybe he's the one helping me."

This girl is absolutely nothing like Airhead Ani, and without my consent, my entire body leans toward Erica, just enough so I can smell the floral scent of her hair. I know without sniffing it that my own hair smells of dust and sweat. Erica's jeans are spotless and tailored perfectly to her body; mine have a broken belt loop and fall too low on my hips, bagging around my ass. Erica's teeth are white and even; mine are ocher and, because I don't wear my retainer, they're growing more and more slanted each day. Erica's skin is smooth and soft; mine is sallow and shiny.

'Madame Leila's' words drift through my mind again. Erica is so different from me, I don't think it's even possible to learn enough from her to change myself for the better. I wouldn't know where to start.

"Keely?" Erica says, startling me out of my trance. "Are you okay?"

"Yeah," I say. "Why wouldn't I be?"

Erica shakes her head. "No reason, I just thought, for a second there, well, you looked like you might cry."

"Nope," I say.

"Just checking," she says, smiling. I'm doomed to fail if learning from her also means I have to pretend to be interested in other people's emotional states. Then again, that kind of compassion—real or not—could be what got her into Hughes. Bedside manner is important, after all.

I need to get the attention back on her so she can tell me something I can use. If there's one thing Mother drilled into my head, it's that I need to exploit other people's weaknesses. If somebody is stupid enough to show you where they are vulnerable, then you have to be smart enough to use it to your advantage. She does it to my father all the time.

"Anything else bothering you?" I ask.

"Dang, this is turning into Erica's therapy hour," she says. "Sorry for all the venting, but it's just so easy to talk to you. You seem… I don't know, older than your years or something."

"No, no, don't be sorry," I say. Not yet, at least. One day soon, she'll be plenty sorry for all the anguish she's caused me. "Just let it out. I'm happy to listen."

So sighs. "I guess there's this girl in my lab, Judith, and she's kind of… how do I put this gently—"

"Don't worry about putting it gently, just tell me the truth." The hands of the Healy clock have almost made a full rotation since I met Erica for lunch; we don't have much longer. The last thing I need is Airhead Ani wondering where I've been and making me look bad to the Jesuits.

"She's a huge bitch, honestly," Erica says. Her relief at getting the words out is palpable. She takes a colossal bite of her sandwich and chews vigorously. "She's constantly on my back, even though she's only one year ahead of me, and she acts like she's my boss, which she most definitely is not. She's always micromanaging every single thing I do, and in the off chance I make even the tiniest mistake, she always sees it and gives me hell for it."

"She sounds awful," I say, taking a careful sip of water to wash away the taste of the Hot Chick. "Do your other lab mates like her?" Not that I care, I just want to keep her talking. She'll eventually say something I can use against her. People always do.

"God, no," she says. "Everybody pretty much hates her. She's even tried to boss around the grad students a few times, and they just sort of grumble but ignore her. Me, I feel trapped. Even just this week, I made a few tiny errors, and she's right there, over my shoulder, telling me I've got two strikes, and if I get another one, she's going to talk to Dr. Gunderson. As if she's never made a goddamn mistake!" Her cheeks are hot and her breath is coming in shallow bursts. I wonder if her chest hurts, too, when she pants like that.

I'm on Judith's side, of course, but I can't let Erica know that. Enemy of my enemy, and all that. When she pauses to take a breath, I drop my bomb to test the waters: "Damn. She sounds like a real cunt."

Erica looks shocked for a second, but then recovers. Of course she does—she's not really a nice girl, she just tries to make people think she is. She almost had me fooled, with all that 'Are you okay' shit, but only for a second… unless she's just trying to brush the c-word aside so that she doesn't make me feel uncomfortable for saying it. "She's not great," she finally says.

"You know what you should do?" I say.

"What?" she asks, finishing off the rest of her Coke with a violent gulp.

"You should beat her to the punch," I say.

"What do you mean?"

"She's trying to get you ousted, so you get her ousted first," I say, hoping Erica can put two and two together from here and come up with her own plan to hang herself while trying to frame her lab mate.

"How would I do that?" Her emerald eyes are wide, but one eyebrow is raised in what could be amusement.

"Maybe she makes her own mistake that isn't so little, and you happen to see it, and then you tell the right person. I'm guessing Dr. Gunderson."

"Unfortunately, Judith doesn't really make any mistakes."

"Eventually, everybody makes a mistake," I say, letting the masklike smile sit on my face and melt like ice cream.

Finally, Erica gets it. "Do you mean, like, frame her or something?"

No, Erica, I don't mean 'like' frame her, I mean frame her. "Give her a little push. I'm sure everybody would appreciate it."

For a second, I'm worried she'll reject the idea outright, but then the wheels in her mind start turning, and soon she's thinking of all sorts of ways to destroy this girl's life, without realizing, of course, that she'll be destroying her own, too. This is my insurance policy; if I can't take Erica down myself, I'll let her take herself down. Fun in a different way, and hopefully just as effective.

"Like what? Like… turn the temperature on the specimen incubator up so everything dies? Or leave the deep freezer door open so all the reagents spoil?" She chuckles, and I can't tell if it's diabolical or incredulous.

"Now you're thinking," I say, trying to push her in the right direction. "You'd just need to make it look like it was Judith. You're a smart girl. I'm sure you can do that, right?"

Erica starts to nod slowly, but I still can't tell exactly what she's thinking. "Hmmm," she says. Then, before I can add anything, she lets out a loud laugh, sending my heart racing. "Oh Keely, that's pretty hilarious."

"Um," I say, caught completely off guard. "What?"

She shakes her head. "It's fun to think of ways to get back at Judith. Thanks for the comic relief." Before I can say anything else, she stands up, collecting her trash. "Let's do this again sometime."

She walks away, leaving me staring at her swinging ponytail. What the fuck just happened?

CHAPTER TWENTY-EIGHT

Is This Friendship? Or Something Else?

The large black rat sits squirming in the tight cage trap, its eyes fierce. Together with the other rat I caught earlier, I've got everything I need to perform the parabiosis operation again. This time, I'll be successful. My lunch with Erica may have rattled me a bit, as much as I hate to admit it, but this is the perfect activity to get my mind right again.

"Don't worry," I say aloud. "You'll be joined with your brother soon enough. Just think—you'll never have to be alone again!" A loud squirt of laughter jets from my mouth, and the rat struggles harder, to no avail.

Now that I'm back in the tunnels, examining my new experimental subject, it occurs to me that Erica never mentioned being here and seeing somebody operating on rats. She was happy to unload about her rapist boyfriend getting cuddled, the weird ideas she's absorbed from her parents, and her lab mate who sounds like she's just trying to bring Erica down a peg—something she sorely needs. I can only think of two reasons why she wouldn't talk about her experience in the tunnels: either she isn't that troubled by it, or she thinks it might have been me she saw and doesn't want to give anything away. I thought she was easy to read at first, but after our lunch, I'm not so sure. I need to keep an eye on her.

My new rat is obese, probably from gorging on the bounty of the

Georgetown Dumpsters: pizza crusts; half-eaten muffins from Uncommon Grounds; bits of Georgetown Cupcakes; leftover Sweetgreen salads; sandwich ends with little bits of rancid meat still clinging to the bread. In contrast, my other specimen is thin and wiry, probably the runt of the litter, surviving on the smallest of scraps left behind by the bigger rats. They're an absolutely perfect pair.

"Did you know," I say to the rats, "some of the most seminal parabiotic experiments discovered the role of the hormone leptin, which inhibits hunger and helps regulate the balance of energy in the body. Those experiments usually used obese and diabetic mice, but hey, we all work with what we've got, and what I've got is you two. Timon and Pumbaa. Who knows, maybe I'll discover something fascinating. At the very least, I'll be able to say I can successfully connect the circulatory systems of two separate animals. That's the jumping off point I need to delve into more exploratory research." The rats aren't paying attention, but I don't care.

Secure in the knowledge that my underground operating theater is protected by several deadly booby traps, I dose both rats with Jif and crushed Klonopin from my stash, giving obese Pumbaa a bit more than tiny Timon, and secure them to my metal trays. A delicious calm settles over me as I spend the next two hours slicing, stitching, manipulating, and sewing the two animals. I don't stop until I tie off the last stitch, transforming the two rats in front of me into a single specimen. Two heads are tipped back toward the metal; two furry bellies stare up at the ceiling; eight paws jut up into the air. Standing over my subject, I'm panting with exertion, and my muscles are nearly shaking from the effort it took to steady them for so long. These next few hours are crucial. As with my first attempt, if the specimen continues to breathe until midnight, there's a high likelihood it will survive—at least as long as I need so I can study the effects of the surgery.

On the tray, the conjoined rats are both still high on Klonopin, their greasy eyes closed, their mouths shallowly sucking in air. There's a single moment where Timon starts to develop a hitch in its respiration, and I hold my breath. Before panic can build up in my throat, Timon's breathing evens out, and I empty my lungs in relief.

Far above, the Healy clock chimes twelve times, midnight at last. My specimen is still alive. A victory whoop comes crashing out of my mouth, echoing around the small chamber. I've done it. I've really done it. Suck it, Professor Demetri, Dr. Gunderson, and, of course, Erica.

I spend the rest of the night taking meticulous notes in my lab notebook—what protocol I followed, physical descriptions of the specimens, surgical outcomes at different time points, that sort of thing. Documentation equals proof, and proof is what I need to show Professor Demetri, to show Erica, to show Mother—to show them all exactly what I can do. I can't help imagining how I'll write my med school entrance essay, how I'll craft the descriptions of my cutting-edge surgeries. Now that I've performed a successful parabiosis operation, no one can stop me. No one can even try, especially not naïve girls like Erica.

I feel invincible—so invincible I drift into a pleasant sleep on the floor without remembering to tie the rope around my ankles.

*　　*　　*

I have got to get control of myself. This has happened so many times now, annoyance replaces panic. The soft feel of an unfamiliar bed, the welcome warmth of a body pressed against mine. I can only hope this dude is a heavy sleeper. I don't want another Tom Carlson on my hands.

I suck in a deep breath through my nostrils, steadying myself for my escape.

That's when I smell it: the heavy floral scent. I recognize it right away, of course. I spent the entire lunch hour alternating between sensory landmines—the foul taste of the Hot Chick and the heady smell wafting off of Erica's hair.

My exhale slips between my lips, and I let my breath tickle Erica's cheek, which I can just make out in the dim light. I guess I got my wish;

she seems to be a heavy sleeper.

I'm spooning Erica, with my stomach pressed against her back and my thighs kissing the backs of hers. My arms are curled into a tight mound that separates my chest from her shoulder blades. I wonder how it would feel to let my arms unfurl, to send one hand creeping over her hip while the other pets her soft hair.

Erica is facing the wall, thank God, and my back is to the rest of the room. A snort breaks the silence, and Erica shifts onto her back, her shoulder digging into my collarbone. From this angle, I can see the planes of her face, peaceful in sleep. The scent of toothpaste drifts into the air, mingling with the odor of shampoo.

I should leave. I should get up right this second and slide out of the room like a ghost. How did I even get in here? Surely the door was locked, given that the Cuddler is on the loose, as far as the girls in this townhouse know?

I may never know the answer, and I have more important things to consider right now. I was stupid to trust myself and leave my ankles untied when I fell asleep in the tunnels, but I'm even more stupid to linger here when the stakes are so high. Erica knows who I am, and I'm sure she wouldn't hesitate to turn me in if she gets a good look at me.

Yet—I can't make my body move. Erica feels different than the boys I cuddled. She's soft where they were hard, smooth where they were rough, sweet where they were sour. My eyes easily pick out her form in the dark; watching her sleep, I feel less like a voyeur and more like a partner trusted to keep watch. Maybe this is what friendship feels like.

I don't have time to muddle over my feelings, because without warning, Erica's eyes fly open. In one deft movement, I roll off of the bed and make a break for the exit.

Erica screams something unintelligible as I rip open the door and run into the hallway.

Lights are going on under doors as I flee down the hall. As I suspected after spying on Erica and her friends eating dinner, all of the bedrooms in this house are on the second floor. My feet slip and slide down the stairs, and for a second, I think I might fall, but then I'm at the front door, turning the handle. My bare feet hit the pavement outside just as Erica screams, "It was the Cuddler!"

As I did with all the others, I don't stop running until I'm hidden far away from the scene of the crime. This is so typical Erica, ruining something I'm enjoying. I wish for once someone would just relax and let me have what I want. Would that be so hard?

Adrenaline courses through my veins as I breeze past the front gates and the John Carroll statue, which looks at me with judgmental stone eyes. I flip it the finger as I pass.

When I reach the metal door in the side of Healy, I pull it open with such force it bangs back against the brick of the building. I'm nearly to the bottom of the ladder before it swings closed again, the bang echoing throughout the tunnels like a scream.

Navigating the twists and turns and stepping over tripwires, I wonder how much of what just happened was an accident. Maybe some part of me wants to be close to Erica, wants to pull her so hard against me we become a single person.

No, no. I'm sure my subconscious merely wanted to do its part in unraveling Erica—scaring her so much she accelerates her own downfall. She certainly sounded terrified, and I'm confident she didn't see my face. I was turned away and out the door before her eyes could even focus in the low light.

When I reach my operating theater, I slump into the corner. Exhaustion creeps into my muscles like poison as the adrenaline drains out, making me floppy. I can still feel the splendid warmth of Erica's body radiating into mine. The scent of her toothpaste breath and flowery shampoo hovers around my face, and I breathe it in greedily. Even as I wish for the feeling to stay, it starts to fade. The good feelings always do, after all. I learned early that even the heat of a slap dies quickly, leaving you wishing for any touch, any human contact to come your way once again.

I crawl over to the table holding the metal tray. My beautiful specimen is still splayed atop it, but something's wrong. There's no rise and fall as lungs contract and expand, no tap tap tap as hearts beat.

"Fuck!" I scream, my arm flying up and knocking over the tray in anger before I can help myself. The specimen drops to the dusty floor with a wet thump, and I collapse into a sobbing heap next to it.

I've failed. Again. I thought I was invincible, and it made me neglectful. I didn't tie myself up like I should have, and I abandoned my specimen when it needed me most.

Without thinking, I pull the conjoined rats close. My body forms a scrawny comma around the failed experiment, whose odor chases away the memory of Erica's sweetness. There's the tiniest bit of warmth left in the bodies, and I cling to it. I want to keep the heat of connection alive for just a little bit longer.

CHAPTER TWENTY-NINE
The Cuddler Got a Girl This Time

I'm stealing packets of honey from the coffee bar at Uncommon Grounds so I can cover Airhead Ani's keyboard with stickiness in an attempt to give myself a thrill and jolt me out of feeling like a walking bag of medical waste. I finish stuffing the packets in my jeans pocket just as the barista calls out, "Venti mocha latte for Erica!"

My body freezes as though I'm about to be caught red-handed, but then I relax. Erica didn't see me last night, and these packets of honey are free—if you buy coffee, at least. Oh, well.

My back is to Erica, and even though I can't see her, I can feel her moving behind me to grab her drink. A mocha latte isn't the world's worst choice; at least it's not a coffee milkshake like Airhead always gets.

I both hope and fear Erica will spot me. Angling my head a little to the right, I can barely make out the swish of her glossy hair. She says "Thanks so much," to the barista, her voice sunny and unbothered. She's starting to seem like one of those Weebles dolls—no matter how many times I try to knock her down, she just bounces back up as though nothing can hurt her.

A weird thrill courses through me, setting my heart to racing. I usually don't feel like this unless I'm about to cut something. It's a heady mix of excitement and nervousness, and it annoys me because I don't know what to make of it. The pure hatred I want to feel whenever Erica is around just isn't there.

"Keely?" A soft touch lands on my shoulder. "Is that you?"

I turn slowly, taking in the mascara-ed eyes and the touch of sparkly pink on her cheeks. The only sign that something could be unsettling her are the minuscule lines of red threaded through her eyes.

"Hey," I say, my voice coming out as a croak since I haven't used it yet today.

"Oh my God," she says, "I'm so glad it's you. Something…well, something horrifying happened last night, and I just really need to talk to someone about it."

Okay, so I did get through to her after all. "Um, sure," I say.

"Oh, um, I'm sorry, I know we don't know each other all that well, but you made me feel so much better yesterday… jeez, how silly can I be? You must be on your way to work, right? I'll catch you later."

I grab her wrist with my bony fingers. "No, it's totally okay," I say. "I've got time." In truth, I've only got about ten minutes before I need to be behind the reception desk in the Chaplains' Office, but who cares? Airhead is late every day and nobody says anything. It's my turn to take advantage of the laxity in the system.

Erica breathes out a heavy sigh of relief that sounds dangerously close to a sob.

"Could we sit down?" she says. "Oh, are you waiting for your coffee?"

"No, no," I say. "I just finished breakfast"—a lie, of course—"so we can go sit."

We find a table just outside the Uncommon Grounds doors in the Leavey Student Center. If we were here during the school year, this place would be packed with students drinking coffee, meeting for group projects, studying, and writing papers. In the dead of summer, it's mostly deserted, except for a few random graduate students sorting through thesis research.

Erica takes a slurp of her coffee. She leans across the table toward me, and for a brief moment, I think she might be about to kiss me, but then she opens her mouth and says, "I was… I was attacked last night."

I would hardly call it an attack, but whatever. "What?" I say.

She takes a shaky breath. "I think whoever has been going around cuddling people was in my bed last night."

Well, she's right enough about that. "No way. Seriously?" I say.

"Seriously," she says, nodding gravely. "I can't help thinking this is karma, after I told you yesterday how I wasn't worried about the Cuddler since it's only guys who've been assaulted. I'm eating my words, I guess."

Oh yes, you certainly are—but it's not karma, it's Keely. "Jeez," I say. "What happened, exactly?"

Erica slurps her coffee again and says in a comically low voice, "I was asleep, and even in my dream I could feel myself getting really hot, which is weird because my air conditioner usually keeps my room frigid, even during the summer. I rolled over onto my back, and I guess I was starting to wake up a little, because I felt air blowing over my face, like someone was breathing next to me. And there was this weird smell…then I realized there was a person pushed up against me, under my covers with me. I was so scared, Keely. I thought something really horrible was about to happen. I thought—I thought—" Erica breaks down, tears spilling out of those red-veined eyes.

Without thinking, I reach up and start petting her soft, glossy hair. "Shh, shh," I say. "It's okay. It's okay. Of course you were scared. It's okay."

Between hitching breaths, she says, "It just felt so… horrifying. Like I didn't have control over my own space. I didn't know what was going to happen."

Of course you didn't. It certainly does feel horrible to have no control over your own space, like when you came into the tunnels and violated my privacy.

"So… what happened?" I ask.

She sniffles and wipes her nose on the back of her hand. "I opened my eyes and started screaming, but before I could really say anything, the

Cuddler was out of my bedroom and running out of the house."

Now for the million-dollar question. "Did you get a good look at the Cuddler?"

Erica sighs and slurps more coffee. "No," she says.

A breath I didn't realize I was holding seeps out of my mouth.

"The person was on the smaller side, but I can't be much more specific than that. I just feel so lucky I didn't get hurt, like Tom."

Yeah, well, Tom deserved it.

"Yikes," I say.

"You know," she says, her voice pensive, "not that I have any real idea what was going on in that person's mind, but I sort of got the feeling the person didn't really want to hurt me, they just... I don't know... didn't want to be alone." She shakes her head. "God, look at me, justifying that person's assault. I guess... I can't help feeling for them. Does that make any sense at all? I mean, everyone's a little bit lonely, right?"

I want to tell Erica how terrified she should be that the Cuddler might come back for her. I want to play up the violation aspect of what happened. I want to freak her out so badly she can't do her research and gets kicked out of the Hughes program so I can take her place.

Looking at her bloodshot eyes, the earnestness so plain on her face, I can't say any of those things. I want to hate Erica, I really do, but I can't. She's got a sort of natural emotional intelligence that's all the rage in medical schools these days, something I've been glossing over in my own self-education both because I want to be a surgeon, not a practitioner who develops a relationship with patients, and because try as I might, I can't access those feelings. My mind replays all of my interactions with Erica, and I start to see them in a different light. Maybe she paid for my vile Wisey's food not out of pity, but out of kindness. Maybe she accepted my lunch invitation not because she was lonely, but because she could see I was.

I imagine myself through Erica's eyes: an unkempt, greasy girl wearing torn clothes covered in spots of dirt. Of course I look like someone who can't take care of herself, someone who is floundering. I look like someone who needs help, and maybe Erica was just trying to offer that to me.

"Keely?" she says. "Does that make sense?"

"Yeah," I stammer. "Yeah, it does. I… I think you might be right."

Erica closes her eyes and smiles. "Thank you for saying that," she says. "You're actually the only person I've told about what happened. Since I didn't get hurt, and I, you know, feel for the person who's doing this, I just… don't know if I should add more fuel to the fire by reporting it to the police. I know that sounds ridiculous."

"It doesn't sound ridiculous," I say. Maybe I was all wrong about Erica from the beginning. There might be some wisdom in 'Madame Leila's' words after all—perhaps Erica wouldn't be the worst teacher for me.

Erica drains her coffee with the loudest slurp yet. "Thank you for listening," she says, reaching across the table to take my hand. Her fingers are warm and soft, just like I expected them to be. My own fingers must feel so cold and crusty to her, yet somehow she can bear to hold them without flinching away.

"Anytime," I say.

"See you around," she says, then gets up and, with a little wave and a smile that leaves me breathless, passes through the glass doors leading directly into Regents.

I sit still for a few moments, relishing in the residual halo of warmth her presence left. When I finally check my watch, I see that if I hurry, I'll only be a few minutes late for work.

When I walk into the office, Airhead Ani is already behind the desk, once again in the better office chair, leaving me the bad one.

"Morning, Keely," she chirps, as though she's never given me any reason to hate her.

Without preamble, I plop into the uncomfortable chair and lean closer to her, making sure she can smell my morning breath. "You know, I heard the Cuddler struck again last night."

Airhead's lashless eyes go wide and she mirrors me, leaning in close. Her nose wrinkles when she catches a whiff of my breath. "Are you serious?"

"Yeah," I say, breathing hard through the word, right into her nostrils. "I heard the Cuddler got a girl this time."

"No," she says, shaking her head.

"Yes," I say. "So, you know, you should probably watch out. You have roommates, right?"

I know full well that Airhead lives alone; she told me so just the other day. Her insultingly wealthy parents insisted she have a one-bedroom apartment all to herself. It's yet another reason I hate her—she took this job from a work-study student not because she needed the money, but because she wanted some padding for her résumé. The girl is majoring in theology, of all the ridiculous things. You can learn a lot about a person by breaking into their phone and reading their text messages while they're in the bathroom. I've just been waiting for the right moment to use the information I've gleaned.

"Oh, God," she moans, leaning back in the good chair. Even slumped, her back looks ergonomically supported. Damn her.

"Oh, yikes, that's right," I say, letting her stew in her discomfort for a moment before delivering my kill shot. "You're all alone."

CHAPTER THIRTY

It Was Death by Frappuccino

Down in the tunnels, the conjoined rats have long since cooled, stiffening with rigor mortis. It won't be long before they start to swell with the noxious gases burped out by opportunistic bacteria in their guts. There are also the flies and maggots that will come, drawn to the stench of death. If you think about it, it's beautiful how there's a whole tiny world right under our noses that bursts into action the moment something dies.

Pumbaa, the larger of the two rats, has coarser fur, whereas Timon is silky. It reminds me of Erica, her shining sheaf of hair flipping from shoulder to shoulder as she walks.

I'm tired, but I've learned from my past failure. I tie the thick rope around both of my ankles before letting myself fall asleep. As I drift off, I can't stop thinking about her and the way her warmth radiated into me this morning, making me the tiniest bit brighter, as though we were the ones with conjoined circulatory systems instead of my rats.

When I wake up, thankfully still in the same place I fell asleep, I untie the ropes and climb out of the tunnels. It's very early as I walk back to Burleith, and a soft breeze tickles my face and lifts the greasy strands of hair off of my forehead. My own scent feels almost palpable—heavy, sticky, clinging. No wonder Erica feels sorry for me.

The water in my shower is cold, but I don't care. For the first time in days, there's soap on my skin. The water that swirls down my body and into the drain is the color of grave dirt.

Out of the shower, I run a toothbrush through my mouth, wincing as the bristles connect with all the soft spots and tender gums I try so hard to ignore. In my medicine cabinet, there's a mostly empty tube of face cream, probably left over from the apartment's previous occupant. I squeeze the last morsel onto my fingertips and pat it across my pale skin. The comb I pull through my hair is clogged with loose clumps by the time I'm finished with my ablutions. Even though I went through this whole rigmarole a few days ago, it feels different this time. It feels more… purposeful, somehow.

The girl staring back at me in the mirror looks almost human. She looks like a girl who could be friends with someone like Erica Harris. She looks like someone deserving of sympathy, of compassion.

Mother's voice sets off an explosion in my mind, scattering my thoughts like shrapnel. "Don't feel sorry for yourself, Keely. People who pity themselves end up dropping out of high school and flipping burgers. Do you want that to be you?"

My fist crashes into the mirror before I have a chance to stop it. At first, nothing happens; then, slowly, cracks spiderweb out from my curled fingers until the mirror doesn't reflect Erica's friend, but rather the fractured, broken person I really am.

My knuckles are raw and red when I pull them away from the mirror, but the cuts aren't deep. If anybody asks, I'll say I scraped them against the sidewalk while picking up some books I'd dropped. It's plausible enough that no one will ask questions—except for maybe O'Meara, that interfering prick.

I wipe my knuckles on my mildewing towel and get out of my apartment before anybody even realizes I'm home. I haven't seen the girls upstairs since I found the tunnels, and I intend to keep it that way.

It's another hot summer morning, I'm on my way to work, and Roger's voice is as loud as ever.

"Keely!" he calls. This time, he's sitting in a patch of dirt that used to be a flower bed.

"What's up, Rog?" I ask, stopping on the sidewalk.

"I made a new friend," he says. Ah, this again.

"Oh yeah?" I ask. Every so often, Roger tells me about his 'new friend,' who might have once been a real person around the time of Roger's accident. Now, Gretchen is entirely imaginary.

"Her name is Gretchen. We met at Pizza Hut."

I know he's going to tell me all about how Gretchen loves pineapple on her pizza just like he does, but I let him get it all out anyway.

"That's cool," I say.

"Do you have friends, Keely?" he asks.

I pause for a moment, seriously considering his question. Last week, I would have said no, absolutely not. Now, I'm not so sure. "To tell you the truth, I think I might. There's this girl named Erica, and I want to hate her, but I can't. She smiles at me. She even patted my hand like she isn't afraid to touch me."

"Gretchen touched my hand, too," he says.

"But every time I think about Erica, all I hear is Mother's voice. 'What's happening to you, Keely? You have important work to do. You need to get into the Hughes program, remember? And then, of course, medical school. Don't get sidetracked. There's not a single person at Georgetown who's really your friend. They all just want to bring you down so they can get ahead. That's how life is.'" My voice ratchets up a notch when I imitate Mother, and it hurts my throat.

"I'm your friend," Roger says.

"That's right, you sure are," I say, realizing in that moment it's true. Roger's the best sort of friend—no maintenance and respectful of my privacy. It doesn't hurt that he can't remember a single damn thing I tell him. "The thing is, though, I used to find Erica so repulsive. I don't know how that ever happened, though. All I can think about is the smell of her hair, the minty freshness of her breath. It all makes me think Mother might be wrong. She always told me I had to be perfect, and nobody was good enough to be my friend. That can't be true, can it?"

"Gretchen split her pizza with me," he says. "And I'm not perfect." I wonder where the real Gretchen is now, if she heard about Roger's accident.

"I think you're pretty great, Rog," I say. He beams. "I'll see you around."

"Bye, Keely!" he shouts, then resumes picking grass out of his lawn.

Before long, I open the heavy door and enter Healy Hall, Mother's voice and Erica's scent at war in my mind. Mother yells, "What is wrong with you? This is not the daughter I raised!"

If I became more like Erica, maybe I could feel less alone and still continue my work. Confusion swirls in my mind, and—

"Keely, where are the extra boxes of pens?"

Goddamnit, Airhead. Silly twits should speak only when spoken to.

I arrange my face into its mild-mannered mask and try to modulate my voice, which wants to snarl more than anything. "Everything is in the supply closet upstairs. Where it always is, always has been, and always will be, Annie."

Airhead looks hurt, which I relish, of course. "Oh," she mumbles, lowering her still-lashless eyes, not even bothering to correct my pronunciation this time. "Well, you don't have to be so mean about it."

Airhead must never have had someone be cruel to her, if she thinks my measured response is 'mean.' She'd really understand 'mean' if she knew about everything else I'd already done to her. The gum on her chair, the Nair in the fake eyelash extension serum, the vomit in her trash can. She's far too trusting.

I rearrange my features into something resembling barely controlled anguish. "I'm sorry," I say. "That was uncalled for. I just, it's been a really hard morning for me, what with my great grandmother dying and all—" I break off, approximating tears as best I can. My eyes stay dry, but Airhead doesn't seem to notice.

"Oh my God," she says, bringing the hand not holding her diet Frappuccino to her glossy mouth. "Oh my God, Keely, I'm so sorry. I can't even—you do whatever you need to do, girl."

She's abysmal at comforting people, but at least I've unnerved her.

"It's okay," I say. "It's kind of hard to care about extra pens when my Gaga just died, you know?"

"Totally," she breathes. Then, like the total piece of moldy dog shit she is, she asks, "Um, how did she die?"

Like my fake great-grandmother's fictional death is any of her business, but I don't mind, because this is what I wanted her to say. I let loose a choking sound, trying to make it seem like a sob. I force earnestness into my voice. "It's so sad," I say. "I mean, we kind of saw it coming, but you're never ready for it, you know? She really loved—well, you wanted to know— she really loved diet Frappuccinos, she was drinking them all the time, and even though her doctor told her all the fake sugar could increase her risk of stroke, she didn't listen. She just couldn't get off the stuff. She was actually drinking one when she had her stroke. She was gone before the paramedics could get anywhere near her."

I've never seen Airhead Ani look so pale. Even her irises look whiter. "Oh," she says, her voice tiny. "I'm so sorry." Then, with a quick thrust of her hand, she tosses her half-empty Frappuccino into the garbage. It's so hard for me not to laugh, because nobody should believe such a ridiculous story. Death by Frappuccino sounds like a parody movie.

"Are you going to the funeral?" she asks, looking at me from the corner of her eyes.

"There won't be a funeral," I say, my voice thick with false emotion. "Gaga didn't want one."

Airhead nods, mulling this over. "If there's anything you need," she says halfheartedly, still pale as a bowl of milk and just as interesting.

"Thanks," I sniffle. I bet with myself: within the week, there will be another diet Frappuccino in her hand. The girl can't stay away, and now I've zapped at least some of her enjoyment. "You could, you know, maybe get those pens yourself?"

"Of course, of course," she mutters, thrusting back her chair—the good one, of course—and makes a beeline for the door.

It'll take her at least three minutes to locate the pens and come back down to the office. That's two and a half minutes more than I need.

The packets of honey are still in my desk drawer where I stored them after running into Erica at Uncommon Grounds yesterday. I rip off the top of one packet with my teeth, spitting the shred of wrapper onto the floor. With one hand, I nudge Airhead's ridiculously large designer tote open. With the other hand, I squeeze the packet of honey, drizzling the sticky mess all over her keys, books, iPad, laptop (I really don't understand why she needs both), can of SlimFast (weird, I didn't know Airhead was a 90's soccer mom looking to lose the baby weight), and reusable water bottle with a sticker that says, "Climate Change Is Real!"

I rip through three more packets of honey, repeating the drizzling until every last drop is in Airhead's bag. Then, I nudge it closed and push it back under her side of the desk. I toss all the honey wrappers in the trash can, cover them with crumpled tissues, then take a seat and wait for her to get back with the damn box of pens.

The phone next to me rings, the sound ripping through the peaceful silence of the office and making me jump in my chair—the bad one, of course. That reminds me: I should switch the chairs before Airhead gets back.

I pick up the receiver and say, "Hello, this is the Chaplains' Office, Keely speaking. How may I help you?"

A familiar voice comes on the line, but I can't place it. "Hello, Keely." The cheer is obviously forced. "This is Rachel Borrister from the student counseling office."

Ah, yes, of course. Rachel Borrister! I wondered when I would get a chance to mess with her again. "How can I help you, Rachel Borrister?" I ask.

"Well," she says, "I wanted to ask if you were still planning on coming in for your appointment."

My lips curl back into a grimace. I completely forgot I had to keep going to that joke of a therapist. I should have figured out how to get out of therapy by now. Maybe Mother was right—I'm losing focus. "Oh," I say. "Right." I glance at the clock. It's 9:05. "What time is the appointment for again?"

"Nine," Rachel says.

As much as I want to tell Rachel Borrister to suck it before slamming the phone down, I know any weird behavior on my part will be immediately reported to O'Meara, who will be on my back all over again. That's the last thing I need.

"I'll be right over," I say.

I'm pulling open the office door to leave just as Airhead comes back with the pens. "I have to go take care of something," I say tersely. "You know, relating to my dead Gaga."

"Right, right," she says, her expression a mixture of discomfort and relief. "Do whatever you need to do. I'll hold down the fort."

I've always hated that saying; it assumes something as unimportant as manning the phones of the Chaplains' Office is as life-or-death as literal war, but whatever. I need to get out of here.

"Cool," I say. "Oh, and before I go—I saw a huge spider on your desk, but it scuttled away behind your computer before I could kill it." Her eyes go wide with fear. "Just so you know."

Airhead's squeal is the melodious background music I need as I leave the office, the door cutting her off as it thuds closed.

CHAPTER THIRTY-ONE

You're Lucky I'm Not That Type of Person

"Hello again, Rachel," I say to the anxious woman behind the reception desk in the student counseling office. The rest of the waiting room is empty, so it's just me and her—perfect.

"Hello," she says, looking at her computer screen instead of me.

"I'm sorry, do I not deserve your full attention?" I say.

Rachel's gaze snaps up to me, and the fear on her face is unmistakable. "Sorry," she mumbles.

"That's better," I say. "Now, I have an appointment, do I not?"

"That's correct," she says. "Christina will be—"

"You know," I say, interrupting her. "Speaking of Christina, maybe I should tell her how disrespectful you were to me just now. I mean, lucky for you there's not anything really wrong with me that would make your actions triggering, but what if I were someone else? What if I were the sort of person who might follow you home after your shift?"

Throughout my little speech, Rachel's eyes get wider and wider. Now, as she stares at me with her mouth open, her eyes are so wide I wonder if they might actually pop out of her sockets and roll across the desk.

"I, um—I—" she stammers.

I give her an ingratiating smile, making sure to show off as many of my yellow teeth as I possibly can. "Oh, Rachel," I say. "Don't worry! I said you're lucky I'm not all of those things!"

"Um—how—"

The sound of a door opening silences Rachel. "Keely?" Christina asks, locking eyes with me. "Are you ready?"

"Absolutely," I say. Before I turn to follow Christina to her office, I whisper to Rachel, "I am the kind of person, however, who can hold a grudge like it's an Olympic sport." One of my eyelids closes in a sultry wink, and then I whip around and leave the waiting room.

Once we're settled in Christina's office, her picking up her legal pad and pen and me trying not to touch the crumbs in the creases of my chair, she gives me that jack-o-lantern smile.

"So, Keely," she says. "How have things been since we last spoke?"

"They've been okay," I say.

When I don't add anything, she prods, "Just okay?"

"Yeah. Just okay."

"Can you tell me a bit more about that?"

I stifle the annoyed sigh in my throat just in time to turn it into more of a ragged exhale. "Well," I say, "I've been using some stress relief strategies that have been somewhat helpful, but certain... events have rattled me more than I would like." That's at least somewhat close to the truth—not that I care about lying to Christina, but I might as well give her something to work with. If I'm going to have to be here for a whole hour, I'd rather make things interesting.

"Okay, naming our feelings is an excellent start. You say you've been rattled. What are the events that caused this feeling?"

Hell no am I going to tell her about Erica and the Hughes kids surprising me in the tunnels, or my failed attempts at parabiosis, or the somnambulism I can't seem to control without tying myself to a drainage pipe, or the increased security and police presence around campus. Instead I say, "Have you heard of the Georgetown Cuddler?"

Her face assumes a somber look that makes her look constipated. "Yes, I have."

"What do you think about it?" I ask, surprising myself with my genuine curiosity.

Christina takes a deep breath. "It's certainly frightening," she says. "I can imagine what those students who woke up with someone in their beds felt—fear, anxiety, panic. It's unsettling to think of yourself as a victim, or even a potential victim. Is that what's rattling you, Keely?"

"That's not what I meant," I say. "I want to know what you think about the Cuddler. Not about the people who got cuddled."

"Oh," she says, blinking. "Well, I can't make a diagnosis on someone I've never met."

"Come on," I goad her. "This is off the record. I'm interested in your professional opinion." As if she could ever qualify as a 'professional.'

She thinks for a minute, then shrugs. "Alright. If I had to offer an armchair diagnosis, I'd say the person everybody calls the Georgetown Cuddler is suffering from either major depressive disorder or schizotypal personality disorder."

I resist the urge to snort in derision at her uninformed 'armchair diagnosis.' "Depressive disorder? Depressed people have troubling getting out of bed, not getting into it."

"That can be true," she says. "I suppose the schizotypal personality disorder might be more likely."

"How can you possibly know that?" I ask, trying to keep the derision out of my voice.

"I can't," she says, shrugging. "I told you, I haven't met the person." She's a really clueless therapist if she fails to realize her subject is sitting right in front of her. She doesn't even suspect what's really going on here.

"Why schizotypal personality disorder?" I ask.

"It's only a hypothesis," she says, and I want to tell her that hypotheses are not shot-in-the-dark guesses, they are informed potential explanations based on observed evidence, but I keep my mouth shut. "People with SPD usually have trouble making friends, showing proper emotion, and thinking clearly. They sometimes think they have special powers, and they can be paranoid and fail to keep up on their personal appearance. Then, of course, there's the possible disruption of normal sleeping patterns."

My heart starts beating a rapid tat-tat-tat against my ribs. I mentally tick off the symptoms: trouble making friends: check. Failure to show 'proper' emotion, whatever that may be: check. Paranoia: check. Disrupted sleeping patterns: check. Unkempt personal appearance: in general, check, but thank goodness I showered this morning.

Mother's voice comes back to me: "Keely, for the last time, you do not need professional mental help. Psychiatry is for people who aren't strong enough to clean up their own messes. Do you want to be a weakling? Do you want to be a failure?"

I'm starting to think Mother has known for a long time there was something off about me. I wouldn't be surprised if she was keeping me away from a psychiatrist to protect herself from the shame, not to protect me.

"Keely? Keely, are you okay?"

I shake my head, trying to fling all the bad thoughts out of it. "I'm perfectly fine," I say. "There is nothing wrong with me."

Christina's gap-toothed smile falters for just a moment, but I catch it. Unless she's truly the world's worst therapist, she's going to see through me. I can't slip up, otherwise O'Meara will know and I'll be out of my work-study job and I'll never get into Hughes and then I'll never be a doctor and then no one will ever look at me with anything but disgust and disdain.

"I made a new friend," I blurt out, distancing myself from the description of a person with SPD.

"That's wonderful," Christina says, still watchful, but nodding for me to go on.

"We had lunch together the other day, then we hung out at night. It was... nice," I say.

"You sound surprised. Do you find it difficult to make new friends?"

"No, not at all," I say, too quickly. "I have loads of friends. I collect new friends like it's my job."

Christina eyes me warily. I need to tone it down a bit to stay believable. "I see."

"I mean to say, I have a good circle of close friends, but I always like meeting new people, that's all."

"That's good to hear," she says.

"I guess I've been a bit lonely this summer, since all of my friends are, you know, back at home right now."

"Right," she says. "Do you think that's making your stress worse?"

"Absolutely," I say, nodding. I hate how obsequious I feel, but keeping Christina in the dark is worth feeling even worse than this. As surreptitiously as possible, I press on the arm wound from my booby trap, letting the pain bring me some semblance of calm. "But meeting my new friend might be helping. Maybe."

"Are you anxious about making a new friend?" she asks.

"No," I say, again too quickly. "I mean, maybe a little. She's almost identical to me in some ways, but extremely different in others. I… don't always know how to reconcile that."

Christina nods as if she has any idea what I'm really talking about. "Sometimes, our differences don't matter. As long as we can connect with someone over the most important things, our differences can fall away."

"That's… interesting," I say, turning the idea over in my head. I don't know if Erica and I connect on the most important things—if she would do anything to succeed, if she would make the necessary sacrifices, like I have. I already know she's not too keen on making lab work her 'entire identity,' so we're not off to the best start there.

"Do you think your new friend is the same as you regarding what matters?"

"I… I don't know," I finally say.

Christina claps her hands together, as though she's solved the riddle of

Keely. Little does she know, it's unsolvable. "That must be what's rattling you," she says. "You found someone who could be a great new friend, but you're not yet sure where she stands on what you find important."

I nod grudgingly, wishing Christina were more off the mark than she is. "That could be true."

She glances at the clock, then makes a sucking noise through the canyon-sized gaps in her teeth. It's not a pleasant sound. "Well, it sounds to me like you need to spend more time with her to determine where your value systems align. I hope things work out, but if they don't, you can cut her loose." Christina claps her hands again and abruptly stands, ready to usher me out the door. No wonder Rachel Borrister doesn't respect the patients in this office—look at the example Christina sets.

I'd be more angry if I wasn't so ready to leave. I stand, too, brushing crumbs from the chair off the seat of my jeans.

"I'll see you next week," Christina says, opening the door to the hallway. "Don't forget this time, okay? Rachel at reception will give you an appointment reminder card."

"Of course," I say, smiling limply at Christina as I pass her and head toward the waiting room. Her door closes behind me as I plant myself once again in front of Rachel Borrister's desk.

"I'd like an appointment reminder card," I say, my voice dripping with fake sweetness. "Can you manage that, Rachel?"

"Y—yes," she stammers, scribbling something on a card and shoving it at me over the top of her desk. "There you go."

"Excellent," I say. "I hope to see you next week, too. Maybe you'll rethink how you treat patients, huh?"

"Mhmm," she mumbles, glancing directly into my eyes before looking down at her keyboard.

"Good girl," I say, then I turn around and get the hell out of the student counseling center.

On the way back to the Chaplains' Office, something Christina said keeps echoing in my head. 'If things don't work out, you can cut her loose.' As the phrase bounces around and around in my mind, the last word falls away.

'If things don't work out, you can cut her.'

'Don't work out, you can cut her.'

'You can cut her.' Would Erica find it as relieving as I do?

Perhaps something useful can come out of therapy, after all.

CHAPTER THIRTY-TWO

This Toast Tastes Less Like Cat Vomit Than I Expected

The bright red oleander waves at me in the morning breeze from its position nestled behind the Mary statue as I walk past Copley Hall. I wave back. It's been a few days since my therapy appointment, and I still haven't made up my mind about Erica. I resist the urge to look over my shoulder, scanning the area for police or campus security.

Most of me wants nothing more than to push Erica down the *Exorcist* stairs so she can never walk into a lab again, while a small but growing part of me wants to return to that blissful moment in her bed and bury my face in the warm nest of her hair. It's hard not to feel like I'm coming apart at my seams when I simultaneously feel two opposite emotions.

My swirling thoughts come to an abrupt halt when I see the object of my mix of anger and desire walking toward a bench in front of the John Carroll statue. Erica is moving strangely, like something is hurting her. When she gets to the bench, she lowers herself onto it carefully, perching her ass on top of one folded leg.

"Erica!" I hear my voice calling out before I can stop it.

She turns, her eyes wide as saucers, like she's expecting to get hit. When she spots me, her puckered mouth melts into a relieved smile. "Keely!" she calls back, waving for me to join her. I'm almost at the steps leading up to the doors of Healy and the Chaplains' Office beyond. I really should get to work, but hey—Airhead Ani thinks my Gaga just died and she told me to take all the time I need, so that's exactly what I'm going to do. I shift course and walk over to sit next to her on the bench. Even at nine a.m., the sun-warmed wood is almost too hot to touch.

"Hey," she says. "How's it going?"

I open my mouth to reply and what comes out is, "Girl, you were walking like you're wearing a too-tight thong! What's up?" I have to try really hard not to howl with laughter, because I've never been the kind of person to address another human being as 'girl.'

Erica coughs, startled and embarrassed at the same time. "Um," she says, "I… uh… I've got a small medical issue. But I'm on medication." She must have seen some sort of imaginary wariness in my face, because she quickly adds, "It's not contagious, don't worry. Just a… um… a feminine issue."

I arrange my features into an expression of concern, but inwardly I'm both disgusted and intrigued, a confusing concoction.

"I'm so sorry to hear that," I say. "Hopefully it's not serious?" Part of me hopes it really is serious; the other part wants her to say it's no big deal.

"No, no, nothing like that," she says. A fat drop of sweat beads up on her forehead and slides down her cheek, nestling in the corner of her mouth. She opens her lips to say something else, and the sweat slips right in. "Hey," she says. "Would you maybe want to go grab some breakfast and coffee right now? As you can probably imagine, this isn't the best day for me."

"Oh," I say, unsure how to answer with my emotions warring inside of me.

She rushes to add, "I know it's short notice, but it's so nice to be able to talk to someone who's not in my Hughes program. It's getting a bit… claustrophobic in there. Plus, with everything that's happened with the Cuddler and all, I need to be around someone who isn't judgmental, who always seems to be above the fray. Like you."

Shit, she really doesn't know me at all. I wanted to be in that Hughes program so badly, and here's Erica treating it like it's a goddamned burden.

She knows I wanted to be in the program, too, and she still doesn't realize her slip-up. A bit of social drama, or whatever it is she's being cagey about, shouldn't matter when you get the privilege of doing cutting-edge research.

"I totally get it," I say, which is the kind of thing people say when they really don't get it at all. "Coffee would be great."

"Awesome," she says, fiddling with the hem of her shirt. "Well, how about Saxbys? I know it's only two blocks away, but it feels like it's off-campus. I need some space from Georgetown right now."

"Works for me," I say.

She smiles and gingerly lifts herself from the bench. It's a short walk to Saxbys, but Erica's waddling gait slows us down. We're mostly quiet, a stark contrast to the way Erica prattled on and on when we went to Wisey's the other day.

When we finally get to Saxbys, there's only one other person in line.

"I'm going to get the Black Garlic and Olive Oil Avo Toast. I know it sounds weird, but it's so freaking good. It's my guilty pleasure," she says, recovering a bit of the pep I've grown used to hearing in her voice.

In truth, I think it sounds revolting, but out of my mouth pops, "I'll have one, too."

"You'll love it," she says. "And don't worry—I asked you to come here with me, so get whatever you want, on me."

Ugh, not again. I'm not a charity case, nor do I want her pity. On the other hand… this might not be pity at all. Maybe this is what kindness looks like.

Erica tells me to grab a table while she orders and pays, so that's what I do. I settle myself into a chair in the back corner farthest from the door, with a wide view of the entire room. The café is sparsely populated, but I don't like being without a clear escape route.

A few moments later, Erica wanders over with two plates of toast balanced on one arm and a to-go coffee cup in the other hand. With the sort of practiced poise I've only ever seen in an operating theater, she carefully sets everything on the table without any wobbles or spills.

"Thanks," I say. The toast on the plate is the same color as Linda Blair's vomit in *The Exorcist*, and the black powder liberally sprinkled on top reminds me of mold. It's far from the most appetizing thing I've ever seen. Erica really has a thing for vile vittles.

She picks up her piece of toast and takes a large bite. Chewing, she leans back in her chair, letting her eyes roll back in her head. "Wow, that's good," she says. "Better than sex, even." She scrunches her nose, as though she's let something slip. "Way better, actually."

"That good, huh?" I say, still having a staring contest with my own plate.

"Let's just say the toast is great, but sex is not," she says. "I mean… that feminine issue I mentioned… it's a urinary tract infection. Tom's fault, again."

"Again?" I'm not surprised that rapist oaf has something to do with this.

Erica takes a swig of coffee from her to-go cup. Black garlic and mocha: talk about a nasty pairing, but she doesn't seem to mind. If I kissed her now, the tang of toothpaste would be completely cancelled out. "It's like, I tell him I'm prone to UTIs, and I tell him there are certain things I need to do to help prevent them, and it's like he doesn't even hear me. He just pushes and pushes and pushes until I give in and then boom, surprise surprise, I get another frigging UTI. I've had five of these in the past six months. I don't even have to go to the doctor anymore, I just have a standing prescription for antibiotics."

"Shit," I say. On the one hand, I enjoy the prospect of Erica being in pain, but on the other, I can't help thinking how horrible it would be to have one painful urinary tract infection after another. I had one once as a kid when I sat around too long in a wet bathing suit, and even though my mom was a doctor, she thought I was malingering until my fever got so high I had to go to the emergency room, where I was diagnosed with a raging kidney infection. It feels very strange to put myself in another person's position, and I'm not sure I appreciate it. I have enough pain of my own; I don't need to be holding on to anyone else's.

"Yeah," Erica says, taking another colossal bite of toast. "Then he'll complain about not getting any for a week while my antibiotics clear the infection. It's so insensitive."

"Why do you even like him then? Why not just break up with him?" I know firsthand how much of an asshole Tom Carlson is. Erica shouldn't put up with his behavior. Being a doormat is not one of my values. I hope it's not one of Erica's.

She swallows and looks at the toast in her hand. "I know I should," she says in a small voice, barely more than a squeak. "But you have to understand, he wasn't always like this."

I seriously doubt that—behavior like his doesn't come from nowhere— but I nod, urging her to go on. I still haven't touched my toast.

"When we first met last fall, he was charming, and smart, and sweet. Oh, and passionate, too, of course. I mean, he's still passionate to the extreme, even with his injured leg, and smart, but the charm and sweetness have just sort of… drifted away. It's like he doesn't think he has to try with me anymore, or even, like, wait for consent, you know? It's hard not to think he's just in this for the sex."

"Do you think you deserve that?" I ask. Christina would be proud—here I am, judging whether or not Erica and I have the same value systems.

"Of course not," she says. Her eyes start to well up, but she sniffs hard, pulling her emotion back inside, where it belongs. "Hey, you haven't even tried your toast yet."

I pluck the toast from the plate as though it's a smushed cockroach, guts dangling from its crushed abdomen. My mouth opens, closing around a minuscule corner of the bread, which is mercifully soft against my nervy teeth. I manage to chew without irritating my gums, swallow, and then, to my shock, take another bite—a bigger one this time.

"Whoa," I say. "This is actually… good?"

Erica laughs. "See? I told you! You can trust me."

I'm not sure that's true, but whatever. Most of the time, when people say 'You can trust me,' they might as well be wearing a neon sign around their neck that says 'Liar.'

Erica takes another gulp of coffee. "Anyway, the antibiotics are kicking in now, so I'll be much better by lunchtime. I took the morning off from the lab, just to take the pressure off, you know. I can't take dealing with Judith on top of everything else right now."

Judith, right—her obnoxious lab mate. "How are things with Judith?" I ask, taking another delicate bite of toast, savoring the sharpness of the garlic, the creamy fattiness of the avocado, and the slick feel of the olive oil. This is so much better than Spam on Wonder Bread, which is high praise indeed.

Her face darkens. She really is so terrible at hiding her feelings. "Awful," she says. "Still. As though I need more shit to deal with."

"What are you going to do about it?" I ask. It's time to find out if she's willing to do whatever is necessary to get ahead. I need to know if she's like me.

She sighs and stuffs the last bite of toast into her mouth. "I don't know. I mean, what is there to do? She sucks, but that's not a mortal sin."

"What about getting her thrown out of the lab?" I say.

She scoffs. "Keely, that was a joke. That's just not how things work," she says. "If I tried to sabotage her, it would just blow back on me."

Okay, she's smarter than I gave her credit for.

"But don't you want to do whatever you need to do to be the best?" There it is, the real kicker.

Erica slurps her coffee, draining it. "If I have to hurt somebody to get there, then being the best isn't worth it."

I feel like I'm short-circuiting. Most of me thinks Erica doesn't know what she's talking about, that she isn't driven enough, that she's cowardly and dimwitted. Part of me thinks maybe, just maybe, there's truth to what she's saying. Mother always told me, "It's not even worth trying if you're not the best, Keely." Or, "Be perfect or be prepared to go hungry until this A- becomes an A." Or, "Don't let anybody talk you into stepping away from your goal. People used to tell me it was no use trying to become a doctor, especially as a woman. I'd probably be dead in a gutter right now if I'd listened to them." Maybe there's an entirely different way to live, one that doesn't involve pushing so hard to be the best that I push every single person away, too.

Erica is staring at me with warmth in her eyes and my protective mask is slipping away. I've seen my own face in a mirror when I'm totally bare, and I know what I look like. There's nothing behind my eyes, just a disarming blankness that's deep and heavy. My muscles are slack, my eyelids slightly lowered. I've almost scared myself while looking in the mirror.

"Anyway, thanks for listening," she says. "Normally I'd talk to my mom about all this stuff, but she and my dad are in Nepal until November researching local shamanic rites and trying to climb Everest. They're completely out of reach."

My mouth opens in shock, and a masticated bite of toast almost falls out. It's jarring enough that Erica's parents are rich and free enough to go climb Mount fucking Everest, but it's even stranger that Erica would talk to her mother about what's going on in her life. I cannot imagine speaking to Mother about boys, sex, or anything that was actually bothering me. It does not compute. Even attempting to have a conversation like that with Mother would elicit an impatient wave of her hand and a comment along the lines of, "Keely, I don't need to be hearing about your problems. You shouldn't be focusing on boys, anyway. Go study, for Christ's sake."

Because I have to say something to fill the silence, I say, "Wow."

"Yeah," she says. "I miss talking to my mom, but I'm glad my parents are going on such a cool adventure."

"Right," I say, struggling to corral my buzzing thoughts.

Erica sighs. "Still, I wish I could call her. It's been a crazy week, between Tom getting attacked, me getting cuddled, the UTI... and some other things."

My ears perk up. This is the first time she's even hinted at what she saw in the tunnels. I guess it made some impression, after all.

"What other things?" I ask, both anticipating and dreading the answer.

She waves her hand as if she can shoo this line of conversation away like an annoying fly. "Oh, it's nothing," she says. "Just something I thought I saw, but I must have been mistaken. Not worth mentioning." She looks down at her watch, then says, "Dang, is it 10:45 already? I've got to get to the lab."

"Oh," I say. "Okay, sure."

"Thanks again for listening, Keely. I'm not sure if it's you, the toast, the caffeine, or the antibiotics, but I'm feeling so much better."

"Excellent," I say, my mind reeling. "Thanks for the toast."

"It's good, right? Like, I wish I could eat it every day."

I do, too, but mostly because it's soft enough that it doesn't send zingers of pain through my molars. "Girl, me too," I say, offering my best attempt at a smile. I don't quite get there, because my preposterous use of the word 'girl' makes me laugh out loud this time. It doesn't come out quite right, though. I can feel my face growing red, and my chest starts to tighten. I've never been able to master laughing like a normal person.

Erica freezes, a hand going to her open mouth. I want to say something else, anything, to break the tension, but then she stands up straight. Her face is ashen—perhaps those antibiotics haven't kicked in quite yet.

I'm about to say something to that effect when she mumbles, "See you," and whirls around, no parting smile this time. In a few loping strides, she's at the door, then out on the sidewalk. When her feet hit the pavement, she breaks into a run, heading toward campus.

Making sure nobody is watching, I breathe into my hand and give it a sniff. Dear God, that's repugnant. No wonder Erica ran away. It's funny, we can eat the same thing, yet her breath still smells fresh while mine reeks like a dead animal. Her excellent self-care clearly includes dental hygiene.

Oh well, I've got a long afternoon in the Chaplains' Office with Airhead Ani —but at least I'll have fun watching her scratch her head with honey-clogged fingers as she tries desperately to understand what happened to her precious designer bag.

CHAPTER THIRTY-THREE

You Don't Wear a Thong with Spandex

"Anyway, so then I got iced. No way, you don't know what that is? C'mon, Mom, it's where somebody hides a Smirnoff Ice—what? It's like flavored vodka—and if you find it, you have to go down on one knee and chug the whole thing. It's funny, Mom. Stop being weird."

It's 10:30 in the morning and Airhead Ani has been on the phone with her mother for the past thirty-seven minutes. She tried to act apologetic in the beginning, talking in a hushed whisper and shooting me 'I'm sorry, this'll only take a minute' glances. She dropped that act about ten minutes into the conversation, and has been openly chatting ever since, as though her job here is secondary to catching her mother up on whatever foolishness Airhead's been getting into. I cannot imagine ever speaking so openly with Mother. Maybe this is how Erica speaks with her mother, too.

"Yeah, yeah, I got the new Louis Vuitton tote. No, I don't know how my other one got ruined. It must have been detective or something." Her voice is thick with frustration and unshed tears, and I can't help smirking. Then again, though, my trick probably didn't really matter if everything I destroyed of Airhead's is easily replaceable thanks to Mommy and Daddy. She may be a little upset now, but it won't last, unfortunately.

"Don't just blame things on me, Mom! I mean, I guess it's possible some maple syrup packets from breakfast burst open in my bag, but that's not my fault!" Nothing ever is, is it?

Her lashless eyes squint in anger as she listens. "Yeah, my eyelashes are starting to grow back in. I think the stuff is working." That's a total lie, but I'm not going to be the one to point it out.

"The shipping notification says the new iPad and laptop will get here by the end of the week. Yeah. Okay. Bye, Mom," Airhead says and removes the phone from her ear. I'm half surprised it doesn't stick there. "Sorry about that," she says to me.

I fix her with my biggest sad sack eyes and say, "I wish I could still talk to my great-grandmother. We used to talk on the phone every day."

Airhead's own eyes go even wider than mine and she says, "Oh my God, Keely, I am so sorry. I can be so freaking insensitive sometimes!"

No disagreements there, although I am amazed Airhead knows a word as big as 'insensitive.' Instead of responding, I snuffle and nod, then turn back to my computer.

As if to make amends and stuff her faux pas under the proverbial rug, she blurts, "Did you see the newest article in *The Georgetowner* about the Cuddler?"

My body goes rigid, and my fingers creep to the nearly healed wound on my arm, pressing harder and harder so I can retain my composure.

Airhead digs around in her enormous purse—new and shiny, I notice with disdain—before pulling out a crumpled wad of newspaper like a peace offering. I snatch it out of her hand, flipping to the front page.

"Whoa," she says, "chill."

I ignore her and start reading.

*   *   *

Georgetown Cuddler Attacks Another Student
By Cynthia Vauxhall

Police are still searching for the perpetrator known as the 'Georgetown Cuddler' after a fourth victim came forward late yesterday. Erica Harris, a rising sophomore, told detectives she awoke in the middle of the night to find a stranger in her bed, pressing up against her—consistent with the three other reported assaults.

"I screamed, and the person ran away before I could get a good look," Harris said. "But whoever it was, they were small. This was not some big guy."

Harris's report stands in stark contrast to that of Tom Carlson, who was struck in the nose and stabbed by the 'Cuddler.' Carlson alluded to the perpetrator's significant size and overwhelming physical strength, making police wonder if there's a copycat at large.

The theory is plausible, considering Harris's assault is the first reported by a female victim. Typically, serial perpetrators target a specific victim type, making Harris an unusual target.

"I don't know if it's the same person doing all of this," Harris said. "All I do know is that while I'm grateful I wasn't injured, what happened to me was still disgusting and violating. Whoever is doing this needs to be caught. A normal person does not do this."

Police are still actively collecting tips that could lead to the identification of the 'Cuddler' and any possible copycats.

*　*　*

I'm not even aware there's a thin moan, like a train whistle, coming out of my mouth until Airhead waves her hand in front of my face and says, "Keely. Keely! Are you okay?"

I suck my lips closed with a smack, cutting the moan off as abruptly as possible. My eyes lift from the paper to Airhead's face. "Fine. Just fine." My chest tightens threateningly.

She shrugs and turns back to her phone, busying herself with texting or scrolling or whatever the hell it is she does on that thing, leaving me to stew in silence.

I thought Erica and I had an understanding. She 'felt for whoever is doing this.' She had empathy. She was going to tell only me and not go to the police, much less the press.

Something has changed, and I don't know what it is. In the back of my mind, Mother cackles, insisting she was right all along about the impossibility of me having friends.

There's a vibrating rattle and then I hear, "What is it, Mom? Did you forget we just talked?"

Airhead's voice careens into my thoughts, scattering them in pieces all over my brain. Nobody should be comfortable talking to their mother this much.

I'm about to rip the phone from her manicured claw and throw it across the room when O'Meara walks in—as if this day could get any worse.

"Hello, girls," he says, his voice quiet but jovial.

Airhead is so invested in her conversation, she doesn't notice his presence at first. She's turned around in her chair, facing the window, her phone still clutched in her hand.

"Mom, why would I even do that? You don't wear a thong with spandex. You just go commando. Everybody knows that. Seriously, I—"

"Excuse me?" O'Meara says, his mouth torqued in a grimace of embarrassment.

Airhead turns around in a panic, the phone falling from her fist to the floor with a thud. O'Meara is staring at her with a raised eyebrow. She looks like a raccoon caught in the headlights—unsure, scared, frozen. I sit back, enjoying the spectacle. Maybe this day isn't complete garbage.

The atmosphere in the room is so still, we can all hear Airhead's mother's voice on the phone, just as grating and unpleasant as her daughter's. "Hello? Hello? Honey, please, just wear the damn thong!"

With an anxious chuckle, Airhead leaps down to retrieve the phone, frantically pounding at the screen to end the call. Her face is as red as a swollen spider bite.

She opens her mouth, then closes it, then opens it again, like a fish. The girl can't think of a blessed thing to say, but that's not too surprising. There's really no coming back from that.

"I suppose I don't need to remind you that taking personal calls in the office isn't the best use of your time," he says. I hold in a snicker.

Airhead blanches. "Of course, of course. I'm so sorry, Father. It won't happen again."

"Please see that it does not." I've never seen this side of O'Meara before—stern, commanding, authoritative. On the one hand, I'm happy all that imposing energy is focused on Airhead; on the other, I hate the idea of it ever coming to rest on me.

"Can I help you, Father?" she stammers, trying to make amends.

He settles himself into one of the chairs in the corner of the office. "I'd love a cup of tea, if you would."

Airhead jumps up, like a well-trained Labrador, to get O'Meara's foul-smelling beverage. I've got to think that much peppermint can't be good for his health—not that I care. In fact, he should have even more.

"Keely, you're looking well," he says, waving a hand at my relatively clean clothes and hair. He leans in close, once again under the erroneous impression that if he speaks quietly and Airhead is making his tea, then she can't hear him. "It looks like therapy is working for you."

I smile so wide it feels like my wiggly molars might fall out into my lap. "Oh, absolutely," I say. "It's going so well I might not even need to keep going."

His smile fades. "Now, let's not get ahead of ourselves. The most important part of staying healthy in therapy is regular maintenance."

I'm about to tell him exactly where he can shove his 'regular maintenance' when Airhead pops over with his mug of tea.

"Here you go, Father," she says, overly obsequious, even for her.

"Thank you," he says. He glances at his watch. "My next appointment should be here soon."

Holy shit, I completely forgot. Erica made an appointment to talk to O'Meara. She's the one he's about to see—and I bet she has a lot to say. I bite my lips so hard I draw blood.

One thing is for sure: I'm going to be listening to every word of that conversation, one way or another.

Airhead tilts toward me and whispers, "I didn't know you were in therapy." For the love of all things holy, I need to make a public service announcement: Speaking quietly does not equal privacy, assholes!

"My fucking mom died, remember?" I hiss at her. O'Meara doesn't seem to be listening to our conversation; he's absorbed in his tea.

"Wait, I thought it was your—your great-grandmother?" Airhead says.

Of course she would pick this moment to actually listen to me. "Right. That's what I said," I whisper.

Airhead leans back in her chair, chastened. I swallow the blood leaking into my mouth from my chewed lip. I've gotten so complacent, so sloppy lately. If I slip up in front of Airhead, there's nothing to stop me from making a mistake in front of someone who actually matters.

A tense silence descends over the small room. Instead of dissipating, it seems to thicken as footsteps pad across the red carpet of the Healy foyer and a hand pulls open the door to the Chaplains' Office.

CHAPTER THIRTY-FOUR

I Have Never Met Someone Who Is Actually Possessed

When Erica appears in the doorway, she's pale and sweaty. I'm not a doctor yet, but I can't help thinking those antibiotics are not working.

She steps into the room, pointedly avoiding looking at me. "Erica!" I chirp. She jumps a little, as though I've startled her. Her eyes flick to mine, and then skitter away again, back to the floor. She doesn't notice O'Meara sitting in the corner.

"Keely," she says, the word more like a squeak. The thin-lipped smile on her face looks more like a grimace. Maybe that UTI has progressed to a kidney infection, or she's feeling guilty about leaving her compassion behind and selling the Cuddler out to *The Georgetowner.*

"You must be here for your appointment. Father O'Meara—"

"Is right here," O'Meara says, cutting me off. Erica spins around to face him. His fingers are still clasped around his mug.

"Can I get you anything?" I ask Erica. Something is clearly wrong, but I can't pinpoint exactly what it is. Not being able to read her is making my eyeballs itch.

"No, thanks," she says, still not looking at me. She could just be in serious pain... or she could be afraid.

To O'Meara, she says, "Nice to see you again, Father." Her voice cracks on the last syllable.

"And you as well," he says, pulling himself upright. He places his empty mug on my desk with a nod. "Shall we?"

He holds the door open, gesturing for Erica to head into the hallway in front of him. He follows, and the door thuds closed behind them. The smell of sweat and peppermint tea wafts toward me in the door's wake.

"She didn't look so good, huh?" Airhead Ani says, ever the tactful one.

"Hey. Have a little respect, Annie," I snarl, and Airhead leans back, as if slapped.

"Jeez," she says.

I need to know what is being said right now in O'Meara's cushy office. My entire body is vibrating with urgency.

The empty mug in front of me catches my eye. I slam my chair back, catching Airhead's arm in the process.

"Ouch!" she yelps. "Come on!"

"Whoops," I say, picking up the dirty mug. "I'm going to go wash this."

"Take your time," she says, her eyebrows bunched together in irritation.

My feet are light and quick on the stairs. I stop into the kitchenette on the second floor to fill the mug with tap water. If anybody sees me, I can say I'm delivering a beverage to my favorite Jesuit.

A few seconds later, I'm crouching outside the closed door of O'Meara's office, pressing my ear to the thick wood. Their voices are muffled, but I can still make out what they're saying.

Erica says, "…everything's gotten so weird lately, with my boyfriend getting attacked, then me, then with what I saw in the tunnels—"

Goosebumps pop out all over my arms like tiny tumors. If she tells O'Meara about the tunnels, he's going to send people to investigate.

"Whoa, whoa," O'Meara says. "Miss Harris, please, slow down. Start with what happened to you."

"You've heard of the Cuddler?" O'Meara must be nodding, because she keeps talking. "Well, whoever it is came for me the other night, and it was horrible."

"That's a very frightening situation," he says gravely. "Can you tell me what happened, exactly?"

Listening to Erica describe our beautiful moment together as disgusting and violating yet again inflates a bubble of rage in my throat, hot and painful. She must have told somebody else about what happened, somebody who twisted everything around and confused her, made her think she had to go to the police and the press. That prick Tom Carlson, most likely.

After a beat, O'Meara speaks, breaking into my swirl of panicked thoughts. "Well, I'm very sorry that happened to you, Miss Harris."

"Me, too," she says.

"Where do we go from here? Have you spoken to the police?"

Erica lets loose a ragged breath that could also be a sob. "Yes," she says. "They still don't have any leads." That's a relief, at least. "I don't know how to get over what happened."

Erica, I thought you were stronger than that. You have know idea how many times I've been pinched, screamed at, pushed, and degraded, but instead of wallowing, I'm here at Georgetown, doing great. Maybe we're not as similar as I was starting to believe.

"There's always counseling," O'Meara says. That must be one of his stock phrases. Counseling can't solve everything, or, in my case, anything at all.

"Maybe I should try that," Erica squeaks. I wonder if she'll end up with Christina, too, or if O'Meara will threaten her lab position like he threatened my work-study job if she doesn't go to therapy.

"I can make a call," he says. "Connect you with the right resources. Sometimes God puts obstacles in our way to make us stronger as we cross them." That's a sack of crap, but whatever.

"Thank you," she says.

I wish I had a camera on the inside, because the few moments of silence that pass behind that door are excruciating. I quickly scan the hallway around me: still empty.

"What else is on your mind, Miss Harris? You mentioned something about the tunnels?"

Oh, no.

"Right," she says. My body becomes so still, I can feel the individual hemoglobin macromolecules inching through my capillaries. "I know we're not supposed to, but some of the Hughes students and I went into the tunnels last week, and I saw something. Something I can't explain. I've kept it to myself until now because I've been trying to rationalize it, but I can't make any benign explanation fit what I saw."

"What was it you saw?" O'Meara asks.

"There… there was a girl down there, and she was doing something awful with animals. She was—like—dissecting them or something." Wrong, it was a parabiosis operation, but whatever.

"That's a very serious accusation," O'Meara says. He pauses before gently asking, "Miss Harris, had you been drinking?" I want to cheer at the question; the answer will undoubtedly discredit her.

Erica splutters, "No—I mean yes, a little—but that's not the point!"

O'Meara sighs. "Did any of the other Hughes students see this… this dissection?"

Erica's voice is little more than a whisper, and I have to strain to hear her. "No."

"Miss Harris, I really think—"

"That's not everything," Erica cuts him off, sounding frantic. "At first, I didn't know who it was. I only saw her from the back, and I was so scared I ran out of there as soon as I saw the…the animals. But then… then…"

No. No way. She better not be about to—

"Now I know who it was. It was Keely. The girl from the Chaplains' Office. She was doing those horrible things. It was her!"

I stop breathing. I'd rather be waking up in another filthy boy's bed instead of facing the reality that Erica has just exposed my private life to somebody with the power to ruin me.

"Keely? You're saying you saw Keely Rexroth in the maintenance tunnels dissecting an animal?" O'Meara sounds more confused than horrified, so that's something, at least.

Erica sobs. "Yes! I saw her, Father!"

"I'm sorry, you said you didn't see her face… and you admit you'd been drinking. How do you know it was her?"

Good question.

"I heard her laugh," Erica says, her voice rising. "I heard it when we were in the tunnels, and then I heard that same laugh again yesterday—coming from Keely. You can't mistake it!"

Shit—I'd thought she was far enough down the hallway with the other Hughes idiots that she couldn't hear me, but either way, come on. I know my laugh isn't the most normal, sure, but it can't really be enough to identify me beyond a shadow of a doubt. O'Meara echoes my disbelief. "It's possible another person may have a laugh like that, Miss Harris," he says quietly.

"I told you, it's unmistakable! Nobody else laughs like that, like—like they're losing their mind right in front of you!" Ouch. Harsh. "Something is really wrong with her, Father, I think she might even be… this is going to sound crazy, but in other cultures it's totally normal…she might be possessed—"

O'Meara stops her. I almost let my signature laugh loose, but I clamp down hard at the last second. This door isn't as thick as it looks, and I certainly don't need to make her case and be discovered at the same time.

Some of the gentleness has fled from his voice. "Miss Harris, as I said last evening during my talk, I have never met someone who was actually possessed. Now, I know this may be difficult to hear, and you've been wrapped up in all of this exorcism talk, but it's not fun and games, as you all seem to think it is. I know Keely Rexroth. She's been working in the Chaplains' Office for a while now, and I'm well aware of her… peculiarities. Almost all of the time, people who display troubling behavior are experiencing mental health challenges—not demonic possession. Rest assured she is getting the help she needs."

"What, like therapy?" Erica shouts, and I pull my ear away from the door reflexively. "Therapy isn't going to get the demon out of her!"

This is unbelievable. Possession is total and complete horseshit. Bad people do bad things. Sick people do sick things. The end, no demons necessary.

O'Meara's voice is soothing, more controlled, and I press my ear against the door again to capture his every word. "Miss Harris, I think you need to let go of finding the 'true story' in all of this exorcism fiction. I think you've let yourself get too involved. It's not healthy. Focus on your research instead. And perhaps refrain from drinking alcohol."

"Father O'Meara, please. I don't care about the 'true story' anymore, I'm not even thinking about that, I swear. I just need to warn you about Keely. I don't feel safe around her. And I don't think therapy is going to cut it." Well, that explains her refusal to look me in the eye earlier. It was fear, after all.

Good. She should be afraid, after everything she's put me through. Pretending to be my friend, telling me she had empathy for the Cuddler, buying me lunches, confiding in me—it was all a scam. It was part of her plan to take me down, since she saw just how far my surgical skills have come. Mother was right when she told me, "There's no such thing as a friend when success is at your fingertips, Keely. If you lose focus, someone else will snatch away what you didn't have the competence to grab when you could."

O'Meara's voice is stern. "Let me be clear. I will not be performing an exorcism on Keely Rexroth. The girl is not possessed. I will do all I can to help you, Miss Harris, but you need to respect that I'm trying to stop you from going down a bad path that's nothing more than a dead end. Pull yourself back from the darkness before you dig a hole so deep you can't climb out." If I had one of those, I'd push Erica into it.

"Please," she says, sounding so pathetic. "Please, Father, just listen! I've heard so many stories from my parents about just this sort of thing, about people who look like they're normal but really aren't, and so many cultures have entire medicinal and religious systems built around curing—"

"I have listened," he says, cutting her off again. "I will take things from here, but you have to trust me, okay? Keep your thoughts about Keely to yourself and let me handle it. In the meantime, I'd like to set you up with an appointment at the student counseling center."

It's clear the show is over, and my neck is starting to cramp. Without waiting to hear Erica's response, I run through the hall, down the stairs, and straight out the Healy doors into the muggy sunshine.

I've never felt so betrayed. *The Georgetowner* article was bad enough, but serving me up on a platter to my enemy, exposing my secrets and vulnerabilities as if they're not worth protecting, is too damn much. I'm still clutching the half-full mug in my hands. I throw the contents out over the flower beds behind John Carroll, relishing the wet slap as the water hits the ground.

I was foolish to think there was a possibility of a different life out there for me: one where my hair didn't always smell of rat urine and my clothes weren't covered in mysterious stains; one where I laughed with friends over bowls of pasta and slices of garlic bread dripping with butter; one where I spent my days in a research lab and my nights with like-minded scholars; one where Mother's voice didn't echo constantly in my head, making me hate myself and everybody around me.

Nobody has my back. I'm utterly alone, just as I've always been.

Without thinking, I throw the mug to the ground, where it smashes into a handful of sharp chunks. I run to the side of Healy, rip open the gray metal door, and barrel down the ladder, the door slamming behind me. It's a risk to enter the tunnels in broad daylight, but now that O'Meara knows about my sanctuary, it won't be long before my privacy is destroyed for good. I must enjoy the last dregs of it while I can.

In my special chamber, the carcasses on the walls have slipped into various states of decay. I sit in the middle of the floor, surrounded by all of the animals I've dissected, along with all the rats with unsuccessful circulatory system connections. The floor and walls are stained crimson, making what should be an operating theater feel more like a slaughterhouse. The smell permeating the room is all-encompassing, burying itself in my nostrils so deeply it eradicates Erica's sweetness, which was all a lie, in the end.

Erica. Erica is the one who's done this to me, but she's not my main concern right now. O'Meara told her to keep her mouth shut and let him deal with me. He's more dangerous than she is, at least for the moment.

That means he's got to go—but I have to handle this situation delicately. I need to get rid of him without having a single finger left to point back to me.

The idea comes to me all at once, fully formed and beautiful. I have to point that finger at someone else, and I know exactly how to do it.

I see what I have to do scene by scene in full technicolor: the crimson petals of the oleander behind Mary's statue; the white porcelain of O'Meara's ever-present mug of tea; the mold-blue of Airhead Ani's wide eyes.

You can kill an adult with a single oleander leaf, you know.

CHAPTER THIRTY-FIVE

It's Easy to Poison Someone When You Know What You're Doing

It's shockingly easy to poison someone when you know what you're doing. I wait until nightfall, that empty space of time when all the professors and research students have gone home and the Georgetown residents are eating dinner, then I creep over to the statue of Mary in the corner of Copley lawn.

I've got surgical gloves on under a pair of thicker gardening gloves, and my pockets are laden with sharp scissors and a few plastic baggies. I approach Mary reverently, my head bowed, then kneel in front of her. The campus population is sparse right now, but, should anyone walk past and see me, I just look like a devout Catholic praying to the Virgin.

The oleander flowers are so red they're obscene. They rest in clusters all around Mary, perversely beautiful. They're not unlike Erica: enticing, but dangerous.

This is going to be a busy night, so there's no time to waste. I take another look around the lawn; seeing no one—so much for that increased Cuddler security—I slip the scissors and baggies out of my pockets and shuffle closer to the crimson blooms.

Oleander has been dubbed one of the most poisonous plants in the world. Every single part of it can kill you, from the seeds to the flowers to the leaves. Each fiber of the oleander is laden with toxic glycosides—

chemicals that slow the heart rate until it stops altogether. Even the smallest dosage of oleander, a single leaf, can kill a human. You can even die from inhaling the smoke coming off of burning oleander. Even in its death throes, it can hurt you.

I don't know why Georgetown planted oleander, of all things, behind a statue of Mary, but perhaps it's an unintended metaphor for the violent realities of organized religion. You're expected to give your soul to a deity, to dedicate your entire life to faith, but all you get in return is a poisoned understanding of your own nature and your place in the world. That sounds about right.

It's a bit tricky to grasp the scissors and oleander while wearing two sets of gloves, but after a few nerve-racking seconds, I manage to corral several leaves into one baggie and a small bouquet of scarlet flowers into another.

Now I just need to execute.

After spending the entire afternoon sitting in relative silence with Airhead Ani—broken only by her occasional inane question or the buzzing of her phone—I'm feeling antsy. I didn't see O'Meara after his appointment with Erica, but after she admitted she'd been drinking and no one could corroborate her story, I don't think he'll send people into the tunnels without speaking to me first. I'll have at least some warning to make all evidence of my sanctuary disappear; if not, nothing down there ties back to me. All the blood and DNA are from the rats, after all.

I know it's risky to go back into the tunnels tonight, but I have to work with what I've got, which is a room full of dead animals, three Viet Cong booby traps, two baggies of oleander, a pair of gardening gloves that can't be traced back to me, surgical glue, a half-empty box of peppermint tea bags I swiped from the Chaplains' Office, and Airhead's address. Into the tunnels I go.

It's also shockingly easy to crumble oleander leaves, slice open peppermint tea bags, funnel in the toxic green crumbs, and seal the bags back up with surgical glue. You'd never know the bags had ever been tampered with, unless you looked really, really close. Damn, I'm good.

Oleander leaves are bitter, but the herbal fug of peppermint should mask the taste enough for O'Meara to chug it down anyway. I stuff the poisonous bags back in the stolen box, remove the outer pair of gardening gloves, and turn to the next item on my to-do list.

I crack open my black doctor's bag and dump it upside down on one of my metal trays. Scalpels, small glass vials, and the trepan I still haven't had a chance to use come clattering out. Into the now-empty bag go the box of oleander teabags, the gardening gloves, the baggies of leftover leaves and bright red flowers, and the surgical glue.

I clamp the handle of the doctor's bag between my teeth, ignoring the pain in my dental nerves, as I climb the ladder up and out of the tunnels. It's full dark now, nearly midnight, and the light pollution from the District obscures the stars.

Airhead's apartment is on the ground floor of a townhouse on Prospect Street, not far from the *Exorcist* stairs. Like most silly and senseless people, she keeps a spare key under her doormat—a detail she readily forked over when I lied and told her "I've lost my key, how in the world do people keep track of those things?" I lift up the moldy rectangle, my hands still encased in my surgical gloves, and there it is, glinting in the yellow light from the street lamps.

This is the most dangerous part of my plan so far, but I'm not anxious because this needs to happen, one way or another. Airhead's lights are off, and when I twist the key and pull the door open delicately, nothing disturbs the stillness of the apartment. I step inside and push the door closed.

I'm in a small foyer, and my well-honed eyes instantly adjust to the darkness. There's a line of hooks along the wall to my right, coats, hats, purses, and scarves hanging from every inch of space. I don't understand why one person needs four black North Face coats, or three tartan Burberry scarves, or five Kate Spade crossbody bags in varying shades of beige. I think, briefly, about taking one of each and showing up to work one day wearing them all, just to see if Airhead will recognize them as her own.

In front of me, a light on the bottom of the microwave dimly illuminates a small kitchen. To the right of the kitchen, I can hear the mechanical whir of a box fan. I listen more closely and can just make out the phlegmy rise and fall of Airhead's snores.

It's time to move. In a few stealthy strides, I'm in the kitchen, setting my doctor's bag on the center island. I crack it open, pulling out the box of tea bags, the baggies of leaves and flowers, the gardening gloves, and the surgical glue. The first kitchen drawer I pull out is full of half-empty tubes of Kylie Cosmetics lipstick. Into the jumble go the gardening gloves, tainted with plenty of residue from oleander, but none from me. The next drawer holds a rattling array of bottles of herbs and spices, most of them unopened. That makes sense; I never took Airhead for much of a chef. Into this drawer goes the baggie of remaining oleander leaves. The third drawer is home to a sheaf of takeout menus, paper-wrapped chopsticks, plastic utensils, squishy maple syrup packets, and a few sets of tiny salt-and-pepper shakers. I shake a few of the adulterated oleander teabags into this drawer along with the little bottle of surgical glue, then shove it closed.

For the final touch, I need an appropriate vessel. I find it under her sink: a tall, thin vase still crusted with the moldy residue of whatever flowers were in here first. I fill it up with water, then maneuver the baggie holding the flowers into various contortions until the stems are resting comfortably in the vase, the flowers a riot of color on Airhead's kitchen table. I wonder if she'll even notice. She's not the most observant.

I put the box of the remaining teabags back in my doctor's bag and flee her apartment, being sure to lock the door behind me and replace the key under the mat. All the way back to my own apartment, I practice what I'll say when the police come asking about Airhead.

How about: "She's always hated Father O'Meara, ever since he caught her talking on the phone during work hours. He wasn't even that upset about it, but clearly, she was!"

CHAPTER THIRTY-SIX

Popping My Murder Cherry Doesn't Hurt At All

The box of adulterated teabags is sitting unobtrusively next to the electric kettle when Airhead Ani prances into the office this morning. There's a pep in her step that's quickly explained when she says, too loudly for the small room, "Oh my God, Keely, Brayden did the sweetest thing!"

The funniest part about all of this is that she thinks I care. I don't say anything, but she forges on as though I've begged her to tell me exactly what Brayden did.

Airhead swings her enormous new tote under her desk and plops into the bad chair. I'm comfortably nestled in the good one, which I've managed to de-gunk. She shifts around a bit, frowns, then gets on with her story. "So, I woke up this morning, and I went to the kitchen to get some low carb oatmeal—you know, watching my weight for hot girl summer and everything—and right in the middle of my kitchen table was a vase of these gorgeous red flowers!"

I don't think it's possible to have low-carb oatmeal, but I remain silent. She doesn't.

"I don't know what type of flowers they are, but they smell kind of like apricots."

I hope she got close enough for the toxic blooms to tickle her nostrils.

As if answering my unspoken wish, Airhead rubs her nose, which I now notice is red and slightly irritated. Goddamn, this is excellent.

Now seems like the right time for me to actually open my mouth. "Don't you think it's a bit creepy that he broke into your apartment while you were sleeping?"

She stops fidgeting with the height settings on the bad chair and smirks. "Of course not. I know this might be a bit tough for you to understand, since you don't have a boyfriend or anything, but when a guy leaves flowers in your kitchen, that's romantic. Not creepy."

"Right," I say. "How can you be sure it was him?"

"Who else would it be?" she scoffs. "Plus, I texted him this morning thanking him for the flowers and he said 'You got it, babe.'"

I stifle my laughter. Of course this dude would claim credit for something Airhead is so obviously excited about. When the police come to question him, he'll admit he didn't put the flowers there, making her look like even more of a liar. This day just keeps getting better.

"Right," I say again. "Good for you."

A self-satisfied smile settles on Airhead's face like a fly landing in a sticky puddle of syrup. She's about to say something when the door opens and O'Meara walks in, looking haggard. The dark circles under his eyes belie a night of sleeplessness and, I hope, nightmares.

The snarky little grin on Airhead's face morphs into one of fawning submission. She jumps up from the bad chair, which gives a metallic squeak of protest, and says, "Father O'Meara, good morning. Can I get you your tea?"

"That would be lovely, thank you," he says.

Showtime.

He leans in close to my desk while Airhead prepares his tea, and it's a struggle to keep my attention on him as she plucks a poisonous teabag from the box, oblivious to the way it's been tampered with. She drops it in a mug, then covers it with boiling water from the electric kettle.

"Keely," O'Meara says. This close, I can see the burst capillaries peppering his nose. "I'd like to speak to you in my office, please."

"Alright," I say, my voice nearly shaking with anticipation as Airhead hands O'Meara his mug.

He blows on it, sending spirals of toxic steam wafting through the air. I hold my breath as he brings the mug to his lips and takes a long sip.

He pulls the mug away from his mouth and grimaces slightly. "Is this a new kind of tea?" he asks.

"No, it's the same peppermint tea I always make for you," Airhead says, the perfect little sycophant.

"Hm," he says. "I must be imagining it, then. I didn't sleep well last night."

"Is there anything else I can get you, Father?" she says.

"No, no," he says, waving her off. He directs a pointed look in my direction. "Keely, shall we?"

My body is vibrating with excitement as we climb the stairs, because O'Meara has unwittingly offered me a front row seat to watch him poison himself. I haven't felt this level of arousal since I found myself in Erica's bed, surrounded by the intoxicating scent of her hair.

When we get to his office, he sits behind his desk and gestures for me to make myself comfortable in one of the cushy chairs across from him.

He takes another big sip of his tea, grimaces again, and clears his throat. "Keely," he says. "This is not an easy conversation for me to have, but we need to talk more seriously about your future."

At least I actually have a future—in a few hours, O'Meara's will evaporate as his body succumbs to the oleander. "What do you mean?" I ask, all wide eyes and supplicating frown.

He sips his tea again. Just keep drinking, you bastard.

"I—I heard a troubling allegation about you yesterday," he says. "Someone said you've been performing some… unauthorized experiments in the maintenance tunnels. Is that true?"

"Unauthorized experiments?" Now I can better understand why Erica uses this pattern of repetitive upspeak—it's very effective in obfuscating the truth.

"Yes," he says. "Now, I'm not one to believe idle gossip or rumors, so I want to get your side of the story. Have you been in the tunnels?"

Soon, it won't matter what he knows, so I say, "Yes. I have."

O'Meara sighs, as if with relief. "Okay. Thank you for telling me that. Can you tell me what you were doing?"

"I was performing my scientific research," I say.

"And why did you feel you needed to do that in the tunnels?"

"The tunnels are private," I say.

"I see," he says. He stares at me, as if trying to bore into the real me behind my mask. The silence stretches on, broken only by O'Meara's slurp of tea. "Keely," he finally says, "I'm going to be brutally honest with you. I am sincerely worried about you, both for your sake and the sake of your classmates. You haven't been taking care of yourself, and I see now that the student counseling center doesn't have the resources you need."

He's right about one thing: the student counseling center doesn't have a damn thing to offer me. "The resources I need?" I say.

He sighs, then takes another sip of tea to fortify himself. "I'd like to offer you the opportunity to join an outpatient treatment program for young women facing the same sorts of… challenges and stressors that you are."

"I don't understand."

"Keely, what I've heard about you is gravely concerning, and what I've seen with my own eyes tells me you are in need of intensive help. I'm worried you might hurt yourself, more than you already have, and I can't let you continue to work here if there's a chance of injury to yourself or to someone else."

Even though I knew there would be some sort of fallout from Erica's tattling, I'm unprepared for the naked anguish on O'Meara's face. Without my consent, a single traitorous tear slithers out of my right eye, tracing a sticky path down my cheek.

"Keely," he says again, his voice gentle. "I know people who can give you the support you need. I can take you to the outpatient center today."

Another tear snakes out of my other eye. "I can't leave," I say. "I have work to do." It's the truth, but I'm sure O'Meara doesn't understand exactly what type of work it is. It's certainly not pushing papers in the Chaplains' Office.

"You'd have to take at least the fall semester off," he says uneasily. "But we would hold your place for you. You can come back when you're feeling better."

I'm never going to feel better. More tears are sliding down my face, pooling at the corners of my mouth. The salty taste makes me feel sick. "Med schools would never accept me with a missed semester on my record," I say. "They'd want to know what happened."

O'Meara tilts his mug back, finishing off the tea with a gurgle. "They'll be more understanding than you think," he says, as if he has any idea at all. Nobody wants the doctor who can't keep her life together. "Keely, you don't have to be perfect." It's like he's taking a page out of 'Madame Leila's' little book of clichés.

Mother's voice slips back into my head, the ever-present uninvited guest. "If you can't be perfect, you can't be my daughter. Mistakes are for failures, and no daughter of mine is a failure."

"Yes, I do," I whisper, my chest starting to tighten.

"I know this is a lot to process," he says.

"You don't understand," I say. Pain shoots through my sternum like a lightning strike. Without a mother like Ellen Rexroth, nobody can understand why I am the way I am. I don't even understand myself, and I've never been in anybody else's brain but my own.

"I understand you're scared and probably very overwhelmed," he says. He's not wrong. "But I can't sit by and watch you destroy yourself. Not when I have the power to help you."

That's where he veers off-course. No one has the power to help me. Even if I wanted to go to his silly treatment program, they wouldn't be able to do a damn thing. There's no fixing me. Plus, O'Meara will be dead before he can force me out of Georgetown.

"Can I think about it?" I ask.

"Of course," he says. "But we need to resolve this by the end of the day, please. And if you have any questions, you know where to find me."

I get up to leave, but he stops me. "One more thing, Keely," he says warily. "If there's anything still in the tunnels, clean it up. Stop whatever you're doing before anybody else finds out and gets you into the sort of trouble you can't escape."

"Alright," I say, staring at his empty mug. I'm already cleaning things up, he just doesn't realize it. By the time he does, it'll be far too late.

*   *   *

As I exit O'Meara's office—hey, I'm probably the last person to see him alive—there's the tiniest part of me that feels not bad, exactly, but sort of unsettled over poisoning him. The anguish on his face was real, I know, but even if he was genuinely trying to do something nice for me, his death can't be helped. It's like that saying, play dangerous games, win dangerous prizes. That's just what happens when you mess with things that don't concern you. He's caught in the crossfire between me and Erica.

Thinking about her makes my hands cramp in fury, and I grip the banister far too tightly as I descend back to the first floor of Healy.

First, she took my spot in the Hughes program. Then, she took my sense of safety and privacy in the tunnels. Then, she took away my focus and drive. Now, she's betrayed my fledgling trust, exposed my secrets to a third party, and left me no choice but to commit my first murder. Little Miss Erica Harris, who's never had to worry about not being enough, is going to pay for what she's stolen from me.

I take my time descending the red carpeted stairs, feeling the plushness under my feet.

'Madame Leila' was right, in a way. She told me to learn from Erica. I can, but not in the way she seemed to suggest—I've learned people like Erica have nothing to offer me except obstacles to overcome. There's not enough room at Georgetown for the both of us; instead, I'm going to slice

Erica right out of her own life and insert myself into the empty hole. I'll be the one stuffing my face with fettuccine and laughing with my roommates. I'll be the one pipetting samples into agarose gels. I'll be the one delivering research talks in front of professors and adoring students. I'll be the one getting preferential treatment from medical schools. As the vision forms in my mind, the pain in my chest finally starts to relent.

I'm almost back to the Chaplains' Office. I can hear Airhead Ani humming to herself, extremely off-key.

I can be the bigger person here. I can admit Erica is the sort of daughter Mother always wanted: clean, smart, driven. Mother might not like Erica's sociability, but look at where it got her—in Hughes, a real smile permanently plastered on her face.

I'm not going to just learn from Erica. I'm going to take her place.

CHAPTER THIRTY-SEVEN
I'm Glad I Killed Him

The first thing I do when I get back to the Chaplains' Office is send Airhead Ani on a wild goose chase for stamps, insisting Father O'Meara asked her to get them for him. Then, I use her computer to send cancellations for all of O'Meara's meetings for the rest of the day, ensuring nothing can be traced back to me. He doesn't have many meetings, but the last thing I need is someone finding him before the poison takes effect. Oleander poisoning is insidious—he'll start to feel confused, then dizzy, then unbearably weak. Fatigue will swamp him, and he'll grow weaker and weaker. By the time he realizes something is seriously wrong, he'll be too feeble and dazed to even dial 911.

When Airhead gets back, she spends the rest of the day scrolling on Instagram, which is fine by me. It keeps her quiet, distracted, and docile, just the way I like her—not that I like her much at all. There's a single close call, when she gets up and starts the electric kettle. "You think this tea is any good? Father O'Meara is always drinking it, maybe I should give it a try."

With great care, I keep the panic out of my voice. "I don't think you should do that," I say. "He brings that tea special, from his home. Haven't you ever noticed?"

"Chill, Keely. I'm pretty sure he just buys this from Safeway."

I shrug, feigning nonchalance. "Do what you want, but you're kind of already on thin ice with him, remember? He's caught you on the phone. You want to add stealing his special tea to the list?"

Airhead grumbles and turns off the kettle, then sits back down. As much as I'd love to give her the same cup of death she handed to O'Meara, I need my scapegoat alive and kicking for a little longer.

The hours pass slowly as I pray to the God I don't believe in that O'Meara stays in his office, suffering in silence like a good Catholic. My plan plays like a movie in my mind on repeat. O'Meara drank the tea without protest, so that's phase one complete. In a few more hours, I'll go check on him. It's risky, but I'll need to gain access to his laptop. As his de facto assistant, I have unrestricted access to his calendar, but that doesn't extend to his personal email, which is what I need to use to lure Erica close enough so I can take her out. The girl is so befuddled by her parents' nonsense that she thinks I'm possessed, which means she's going to keep her distance. It also means she'll grab onto anything O'Meara asks of her like it's a lifeline. I'm counting on it—everything else depends on Erica running right into my spider's web.

When the clock reads 3:30, Airhead stands up and stretches. "I'm taking off," she says. "It's been so freaking slow today. Unless…" She gives me an uneasy look. "Unless you think Father O'Meara will mind?"

I don't protest, because as soon as she's gone, I can go check on O'Meara. "Not at all," I say. "It has been really slow. We don't both need to be here. I'll cover for you."

She smiles gratefully, her still-lashless eyes crinkling. "Thanks, Keely."

As soon as the heavy wood front door of Healy thuds behind her, I'm up and out of my seat like my ass is on fire. When I reach O'Meara's floor, the hallway is eerily quiet. Long shadows stripe the floor, contrasting with the orange light falling through the tall windows. As I creep toward his office, I'm alternately bathed in gold and thrust into darkness, never staying in one state for long.

O'Meara's door is slightly ajar, and it squeaks when I push it open.

"Father?" I whisper. Before going inside, I glance around the hallway again: still empty. I slip into the room and close the door behind me.

O'Meara is slumped facedown on his desk. Next to an overturned cup of pens is a small puddle of greenish vomit, which gives off a bitter reek that fills the office like incense. I squat next to his desk to get a better look at him. His skin is pale and waxy, his lips the color of a winter sky. His eyes are open, but glazed over and unseeing. Just to be sure, I press my fingers into the flabby, cold skin of his neck, searching for the jugular and carotid. There's nothing, not even the faintest thump.

"Calling it," I say. "Time of death, 3:42 pm." In reality, he's probably been dead for at least an hour, but I've always wanted to say that. I know I need to move quickly, but I can't stop myself from pausing over his body, marveling at the mystery of death. A dead human is so different from a dead rat or a dead squirrel. My fingers itch to write observations in a lab notebook, but I don't have the time. I'll have to content myself with taking a mental snapshot of this moment, a crucial piece of my medical training: my first up close and personal look at a human corpse. I guess O'Meara has helped me more than he could ever know.

The moment of stillness passes. There's a twinge of regret upon finding O'Meara dead, but mostly I feel a profound, almost sexual relief. If I'd known killing people felt this good, I might have tried it earlier.

I spy his laptop on the left side of his desk, open but asleep. I turn the thin fabric of my shirt into a makeshift glove and run my covered finger over the trackpad, waking up the computer. Shit—it's password protected. O'Meara wasn't the smartest, but I'm guessing his password isn't 'Jesus.'

I'm about to start searching the desk for password clues when I see the small black square in the upper right portion of the keyboard. It's a fingerprint pad, which shouldn't surprise me in the least. Of course the Jesuits have the newest, fanciest MacBook Pro computers, despite the whole 'vow of poverty' thing. I asked my parents for a laptop like this at the start of last semester since mine is half-dead, but I was flatly denied.

Report cards had just come out, and when Mother saw the A- I got in chemistry, she said, "Why do you need the best laptop when you're not doing the best work?" Even after finishing the spring semester with straight A's, Mother refused to replace my old computer, and my father was too weak to challenge anything she said.

I move the laptop over to O'Meara's right side, and with my fingers still encased in my shirt, I lift his right index finger. His body hasn't entered rigor mortis yet, so it's still pliable. I press his finger onto the black square and, like magic, the computer flashes to his home screen, where his email is still open.

While I have the opportunity, I scan his inbox. There's nothing particularly interesting, and I'm about to move on to the next part of my plan when I spy a (1) next to his Drafts folder.

I double click on the message and find this:

```
To: donna@meadowsrehab.org
From: omearasj@georgetown.edu
Subject: Re: Student in need


Dear Donna,
Thank you for your patience and understanding.
I spoke with Keely today, and she's agreed to
enter your facility. This young woman has clearly
had her share of difficulties, but I'm confident
you and your team can provide the care and support
she needs to get healthy. I've told her she'll
need to take a semester off, but please be advised
that she may need more time than just a few
months. I've heard some rather troubling things
about her lately, and I believe issues as deep-
seated as hers will need the most in-depth care
your facility can provide.
```

>   If it's acceptable to you, I'd like to arrange for
> Keely's transport to Meadows as soon as possible.
> Let me know when you can be ready for her.
>   Yours in God,
>   Rev. Randolph O'Meara, S.J.

Wow. I need a minute to process everything I've just learned. O'Meara clearly thought I was going to agree to his plan. He was so confident he already typed up this little ditty for this Donna person. If I didn't end up agreeing, I bet he would have tried to get me expelled, or at the very least, fired.

Then there's that armchair diagnosis about 'deep-seated issues.' O'Meara's no doctor; he doesn't know what's wrong with me. I'm glad I killed him. That tiny piece of me that felt the littlest bit of regret is dead now, just like him. I resist the urge to kick O'Meara's lifeless body.

I delete the entire draft of O'Meara's email and type this instead:

>   Dear Donna,
>   My apologies for wasting your time. I spoke
> with Keely today, and it seems there has been
> a grave misunderstanding. We had a lovely,
> enlightening conversation, and my concerns have
> been satisfactorily addressed. I won't be needing
> your services, so please fool free to release the
> spot you were holding at Meadows.
>   Sincerely,
>   Rev. Randolph O'Meara, S.J.

I click Send, then I delete my response from his Sent folder, along with every other sent and received email in this chain with Donna. Then, I go to his Trash folder and delete the messages from there, too. None of this will stand up to expert computer forensics, but I'm betting nobody will even look. Most people would probably feel uncomfortable digging into a priest's private emails.

I take a deep breath. Goodbye, Donna, goodbye, Meadows, and goodbye, O'Meara and your meddling. That was one more bullet I managed to dodge. Let's hope my luck continues.

I open up a new email and type as rapidly as I can with my shirt covering my fingers.

```
To: eharris@georgetown.edu
From: omearasj@georgetown.edu
Subject: Meeting


Hello Erica,
I have a rather urgent follow-up question to
our meeting today that I'd like to ask you. Can
you meet me in my office at 8pm? I know it's late,
but it's the only time I have available.
Yours in God,
Rev. Randolph O'Meara, S.J.
```

While I wait for Erica's reply, I busy myself with setting the scene. I nudge O'Meara's mug with my shirt-covered knuckles front and center on his desk. If the police are smart enough to analyze it, they'll find O'Meara's prints, of course, but also Airhead Ani's.

Another ping echoes out of the laptop's speakers. It's an email from Erica:

```
To: omearasj@georgetown.edu
From: eharris@georgetown.edu
Subject: Re: Meeting
```

```
Hi Father O'Meara,
Yes, absolutely. I'll see you at 8.
Sincerely,
Erica
```

This is so delicious it's giving me a stomachache. Everything is going according to plan. Now, all I have to do is wait for Little Miss Erica Harris to show up.

I delete the email to Erica along with her reply, then exit O'Meara's email and close his laptop. I could pick up the phone and call 911, pretend I just found him, but I'm not going to do that. If his body is found right now, this place will be crawling with uniforms for the next few hours, and Erica will see something is up.

Somebody else will find him soon enough. In the meantime, I have to prepare. As Mother would say, "If you're not two steps ahead, then get out of my sight because you're already way behind."

CHAPTER THIRTY-EIGHT

Don't Threaten Me with a Good Time

The sun is low over the horizon, dissipating into the Potomac, not unlike a drop of poison into a cup of tea. My palms are prickly with anticipation as I crouch in the shadows of the Healy foyer, just inside the heavy wooden doors. There's a box cutter in my pocket, pressing against my leg like a lover.

Erica is punctual. She pushes open the Healy doors just as the clocktower starts to chime eight times, its ring reverberating like a death knell. The sound distracts her, and combined with the shock of leaving the golden light of the quad for the darkness of Healy, she's rendered helpless for a few moments as her eyes and ears adjust.

That's all the time I need. Before she can walk toward the stairs or spot me in my hiding place, I lunge and latch on to her arm, clapping my other hand over her mouth. Her squeal barely whistles through my tightly clasped fingers as I pull her into the shadows with me.

Instead of struggling, she goes rigid in my arms, her back pressed against my chest. Clearly, Erica's fight or flight response is more of a freeze, which works fine for me.

"Hello, Erica," I coo, whispering directly into the tender shell of her ear.

She lets out a little moan, but my fingers prevent her from supplying any sort of intelligible response.

My signature laugh rips from my throat, the accompanying spittle falling on Erica's hair like morning mist. "You're right, you know," I say. "Therapy doesn't work."

I can't see her face, but I can feel the tears gushing from her eyes as they run over my fingers. Her lips are petal-soft, and I indulge myself by inhaling the scent of her hair. Even mingled with the sweat of utter terror, it smells divine. Too bad all of that beauty and compassion can't save her now.

"Time to go," I say, taking my hand from her mouth to quickly pull the box cutter from my pocket and press it against her throat.

Erica shakes like a newborn fawn, all awkward limbs and elbows. I can feel a thick glob of snot travel from her nostril to her upper lip, then down to her throat. She moans again. I wonder if this is how she sounds when she's with her monstrous boyfriend.

I keep one hand wrapped around the box cutter shoved against her throat and tighten my grip on Erica's arm from behind so she can't wriggle free. In the unlikely event anyone else happens to intrude, I'll move the box cutter to her kidney, and they'll think I'm supporting a despondent friend in need.

My knee nudges hers, first gently, then more forcefully, pushing her into a slow march. After some prodding, she opens the Healy doors onto the quad, which has descended into dusk, when visibility is poorest. Perfect.

When we get to the top step, I feel Erica tense next to me, coiling her muscles like a spring. It's obvious she's getting ready to run—that flight response has finally kicked in. She won't go without a struggle, but I've got the trump card.

Before she can put her foot onto the step below, I extend the blade of my box cutter and press it to the small of her back.

"You listen to me," I hiss. "No screaming, no running. If you try anything, I'll plunge this blade right into your L1 vertebra. You'll never walk again and you'll have to piss and shit in a bag for the rest of your life."

She turns to face me with her big doe eyes, their surfaces rippling with tears. "Keely," she whimpers, clearly trying to play to emotions I don't have.

"Think I'm kidding?" I say. Time to lay all the cards on the table. "You've seen me in action, Erica. You know exactly what I'm capable of."

There's no sense wearing the mask of normalcy anymore. Erica knows who I am, and now she knows I know, too.

"Please," she whines.

I tighten my fingers around her arm and pull her down the stairs. It's incredible how Erica thinks some halfhearted whimpering and begging will get her whatever she wants, will let her escape the mess she's made for herself. That must work with Mommy and Daddy. It won't work with me.

I tug Erica toward the corner of Healy. There's some resistance, but a good healthy yank gets her moving. I squeeze my grip on her arm even more and continue to press the tip of the blade against her spine, making sure she can feel it through the thin fabric of her shirt. If she's going to try anything stupid, now would be the time. Unfortunately for her, there's no one around to help. I half-push, half-drag Erica toward the innocuous metal storm door.

"Keely, please," she tries again. I push the blade in a little harder, drawing a pinprick of blood that blooms like a poppy on her shirt. "You're hurting me," she says.

"Don't threaten me with a good time," I say, and the smile spreading across my face is completely genuine.

We take a sharp left down the walkway between Healy and Copley Halls. I can feel Erica realize exactly where we're going by the way her entire body tenses and her heels dig into the asphalt. "No," she whispers. Her lungs suck in a greedy gulp of air, and I can tell she's about to scream. Bad idea.

I push the knife in deeper as I move the hand gripping her arm to her lips. "Stay quiet and you get to keep the use of your legs," I say. Erica's breath is hot and moist on my palm.

We're at the metal door now, the one that leads into the tunnels. I rip my hand from Erica's mouth, relishing the terror coming off of her in waves.

I open the door in one swift movement, the yawning abyss impenetrable in the dusky light. Erica starts to shake. "No, no, no, no," she says.

"Yes, yes, yes, yes," I say. "Now—"

This is when Erica does something absolutely senseless. Despite my warnings, my threats, my very sharp knife in her very vulnerable back, she still thinks the little things she learned in her stranger danger classes will help her. She jerks herself away from my knife and turns to face me, putting her back to the open doorway. She pulls in another lungful of air, ready to scream, and I can see she thinks she's smarter than me, quicker.

She's wrong.

I shove Erica through the doorway just as the first high-pitched whine of a scream comes out of her mouth. It's swallowed by the darkness as she pitches backward into the tunnels, the sound getting smaller and smaller as she falls, like a rat plummeting down a deep well. I shudder with pleasure when I hear the sticky crunch of her body hitting the concrete below.

I slip in behind her and the storm door closes, plunging us into velvety blackness.

CHAPTER THIRTY-NINE

We're Not Friends

It was challenging dragging Erica through the tunnels and lifting her over the tripwires into my operating theater, but now that she's here, everything is falling into place. I'm cleaning my scalpels, humming to myself, when I hear her groan in agony.

I turn to face her. "Ah! You're awake!"

She's lying awkwardly on her side with her face pressed against the bars of the dog cage. I knew that would come in handy one day, especially since I reinforced it with a padlock. Even if Erica could walk out of here, she can't get past that lock.

"You had a nasty fall," I say, licking my lips.

Her eyes are squeezed shut, as though she can blink away the reality of the shitstorm she's brought upon herself by sticking her nose where it doesn't belong and getting in my way. She moans again, louder this time.

"Don't worry, Erica, I'll take care of you."

A gurgling sob barrels out of her throat, and she finally opens her eyes, slowly prying the eyelids apart as though they're welded shut. She blinks several times, then turns her head wildly around, taking in her cozy accommodations.

"I can't feel my legs," she says in a tiny voice.

"Well, that's probably for the best," I say. "You know, with them being broken and all."

Panic lights up her face and she tries to scrabble around to get a good look at her lower body, but the confines of the cage keep her wedged in place. She sucks in a noisy breath to scream, but I cut her off before she has the chance. There's no point in making things unpleasant.

"Come on, Erica, there's really no use in screaming. You know where we are, right? Nobody can hear you."

Without warning, vomit spews from Erica's mouth, coating the bars of the cage and dripping down her shirt.

"Erica, Erica, Erica," I say. "Don't be scared." Of course, when people say that, you should absolutely be scared.

Erica makes a garbled choking sound, which makes me laugh.

When she speaks, her voice is thick with the remains of the vomit in her throat. "Why?"

I whip around to face her, clutching my clean scalpels to my chest. "You know something, Erica? When I held you, when I breathed in your flowery shampoo and your minty breath, when I pulled the warmth coming off your body into my own, I felt better than I ever have in my entire life. I don't believe in God, of course, but it was probably how people feel when they're having a religious experience. It felt like you opened up a window for me, and through it, I could see how my whole life could be different."

Erica says nothing, only spits out a few mouthfuls of bile. If she understands what I'm talking about, she doesn't show it. She won't meet my eyes.

"Look at me," I command, and she lifts her gaze to mine. Her eyes are so shiny with tears, they look like glowing emeralds. "I thought I could be your friend. I really did."

"We are friends," Erica whimpers.

"No!" I nearly scream it, my anger at her lie rushing out in one word. I take a deep breath and reel myself back in. It's dangerous to perform surgery in a heightened emotional state, after all. "No, we're not. I thought we were, but then I read what you said about me in that article. You told that reporter what happened between us was 'disgusting and violating.' You said I needed to be caught. You said a 'normal person does not do this.' For your information, I have a problem with sleepwalking and can't help what happens when I'm unconscious." I pause, considering, then add, "Oh, and your repulsive boyfriend tried to rape me."

Erica's eyebrows shoot up so high they kiss her hairline. "You're the Cuddler?" she says. "It's you? But Tom swore it was a guy! He told me I had to go to the police or else the next victim's blood would be on my hands! And wait—what? He tried to rape you?"

"I thought everything could be different," I say, ignoring her. Of course Tom poisoned her mind like he poisoned her urinary tract again and again and again, and what's worse, she let him. "But I was being ridiculous. You were right. A normal person does not do this. A normal person goes to a mid-level school, earns mid-level grades, gets a mid-level job, has a mid-level life. That will not be my life. I'm going to be a world-renowned surgeon."

To my utter shock, Erica laughs. She actually dissolves into uncontrollable giggles, knocking her head on the bars of the cage as she shakes. Before I can say anything, the hysterical mirth turns to dread, and then she's crying again. "You're out of your mind," she says, glancing around the room as though seeing it for the first time. Her gaze locks on the dissected animals decorating the walls. "You're completely fucking insane."

I run my finger lightly along the blade of one of my scalpels. It's refreshingly sharp and clean.

"No," I say. "I've never been thinking more clearly."

"What are you going to do to me?" she says quietly, through what are now tearful hiccups.

I bat her question away like an annoying mosquito. "You know," I say, "I've been wondering what it would be like to climb inside your skin and live there for awhile. Are you happy with your life, Erica? When you perform experiments in the lab, or go to the intellectual salons with your Hughes friends, or sit down to eat pasta with your roommates, or let your repugnant boyfriend touch you, are you happy? Even with everything you have, look where you've ended up!"

Erica doesn't respond; she just sits silently, letting the fat salty droplets course down her face.

"I've been working on performing a parabiosis operation," I say. "The night you intruded down here and interrupted me, you killed my specimens. I was at a crucial point in the surgery when you decided it was acceptable to invade my privacy and the sanctity of the operating theater. You pulled my attention away when it was needed most, and both of the specimens died on the table. I've tried again since then, but it's just not working."

I gently place the clean scalpels back on the metal tray, readying them for their next surgery. "I've wondered what it would be like to connect my circulatory system to yours. Do you think whatever makes you so clean and perfect would run through my veins, too? Do you think it would make me just like you?"

"I told Father O'Meara about you!" she explodes, her words echoing around the small room. "He knows what you're doing here. He's going to come find you."

Now it's my turn to chuckle. "Oh, Erica," I say. "You still think you're smarter than me, don't you? Always one step ahead?"

Fear transforms her face into a grimace.

"O'Meara is dead, Erica," I say, relishing the shock and outrage that sparks behind her eyes.

"No," she says. "There's no way."

Instead of going back and forth with her over the patent fact of O'Meara's timely death, I say, "You know, most students have to wait until medical school to do cadaver dissections, but not me. I won't let a good body go to waste."

"Jesus Christ," she breathes. "You're going to dissect Father O'Meara?"

"Ah, no, there's been some confusion," I say, happy to correct her. "Have you ever considered donating your body to science, Erica?"

"You can't—"

"Don't worry!" I say, cutting her off again. "It's for a good cause. Just think, you're going to help train the future best surgeon in the world. That's got to count for something, right?"

Erica makes a strangled gasping sound, then, instead of vomiting again like I expect her to, she yells, "I cast you out! I cast you out, demon!" Her face is whiter than the pus of an infected wound. There's no trace of her intoxicating beauty now; fear is the great leveler.

I tilt my head and let her voice echo through the chamber for a few beats. A single drop of hope blooms like a fungus across her pallid features before I let out another one of my feral-sounding laughs.

"Are you trying to exorcise me, Erica?"

The blush of hope fades from her cheeks and she whimpers something unintelligible.

I fix her with a cold, gray stare. "I'm not possessed, Erica. I'm operating on a higher level than everybody else. I thought you could understand that. I even thought maybe there was room for both of us, but clearly I was wrong. People like you can't seem to grasp the truth. I'm a fucking genius, and the Hughes program can't see it, and the girls upstairs can't see it, and the brainless drones in the Chaplains' Office can't see it, either." When I finish, I'm panting like a dog in heat. Each exhalation feels like a cleansing purge, with no hint of my normal chest pain.

In a last-ditch effort to save herself, Erica pleads, "Keely, please! We're friends!"

"No, we're not," I say, fingering the gleaming metal of a scalpel. "Mother was right: I don't need friends." My eye catches the industrial curves of the trepan. Maybe it's time to try that one out—how exciting!

"Yes, we are!" she says, her voice rising to a thin scream. "I didn't realize how much you needed a friend, Keely! But now I do! Don't you see? I can be there for you. It was wrong of me to describe what happened between us as disgusting. It wasn't. It was… it was beautiful. Let me make it up to you. Let me be your friend! Please!"

"I think not," I say, the calmness of my voice such a sharp contrast to hers. "That would be much too vulgar a display of mercy, don't you think?"

My fingers close around the trepan and pick it up. That's when Erica starts screaming in earnest—the kind of horror-movie scream that is rife with hills and valleys of sound, an entire landscape of terror echoing incessantly against the long, hard walls of the tunnels. She takes a short inhale and starts up again, the sound even louder this time. Her scream is burrowing into my skull, sending needles of electric pain through my nerves.

"Shut up!" I yell back at her, barely able to hear myself over her cries.

She doesn't even register my command; she keeps panting and screaming, panting and screaming. I've never been trepanned before, but if I had to guess, I'd say it feels something like this. A migraine is starting to build in the center of my forehead.

"Stop!" I yell again, but my command has zero effect. "Nobody can hear you down here!"

I drop the trepan and slap my palms to my ears. It doesn't really help; the sound still creeps between my fingers, digging itself deeper and deeper into my brain.

I lurch toward the bars of her cage, hoping some display of aggression on my part will shut her up, but she doesn't seem to register me. With each scream, my body feels like a bowstring tightening and tightening until the inevitable snap. I have to get her to stop, one way or another.

I nearly rip the denim of my jeans trying to wrench the padlock key out of my pocket. The pain in my head—nothing like the pleasant pain of controlled bloodletting—is starting to blur my vision, and it takes several tries before I manage to jam the key into the lock and twist. The lock falls off with a heavy metallic thud, and the door of the cage swings open.

"Shut up!" I yell, my face inches from hers. Erica's eyes are squeezed shut, but they fly open when my fist connects with her jaw. Her head dips back from the impact, and she finally stops screaming.

I fall back against the concrete floor in relief, pushing myself over to the wall with my heels. My head is still pounding, but it no longer feels as though millions of microscopic needles are tearing my brain tissue apart. My eyes flutter closed, and I let myself breathe in the refreshing atmosphere of silence.

I only rest for a moment, but that's all Erica needs to try to outsmart me one last time. Somehow, she manages to crawl out of the cage with two broken legs. She's running on pure adrenaline now, I suppose. I don't know what she thinks is going to happen. It's not like she can climb the ladder and run back to the safety of her townhouse.

The concrete is blissfully cool against my back as I watch Erica pull herself across the floor toward the open doorway leading to the rest of the tunnels. I moved the flimsy door aside and haven't yet put it back   something I'm glad of now. It will make for a much more entertaining show. I shift into a more comfortable position.

Erica grunts and heaves, straining to get herself as far away from me as possible. It's interesting how far the brain will push the body to hold on to the slimmest chance of survival. In a way, I find it admirable, this fighting for the impossible. Erica is stronger than I expected, but she's showing it much too late.

She's almost at the door. I'd love to know what thoughts are running through her head, but I keep my mouth shut. It's just about time for the climax.

It's Erica's shoulder that hits the tripwire first. There's a charged moment where she feels the obstruction in front of her and keeps trying to push through into the hallway, but she fails. The tiger board swings down with an elastic thwap, sending a cluster of sharpened spikes right through her head.

I knew those booby traps would come in handy one day.

CHAPTER FORTY

It's No Harvard, But Good for You

"It's been three weeks, Rog," I say, looking into Roger's slightly unfocused eyes as he stands on his front lawn. "Three weeks since O'Meara drank that cup of poison and Erica impaled herself on my booby trap. What a pitiful way to go, really. There've been police officers and detectives swarming all over Healy investigating O'Meara's death, but nobody's come looking for Erica."

"I don't like tea," Roger says.

Then, because I'm itching to tell someone, I unload. "I learned this with O'Meara—it's so simple to make people think you're still alive if you keep sending emails and posting on social media. After Erica got herself skewered, I dug her phone out of her pocket and sent a few emails. There was one to her lab head, one to the head of the Hughes program, and one to the Dean. Side note: you wouldn't believe how good the cell service is in the tunnels. It's better than in my apartment. There's even WiFi."

"I'm not allowed to go on the Internet," Roger says.

"Eh, you're not missing much. Anyway, I used Erica's email to send all three of them something like, 'I'm so sorry, I have a family emergency that requires my immediate and prolonged attention. I need to leave campus urgently, and I'm not sure when and if I will return to Georgetown. For the next semester and possibly longer, I will relocate to a school closer to home so I can be with my family during this difficult time.' Pretty good, huh?"

"My mom is coming to visit," Roger says, picking at a hangnail. He seems more subdued today than usual.

I'm not done, though. This grand reveal is so cathartic. "Then, I texted her top three contacts: that dickhead Tom Carlson, some girl named Penny who I think is one of her roommates, and Kat Saunders, the girl who wanted to talk to O'Meara about exorcisms. They all got something along the lines of 'Hey, I know this sounds sudden but I just found out I have a family emergency that's going to take me away from Georgetown for the next semester, probably longer. So sorry to have to break the news over text, but I'm already on my way to the airport. I didn't even have time to pack my stuff. Talk soon.' It was that easy! And even I know most people who say 'Talk soon' have no intention of doing so."

"Gretchen used to text me," he says.

"Then, the last piece: I opened up her Facebook, Twitter, and Instagram accounts to announce she's 'Taking a break from social media for awhile. Peace out.' Brilliant, right?"

"Social media rots your brain. That's what my mom says."

"Your mom's not wrong. After all that, you won't believe it, I got to use the trepan for the very first time! It was just as wonderful as I imagined it would be. So powerful, so different. But..." I trail off, watching Roger pick his hangnail savagely. Something is definitely off about him.

"But what?" he says, not taking his eyes from his fingers.

"But now, looking back, I don't feel as happy as I thought I would. I don't feel guilty—not in the least. I feel renewed, powerful. I mean, I am powerful, getting away with everything, but I also feel, at times, like I'm trapped deep inside this massive black cloud. I had to kill Erica, of course; she was my competition, plus she was a dirty snitch, and now she's gone. Mother never knew Erica existed, and now she never will... but she also won't ever know the brilliance of my victory."

Roger doesn't respond, and I shake my head to clear it. There's no sense dwelling on the negative. I'd rather think about the positive, like how I no longer have to go to therapy now that O'Meara's gone, or how it's so simple to make people disappear if you're smart and can keep a cool head.

"Oh, wait, I almost forgot—what I did with O'Meara. I didn't want to make him disappear like I did with Erica; the Jesuits would be all over a missing brother, whereas flighty college girls are so unimportant in comparison. Misogyny can be great when it works to your advantage. I also didn't forget the extremely convenient fact that Erica's globetrotting parents are completely off the grid looking for the Nepalese boogeyman and climbing Mount Everest for the next few months. How perfect is that? By the time they get back and find their daughter missing, the trail will be so cold, it'll be frosty."

"Mmm," Roger says, hunching his shoulders. Something isn't right with him, but I'm on a roll, and I can't stop now.

"You know, it took the authorities a lot longer than I expected to find O'Meara's cause of death. Jesus Christ, I made sure the evidence was front and center on his desk, and they still struggled. I know oleandrin isn't on the normal autopsy blood panels, but come on."

"I don't like blood," Roger says, taking a half-step backwards.

"It's not that bad once you get used to it. Then the police interviewed Airhead Ani and me together the day after O'Meara died. A janitor found his body, around ten at night, right when Erica was probably getting impaled. Let me tell you, I was sweating through our whole interview, mostly because Erica's blood was still under my fingernails, and I was afraid the officers would notice. We both gave these bland statements, like 'No, I didn't see anything. No, I didn't hear anything.' Airhead was so flabbergasted she didn't even shed a tear, which played pretty damn well into my plans. Me, on the other hand—I used Visine to get some fake tears going."

"People think I don't see or hear anything, either," Roger says. With a final rip, the hangnail comes free, and Roger stares down at it pinched between his fingers before taking another step away from me.

"Then, just last week, once the cause of death was released and O'Meara's case had been ruled a possible homicide, these detectives, not the same ones we talked to first, came to interview Airhead and me again. They separated us that time, which made things much easier. A detective named Grady asked me if Father O'Meara always drank tea in the mornings, which yes, he did, and I was able to tell him Airhead was the one who made it for him every morning like clockwork. Then, I worked up a few snuffles and told him I thought the tea she made him that last morning smelled a little off, but since he drank it anyway, I didn't think anything of it. Oh, oh, Rog, here's the best part—when Grady asked if there was anything else, I let out this fake sob and said I was so sorry, I should have known, Airhead's hated Father O'Meara ever since he reamed her out for making a personal call in the office during the workday. I told Grady I thought maybe Father O'Meara had threatened to fire her, since she was so upset about the whole thing. Then I told him Airhead scares me sometimes."

"I get scared sometimes, too," Roger whispers.

"There was more about how much Airhead hated O'Meara, how they had a difficult relationship, et cetera. I really drove that shit home. I had Grady scribbling notes like he had to get everything down verbatim. It was awesome. But... but there's been nothing for the past week. No news, no arrests, nothing."

I check the time on my phone. I've got ten minutes to get to the office. Despite everything that's happened, the Jesuits still need tending to, so Airhead and I are still coming into the Chaplains' Office every day, trying to pretend nothing has changed. She hasn't said much about what happened—mostly she's been scrolling on Instagram, burying her face in her phone for the entire workday now that there's not a Jesuit keeping tabs on her. Every now and then, she'll let her eyes stray from her phone long enough to lock eyes on the diet Frappuccino she can't give up despite my fictional great-grandmother's cautionary tale, bringing the straw to her mouth and suckling like a hungry piglet.

I'm about ready to leave Roger staring at his picked skin when he says something that makes my entire body break out in goosebumps.

"You shouldn't kill people, Keely." His timbre is deeper than usual and filled with something that sounds like a taunt.

Time seems to stop right there on that steaming sidewalk. This can't be happening. It's been at least fifteen minutes since we started talking—Roger should not be able to remember what I've told him. Nothing like this has ever happened before, and he's never cast any sort of judgment on me, not once.

Motherfucker. Roger's brain might be healing, after all—and at the world's most inconvenient time.

"What was that?" I say. My voice is way too high and shaky.

He raises his eyes to look into mine, the sun glinting in his bleach blond hair. For a second, I glimpse a sort of playful awareness. Just as quickly, the expression morphs into the typical dull-eyed stare I'm used to from Roger. The goosebumps strain so hard against my skin, they're starting to hurt.

"My mom is coming to visit soon," Roger says, all innocence once again.

We stare at each other for a long time. Roger doesn't move, doesn't change his expression. My hand goes to the keys in my pocket—in a pinch, I could use them to stab Roger's carotid. Not elegant or private, but it would get the job done.

The spell breaks when a dog yips a few blocks away. I give the keys a squeeze.

"It's a beautiful morning, huh, Keely?" he says in that familiar foghorn voice.

In the distance, I can hear the Healy clocktower chiming nine o'clock. I need to leave, but my feet don't want to move. I can't shake the feeling that I'm not the only one wearing a mask; maybe Roger is, too. Maybe he's been wearing one for a long time.

Fuck. That's tomorrow's problem.

*　　*　　*

I arrive in the Chaplains' Office sweaty and disconcerted. I don't know what I'm going to do about Roger, or if I even need to do anything at all. The man has a traumatic brain injury, for God's sake. He cannot form new memories. He doesn't know shit about me.

Unless he does.

Even if he does, nobody's going to believe anything from a man with a brain injury so unusual it was documented in the fucking *New England Journal of Medicine.*

Unless they do.

In front of me, my Georgetown email inbox pings with a new message, mercifully pushing thoughts of Roger out of my head. My entire body goes limp with excitement when I see who it's from: Professor Demetri.

```
To: krexroth@georgetown.edu
From: demetri@georgetown.edu
Subject: Hughes Research Fellowship


Dear Keely,

Due to the departure of one of our current
students, a spot has opened up in the Hughes
Research Program. Your application was impressive,
and I'd like to offer the spot to you, if you're
still interested in being a part of the program.
Please let me know as soon as you can.

    Cheers,

Lynn Demetri, PhD
```

I let out an uncharacteristic "Whoop!" and a gobbet of drool lands on the back of my hand, startling me. I wipe my hand on the leg of my pants and close my salivating mouth. I've done it. I've really done it. I'm going to take Erica's place.

I fire off a quick response to Professor Demetri, thanking her for the offer and accepting the position.

"Dude, what happened?" Airhead Ani asks, popping my bubble of euphoria.

"I'm getting out of this place," I say.

"What, like, you're going home early?" she says.

"No," I hiss. "I just got into the Hughes program. I'm going to work in a lab and make discoveries, instead of sitting in this shitty office making copies."

"Jeez, that's harsh," she says, her scummy blue eyes wide. Stubby new lashes are just starting to erupt from her eyelids. "It's not so bad here."

I ignore her and pop up out of the bad chair, my phone in my hand. The hallway outside of the office is empty, and my fingers are calling Mother before the door behind me fully closes.

The phone rings and rings. Just when I think she's not going to answer, I hear Mother's snippy "Hello" shoot through the speaker like a missile.

"Mother," I say. "It's Keely. I—"

"Keely," she says. "I'm in the middle of finishing my paperwork. Haven't I told you never to call me at work?"

"I know, Mother, but something wonderful has just happened—"

"Did you plan the best tea party for all the papists?" she sneers, trying to stab me through the phone.

"No, Mother, I wanted to tell you I got into the Hughes research program. I'm going to work in a lab. This is basically a guaranteed ticket to the best medical schools in the country. This is a big deal." She can't ignore this— being accepted into the Hughes program is an enormous achievement, one that will be stamped across my résumé for as long as I live.

The line is silent, then Mother sighs. "Oh. Well. It's no Harvard, but good for you, darling." The point of her knife digs deeper and twists, leaving me gasping.

Without saying goodbye, she hangs up.

My back connects with the wall, and I slide down it like a broken egg dribbling to the floor. I've worked so hard, sacrificed so much, practiced so diligently, killed so carefully—and Mother still isn't proud of me. She won't give me a single compliment, not even the smallest molecule of validation.

I am no more than a hollowed-out shell. The last time I felt full was when I was with Erica, before she had to ruin everything by betraying me. Maybe O'Meara was right after all; maybe that outpatient treatment program could have helped me, could have put the yolk back in my shell.

My head falls into my palms. I gave up everything for nothing.

I'm contemplating whether I should jump off of Key Bridge or throw myself down the *Exorcist* stairs when the heavy Healy doors burst open and the hallway floods with uniformed officers. I recognize Detective Grady leading the charge.

Those flesh-ripping goosebumps cover my body again. I should have taken care of Roger when I had the chance, before he could go and call the police. I fucking handed him my confession, every sordid thought and plan I've ever had, and now I'm going down—

Grady stalks right past me and yanks open the door to the Chaplains' Office, the other officers following in his wake.

"What—" I hear Airhead say, but Grady is already talking over her.

"Anica Ableman, you're under arrest for the murder of Father Randolph O'Meara," he says. "You have the right to remain silent. Anything you say can and will be used against you in a court of law…"

Grady finishes Mirandizing her, then clips a shiny pair of handcuffs on her wrists. I heave a huge sigh of relief, the goosebumps slowly receding. They're not here for me. In fact, nobody seems to have noticed me at all, crumpled against the wall like a used tissue. The officers speak freely in front of me.

"I thought Georgetown kids were supposed to be smart," one of them whispers to another. "This girl left fingerprints all over that mug."

"That's nothing," his companion says. "Did you hear she even had some of that oleander in a vase on her table? As if the leaves and all that other tea stuff wasn't enough to incriminate her. Some people just have no sense."

"I guess Georgetown's letting in anyone nowadays," he says. "You might even have a shot, Chuck."

Chuck gives the first guy a companionable shove and they turn to follow Grady, who is leading Airhead out of the Chaplain's Office and back toward the Healy entrance.

"What are you doing?" Her words are barely intelligible as she starts to choke on her tears. "I didn't—you can't—I need to call my mom—" she sputters.

"I recommend you exercise your right to remain silent," Grady growls.

For once, Airhead listens and shuts her mouth.

When the doors thud closed behind the melee, I pull myself up to standing and walk back into the Chaplains' Office. I firmly wedge the bad chair under Airhead's former computer and plop into the good one. I'm tempted to call Mother again, to make her understand, but I know better. Don't I?

Win some, lose some, but all things considered, it's not such a bad day after all.

A splash of yolk drips back into my shell.

AUTHOR'S NOTE

I wrote the first draft of this book when I was nearly nine months pregnant with my first child and revised it when I was nearly nine months pregnant with my second. Clearly, getting this book out into the world was much harder and more time consuming for me than giving birth. Twice. As with my children, this book is a labor of love.

After reading this, it probably comes as no surprise that I went to Georgetown. I graduated in 2015, so any current students or more recent graduates reading this may find that my descriptions of the campus and surrounding areas are slightly outdated—my apologies. It's all in service of the story!

If you're interested, much of what I describe in the book is real. The steam tunnels under Healy Hall are real. The Howard Hughes Medical Institute Research Scholars program is real, and I was lucky enough to be a part of it. The places, businesses, and buildings are all real. Even the Georgetown Cuddler was real, although that moniker has been widely denounced, and the Cuddler was a male.

I'm telling you all of this because the scariest things always have a bit of truth in them, wouldn't you say? If you want more information about all the Georgetown lore, you can find more at my website, www.viggyhampton.com.

I should make it very clear that this novel is not autobiographical. If you're looking for traces of me in these pages, I'm definitely more of an Erica, although that's not to say I have no Keely in me (I do write horror, after all).

Now on to my very sincere thank yous. Thank you to my mom, who has read this manuscript about a thousand times, offering helpful feedback and catching mistakes every time. Thank you to my dad, who has been an invaluable proofreader and editor. Thank you to my editor extraordinaire, Amy Grace Loyd, who helped me really bring Keely to life. Thank you to my husband Ryan, who has always made space for me and who supports me unconditionally. Thank you to my friend Katherine, who served as a wonderful beta reader for this manuscript and is always there to bounce ideas around with me. Thank you to all my family and friends who have championed me and my work over the years. Thank you to Georgetown, which gave me a wonderful place to call home for four years, and to my fellow Hughesies, who made that home exciting and fun. And, of course, thank you to every reader who picked up this book and gave it a try.

Thank you to all the amazing authors who blurbed this book and provided support and encouragement, including Ronald Malfi, Christa Carmen, Angel Van Atta, Gage Greenwood, Rektok Ross, and Alan Shivers. Your kind words helped me believe in myself and empowered me to keep pushing. Thank you to the horror community, which has welcomed me with open arms. A rising tide lifts all boats, and that's what the community of horror readers and writers feels like—a rising tide.

Oh, and if you try the Keely sandwich, please let me know how that goes. I've heard it's incredible.

VIGGY PARR HAMPTON

MPH is an epidemiologist, content marketing strategist, host of the podcast "Horror Humor Hunger," and the author of *A Cold Night for Alligators*. She is a graduate of Georgetown University and Emory University's Rollins School of Public Health. *Much Too Vulgar* was inspired by her time as a Howard Hughes Medical Institute Research Scholar during her undergraduate years.

Connect with her at her website, www.viggyhampton.com
or on Instagram or TikTok @viggyparrhampton